TRIO
IN THREE FLATS

By Eileen Dewhurst

TRIO
IN THREE FLATS

EILEEN DEWHURST

PUBLISHED FOR THE CRIME CLUB BY
DOUBLEDAY & COMPANY, INC.
GARDEN CITY, NEW YORK
1981

Library of Congress Cataloging in Publication Data

Dewhurst, Eileen.
Trio in three flats.

I. Title.
PR6054.E95T7 1981   823′.914   AACR2

ISBN 0-385-17647-3
Library of Congress Catalog Card Number 81-43008

TRIO
IN THREE FLATS

CHAPTER 1

Darling.

I see I put a full stop instead of a comma. Symbolic? Probably just because as soon as I wrote the word I had to stop and think about it. For five minutes I've been half thinking and half watching a couple of women talking in the road below. I find myself, now, envying people whose lives I know nothing about.

I suppose that's because I just can't believe anyone else can be walking round with this poison in them absolutely every minute of the time. When you first told me the score it went into me like an injection, I felt it running down my arms into my fingertips. Now I'm used to it, but there isn't a single moment when I don't know it's there.

Darling. I can't imagine ever using that word and not meaning you, Peter Shaw. But the word darling, so far as you are concerned, no longer means me. I keep saying that to myself, over and over again, forcing myself to accept it, hoping the impact will get less. It doesn't. But today all at once I can write about it.

I keep wondering whether I'd feel better if you'd got rid of me for another woman. I don't think I would, I think then the jealousy and the self-hate would both be worse. I can at least, as things are, tell myself that you no longer want a woman at all, and so that it wasn't because I'm Hilary that you told me to go. And I can't make comparisons.

I really sat down to tell you that I've got a job, and have worked a week of it. I think you'll still be interested, just, in that. It's ironic: I've got more responsibility than you ever gave me, but over things I don't very much like. Believe it or not, I'm managing a tiny modern gallery round the corner from here. I tried a few antiques and old masters with no luck, and then when I was investigating the local shops I saw this man standing in his doorway and he said good morning, and come and have a look round, and while I was wandering about inside, feeling spare because I had just no reaction to any of his stuff, he said, "I don't suppose you want a job," and I said I did. I also said that in a way I might be considered well qualified, but he wasn't interested in what I'd done, he said he had instincts and he thought I was what he wanted and wouldn't abscond with his profits or take too much French leave. I said on the other hand I might be considered badly qualified, because my work with more traditional stuff had developed tastes which were by no means sympathetic to what he had on his walls, but that didn't interest him either. He told me he was opening another gallery in the West End and didn't want to spend much time in this one. It seemed fair enough. There's an elderly woman living in a sort of flat over the back, who cleans the place and can be called on to hold the fort for short moments if I want to slip out for anything. They launch obscure artists, generally one by one, but sometimes if a little "school" is in evidence they'll show a representative selection. At the moment there's the work of an abstract Pole whose surname is all s's and z's and has to be looked up before I can write it. I think the fact that I'm getting a surprisingly good salary is because of this man's flair (I don't mean the Pole, although him I can't judge). Oh, my employer's name I can give you, Stephen Elliott.

The place is all yellows and whites and acid greens, a sort of bright pallor. I find myself mourning the green bobbled cloths and even the stuffed birds. The sort of underexposed look of things. Everything here is over-exposed, thin-textured.

Amazingly, I'm well. Except . . . no, nothing to put into words, nothing I can let myself even put into thoughts. How long is it since you told me? Nearly three months, now, and that was the end, abruptly. I know shock can do unusual things to one's body.

There are single people behind the other three doors on the landing. One is an elderly woman I've learned to look out for, because once one encounters her one can't get away. It's a pity, because she's nice and has obviously done interesting things, only she weights them with lead when she talks about them. The one time I actually accepted an invitation from Miss Prince to go in for coffee (really because I got so stiff standing poised for flight outside her door) it was over two hours before I staggered out. So that now I'm always in a rush when I meet her.

The other female's quite different. The first time I saw her I thought she was a schoolgirl, but she teaches art and paints on her own account. Very fair, with a marvellous complexion and a turned-up nose and a smile that's dazzling when it gets past being diffident.

(Pity I can't take a leaf out of your new book.) If I was feeling anything I'd feel glad I'd met Cathy, except that her breathlessness can be catching. There's always work in progress, very painterly but offbeat so that it couldn't possibly go on a chocolate box. Faintly surrealist, I suppose. I should think she's good and I may eventually suggest putting her in touch with Stephen, if she's interested—I gather she hasn't found any sales outlet yet, not I think that she's looked very hard.

Cathy's naïve. A rather dishy dark man lives in the fourth flat, and in telling me about him she Revealed All in her first few words. He's a detective-inspector in the Metropolitan force, and her Hero. Not her boy-friend, although she sometimes feeds him when he's late and tired, and they look after each other's plants when they're away. (Sweet? Yes. But Neil Carter on his own, I'm sure, is anything but.)

He finds me interesting. He's the sort of man who would find the idea of any woman under, say, forty-five interesting, but I think his interest in me is sustaining a little beyond that, although we've only exchanged the odd word on the landing and in Cathy's hall as we passed one another.

If only the idea of this would make you jealous, but it will make you relieved, which is as hateful as anything I can think of.

The gallery—called the Stephen Elliott Gallery, of course—is closed all day Saturday, that's why I'm sitting in the flat writing to you. I was going to say "at home," but I'm not. It's an easy journey from here by car, and not all that awkward by tube—sixteen stops, I think, and two changes. I suppose this is civilization, wanting to go somewhere one could so easily go, and not going.

I go so often in my sleep I could say now to a psychiatrist, "Well, I have this dream. . . ."

It's always dark, and I take the car and I coast up to Marble Arch because the roads are clear. This part of the dream is patchy, I don't really stick with it until I'm winding up the drive, and then I'm aware of things, the shape of that rhododendron which always taps the car window if you're a bit over to the left, my front-door key going in the lock.

I'm halfway up the stairs, on the flat bit at the turn, when I know something's wrong. I don't want to go on, I can hardly breathe, but I cross the landing, push the sitting-room door (it's half-open), go as far as I can towards your chair, and you're lolling in it and your face is all wrong, and then I scream and scream and you can't hear me because although you're staring at me you're dead and then, thank

God, my screaming wakes me up. Cathy's bedroom is the other side of mine and the first time I screamed she came in via the balcony and when I woke myself up she was tapping on my bedroom door (the balcony doors are brutes to lock and so high up we don't always bother). I've asked her since if she still hears me and she just says, "Oh, never mind," so she obviously does.

It's dreadful, a dreadful dream, and I don't shake it off when I wake up.

People talk about love and hate being the opposite sides of a coin, but the opposite side of the love coin isn't hate, it's indifference. Your indifference, the last time I saw you, was worse than if you'd begun to hate me. Sometimes, just sometimes, I hate you.

I don't know how to sign off. But it doesn't matter, of course, because you won't care what I put, or don't put.

Hilary

CHAPTER 2

He was aware that four or five nights had gone by when he had been late, and no one had appeared on the landing to prevent him slipping straight into his flat. Late again, and tired, he was surprised to find himself standing motionless, his key in the lock, listening to the silence.

One of the other front doors flew open. He withdrew his key.

"Well, Cathy. Where have you been these last few days?"

Pink flooded her face; he knew it was because he had realized he hadn't seen her. She pushed hair off her forehead.

"Oh, I don't know. . . . I heard the lift. Do you feel like a coffee, Neil? And I could do you an absolutely delicious Welsh rarebit?"

"No Welsh rarebit tonight, but a cup of coffee and—have you any of those special little biscuits your mother sends you?"

"I have. I have."

The sudden luminosity of her smile struck him as dazzlingly as the first time he had seen it.

"Very well, then. But only for half an hour. I'm tired."

"Of course. Shut the door, will you." She preceded him across the little hall, so like and unlike his own. "You've been frightfully late this week. As I said, I hear the lift," she added hastily, still presenting him with the back of her gold cap of hair, "and Hilary Fielding and Miss Prince just don't go out at night."

"And Miss McVeigh?" he demanded, sinking into her most comfortable sitting-room chair. Columbine confronted him on an easel, pointing a toe, and Harlequin above her broke a blue sky like paper as he leaned down from among the trees behind the blue. On a corner of the sitting-room wall a pale blue sky had one star in the curve of a crescent moon and beside it a hint of rose betokened dusk or dawn.

"Sometimes I'm out, sometimes I'm in. No pattern." Cathy perched on the arm of her enormous lilac sofa, angling her denim legs. Neil studied the wall.

"I've always meant to ask you, sunset or sunrise?"

"Oh, sunrise! Dawn!"

"Yes, it would be."

"The moon and star," said Cathy. "I know it's impossible, but I was thinking of *The Ancient Mariner*. 'The horned morn with one bright star Within the nether tip.'"

"I see. And I see you've got a bit more company since I was last in."

"You've noticed?" The flush was in her face again, as well as her painted sky. "What do you think?"

A boy and a dog rose from the skirting-board, looking up towards the earlier handiwork.

"Self-portrait?"

"Oh, Neil!" Cathy stared at him in dismay. "Not really?"

"Well, that was my reaction. Did you have a model?"

"Not in the flesh. But I was thinking about brother Robin."

"That would figure. And, yes, I have made a pun although I didn't intend to."

"Oh *Neil.*" One vigorous movement took her to the door, where she turned to glower at him. "You can't really think I look like a fifteen-year-old boy."

"Not entirely," he said, grinning, too unromantically fond of her to let his eyes rest on her evident breasts. "But you did agree with me, when I propelled you both by your blond hairs in front of a mirror."

"That was only because we were both wearing jeans and check shirts. We'd look quite different if I was dressed up."

"Indeed you would." He had suddenly remembered Cathy as she had once let him into her flat for a party, insubstantial in floating white chiffon, eyes made mysterious, lips glowing dark, crystal drops shimmering to each side of her newly fragile jaw. For an instant they had stared at one another, like strangers. "Anyway," he went on, "of course it looks much more like Robin."

"It's my dog Barney. I miss him." She whirled out of sight. "You stay there, being so tired." Her voice floated back to him. "Be vetting your week's activities to see what you can tell me about."

"I'm not that tired." He followed her out to the kitchen and perched on a stool. "I don't think I can find anything to tell you," he said, enjoying the small figure busy about its domain. It always amused him to see Cathy's pleasure that he should follow her vying with the disorder it created in her preparation of refreshments. "That's not because of secrecy," he added, getting to his feet to reach down a cake tin towards which she had made three ineffectual jumps. "Simply that at the moment it's all slog and hardly any result."

"Just one big thing or lots of small ones? Would you like some cheese biscuits first, if you really won't have Welsh rarebit?"

"I really won't, and I wouldn't. It's never just one big thing, I'm afraid. But the biggest thing at the moment, that's inquiries, inquiries, and more inquiries."

"Do you go round yourself?"

"I do."

"Find yourself in pleasant places?"

"At the moment, old suburbia. You wouldn't believe me if I told you how many people can live in one short street of terraced Victorian villas."

"I would if you told me. Now we're ready, if you can believe me. Come on."

She picked up the tray and immediately relinquished it into his extended hands. Neil followed her dancing progress back into the sitting-room.

"Are you still happy in London, Cathy?" He set the tray down on the low table in front of the sofa and resumed his chair. "You don't ever feel you'd like to go back home?"

This was the sort of question he remembered to ask her at intervals, when he remembered her father on the landing the day she moved in, saying how he would appreciate it if Neil could keep an eye on his young daughter.

"Oh, I sometimes do," she said cheerfully, flopping down behind the tray and pushing strands of hair out of her eyes. "And so then I go for a weekend. And then I'm ready to come back. Anyway, Grandma and Grandpa having had this flat for so long—they were the first people to live in it when the block was built just before the war—it's part of home. The first time I ever came to London when I was about five I stayed here and so my first memory of it is of a sort of enchanted place. Gosh, it really was magic. Sometimes just for a moment, now, I can get that feeling back again."

"Perhaps that's why I always feel it's a bit Art Deco in here."

"Yes!" Her response when they reached areas of obvious agreement was inclined to be intense. Neil was never sure whether he found the tendency irritating or endearing. "People were going off Art Deco for the first time round when Grandpa bought the flat, and they brought some of the more extreme stuff up here so they wouldn't be living with it all the time. If I'd come to live here any sooner I'd have probably chucked it all out, but now it's got a sort of nostalgic glow about it. Do you know what I mean?"

"Of course. Period charm. Sunshine windows and malachite. It's a pity they were so skimpy on bathrooms and kitchens in the thirties."

"Nobody had any gadgets then to take up space. Neil, I think it's time I had a party."

"You just had one."

"Nonsense. That was months ago." She leaned towards him with the coffeepot and refilled his cup. He helped himself to a third biscuit. "It's Hilary next door. I had her in for coffee the other day. She's just started a job but she never has any visitors and she seems to be on her own. She didn't say much but she did let me gather something had happened which had changed her life and made her move home. She seems sort of—well, sort of punch-drunk. Did I tell you about hearing her scream in the night and getting into her flat and knocking on her bedroom door?"

"Yes. I gave you a lecture about locking balcony doors."

"I do lock mine sometimes. I still hear the screams some nights. She sounds terrified." Cathy stared at Neil, troubled. "I do hope she's all right. She doesn't look ill, does she? Actually I think she's rather attractive. You must have bumped into her at some point. Did you get any clues?"

She was still looking at him, as always when she spoke to him, but she lowered her eyes to the tray while she awaited his reply, picking up a biscuit and in two bites demolishing it.

"Yes, I've bumped into her. And no, I didn't get any clues, except I would agree with you she could be suffering from shock."

"But attractive, don't you think?" Cathy's glance came briefly up, swooped back to the tray.

"Quite attractive," responded Neil evenly.

"I would have thought she was just the sort of woman who would intrigue you," said Cathy, carrying the war rather waveringly into the enemy camp.

"Anyone who appears to be not quite him- or herself is automatically intriguing to a policeman."

"Yes, I see that, but when as well it's someone so tall and slim and dark. And she has an attractive sort of a husky voice—"

"So you think you'll give a party for her?"

"Not *for* her—oh, well, yes, I suppose it would be. But just a few people, just to offer her a few contacts."

"She has you, it seems. Was she any more expansive in her flat than in yours?"

"Not really." Cathy put her hand out to a lamp, turning the dove-grey sky to navy-blue, then got up and drew the lilac curtains against the last of the spring dusk. "She was a bit less chilly, I suppose, smiled when I admired some of her things. She has some super things, Neil," said Cathy enthusiastically, throwing herself back on the sofa. "Not modern, although she works in a modern gallery. She really did smile when she told me she was working in a modern gallery and didn't like modern art. Then she looked like thunder when she said she used to be in the antique business, so I didn't ask any questions. She's rather clever and knowledgeable. And I think she could be quite fun if she wasn't so—well, you know, intense."

"Perhaps that's just because of whatever it is that's happened to her."

"Perhaps. I will have a party, Neil. Another biscuit? More coffee?"

"No, thank you, child." He ignored her gesture of protest. "I must go. There's a chance, any time after midnight, of my rest being disturbed. Does the lift wake you, by the way, once you're asleep?"

"No." She had blushed again. "Thanks for coming in. I'm glad you like the mural. Shall I give Robin more company?"

"If you really think he needs it."

"I don't know yet but you're right, that would be the only reason. I'll see you, Neil."

"See you, Cathy."

The slightly wistful face didn't linger. When Cathy's door had shut there was utter silence while he found his key. Before using it he looked speculatively towards one of the other closed doors, not for the first time.

CHAPTER 3

Peter.

I've been sitting thinking, and watching a blackbird hopping about on the balcony. Small birds tend to appear from Cathy's direction, so she must be feeding them. When winter comes I'll probably put something out myself.

I had to stop then, at the thought of summer and autumn and winter and spring again, and no you. I had to hold on to the edge of the table while the awful sort of cold wave went over me. Oh, yes, there's one stage worse than the poison, even more physical, but it doesn't come very often and it doesn't last. Well, it couldn't.

I had a letter from you yesterday. No, not a letter, I can't pretend it was that, I had a horrible little note hoping I'm O.K. and enclosing those minute gold earrings I left behind. And then only because I wrote and asked for them. I didn't want them to go on lying at the back of the top right-hand drawer of my dressing-table. Underneath Anthony's bits and pieces.

Exact thoughts like that, of actual physical facts, those are the ones I really pay for.

I see attractiveness in men, now, rather like I see a painting that appeals to me, or a spectacular sunset. Quite objective. Detective-Inspector Neil Carter is attractive. So is Stephen—rather more so than his pictures! I'm glad of the job, although even there there can be too much time to think. But I call on Mrs. Tilsley, the "caretaker," as little as possible, because although she's extremely obliging and so far has come to hold the fort every time I've asked her, it's the devil's own job to get rid of her, she recedes very, very slowly in a tide of talk, and even when a potential customer came in the other day he had to wait because Mrs. Tilsley was still talking. Not a second time, though. I let her go on the first time through sheer amazement, but now I say "Thank you, Mrs. Tilsley," and turn to whoever has come in. Perhaps I'll get to a point of being able to say it even without anybody else to help me! But at least people like Mrs. Tilsley—and Miss Prince on the landing here—they don't want to ask questions and listen to answers. I keep seeing questions looming up in Cathy's eyes, and she only holds them back because her sense of fitness is stronger than her natural curiosity. But curiosity isn't really the right word for Cathy. It's more a sympathetic interest in her fellow creatures, of whom even I am one. (Oh, oh, there's a difference between setting down how absolutely foul one feels, and self-pitying little sarcasms, and I crossed the line there.)

Detective-Inspector Carter looks curious too, of course, but for sure that's merely because I represent the general Enigma of Woman— in tall, slim, fairly youthful form. Stephen isn't curious, and part of that's his egotism, I know, but also he's sensitive and I think he respects the personal barrier I put up from the start. He asked me to have lunch with him on Wednesday at the trattoria next door but one to the gallery, and it was very nice and restful, I shall certainly get interested in his plans, and already Mr. Sz.'s pictures jar less than they did at the start, so perhaps this is a first stage towards appreciating them.

Oh yes, Mr. Sz. actually came in on Thursday, while Mrs. Tilsley was in full flow, and she didn't recede because apparently she's met him before. I soon learned that he too is hard to cut off and I sat back while the battle of the conversational giants raged across me. The result was a draw, because it was me at last, in a rare gap, who said "Thank you, Mrs. Tilsley," and got her away. Mr. Sz. then turned the force of his ideas on to me, very flowing and accented and complex, and it was only the advent of Stephen which brought *that* to a close. One or two of the things Mr. Sz. said have at least given me a start when looking at his pictures (which I shall be packing up in a couple of days anyway), but I can't help thinking there must be something wrong with art which needs so much explanation before people can get at it.

I was thinking of your little Boudin as I said that, no explanation needed of that great windblown sky and those minute but crystally clear figures in the bottom quarter of the picture, trying to be fashionable in the maritime gale. Our next client, I gather, is representational—of "the environment of modern man." We shall see.

Cathy's asked me to supper next week. "Just a few friends." She intends producing an enormous vat of risotto and a complicated salad. I asked if I might help and she said no, she liked doing it on her own, but I could go in next morning (Saturday) to help her clear up and talk it all over. She said in her artless way that Neil was "so good," he was going to do the drinks. Although she talks about people with both men's and women's names I get the impression most of them are in pairs and that she doesn't have anyone particular herself. I wonder if this is because of her passion for Detective-Inspector Carter? She's a very sweet creature, and I'm certain men must at least try to be around.

I catch myself out, sometimes, hoping you'll feel you've made a mistake. Time will never "do" anything for me while I have this hope lurking about. I suppose that's why I haven't got round to seeing my solicitor. I ought to keep reminding myself of your revulsion at the end, nothing could come back after *that*. You really punished yourself with me that last time, didn't you? And I, because you didn't tell me till the morning, I was *particularly happy*. . . . Sometimes I hate myself as much for that, blind idiot, as for being the person you no longer want.

And when I remember that last time I remember . . . There wasn't any warning, I thought you were so carried away. . . . Fool. What a fool.

I had the dream again last night. I've had it several times since I last wrote to you. Always the same progress, the same sight which wakes me screaming. But on different nights I'm aware of different parts of it, as if someone was flickering a torch about and the light didn't always catch the same things. Last night I stumbled on that first outside step, where I came such a cropper a couple of winters ago and bust my shin. (The stitches still show white after two seasons' sunbathing.) I didn't fall this time, I managed to save myself by grabbing the railing, and I remember being sort of shocked even in the dream by the disturbance, as if it might stir up a whole host of ghastly things. Sometimes I find myself actually trying to take notice, to get some sort of a clue—to what? You're always dead when I reach the sitting-room, and I always wake up before I can get close enough to see why you died. Judging by your face across the room you haven't died naturally, but of course I don't know what people

look like after a—a what? A coronary? A stroke? You could be dead
of something like that, I suppose, but in the dream, in our sitting-
room, there's such a sense of evil. I know you always laughed at the
idea that I could have second sight—that anybody could have second
sight—but there really have been times when I knew things. I never
wanted to; I hoped I wouldn't, because it always frightened me, and
it was other people who made a thing of it. Anyway, the sense of
evil, I think that's the worst part of the dream, worse than seeing
you dead. I think that's what sets me screaming, to wake up and escape it.

The vase is on the table. As I used to see it sometimes when I
came in unexpectedly, and found you worshipping.

Your dear brother called to see me last night. Dear, dull old
Arthur. Only last night . . . He called first about a month ago. To
see if I was all right, with the apparent emphasis on my legal situation. We had coffee, and I found myself doing all the work to get
him over his embarrassment. At the time I wondered why he should
be so embarrassed. Anyway, we talked and it came over hot and
strong how much he disapproves of you. Not just because of me, I
don't mean, more I think because of Anthony, and most of all because you're you. Jealousy? It shouldn't be, because Arthur really has
Done Well, nothing precarious about *his* success. But people are attracted by you, all kinds of people, you're bound up in life in a way
Arthur couldn't be in a million years. He's awkward and has no sense
of humour, even after living with Clara. I could much more easily
think of Clara as your sister and Arthur as your in-law than the way
it is; it's so hard to believe you and Arthur had the same parents and
were brought up in the same house in the same way.

And my imagination has always folded completely whenever I've
found myself thinking about Arthur and Clara on their own together. I can imagine Clara, oh, yes, but with Arthur . . . And
Arthur . . . Well, impossible to imagine Arthur with anyone—until
last night. Last night I knew why Arthur had been embarrassed that
first time he came to see me. Because—I don't know why I'm writing
this down, it's so vague the fact of saying anything at all makes too
much of it, and anyway it makes me feel sick—but one minute it was
just dear kind dull old Arthur, leaning over to pat my hand in his
brotherly way, and the next—oh, Peter, it was a *man*, staring at me,
his lower lip all full and trembly, that expression which makes every
man look the same. . . . And then it was gone, and I was praying I'd
imagined it, and then again, just as he was leaving—he kissed me on

the cheek as usual, but for another moment . . . Oh, it's ludicrous, it's obscene, and I know perfectly well I wasn't imagining it.

It's as if every landmark is disappearing or changing. If sometimes I've wished for some sort of distraction, it wasn't anything like *this*.

I'm glad I never got into the habit of telling Clara how I feel, because I couldn't tell her this—this nothing—about her husband. Not that I've seen much of her since you and I split up. Well, I haven't somehow encouraged visits, or been to see her very often, and she hasn't pressed it. Sometimes I wish I had what seems to be the general urge to talk about oneself, it might ease things a bit, but I haven't. I never did talk about myself to anyone but you, which makes it all the harder now.

I suppose, though, I have confided in Clara in a way, because I wept once when she was here. I hadn't been saying anything, in fact we were talking about something quite unimportant, and I didn't say anything afterwards, but I just suddenly started to cry. I think she was as surprised as I was. I was looking at her face, which she was trying to make reassuring instead of anxious, and her lovely big soft front (it always seems wrong that Clara hasn't had children), and the next moment I was weeping. Not a bit like me, and I could tell poor Clara was caught between concern that I should be so out of character, and a sort of triumph that she had got through.

I don't want Arthur to come here again, now, I hate the thought of it, although I just smiled silently when he said he would. I can imagine myself freezing when I hear the bell, then crawling along the hall to look through the spy-hole. And leaning there until he goes away, not being quite sure how he's taking the disappointment because his face will be distorted as if I was seeing it in a fairground mirror. At least I think I know the danger time—when he's on his way home from the office.

Perhaps I ought to tell Clara. She could well roar with laughter and blow the whole thing sky-high. The whole what? Perhaps I am imagining it all.

No, I am not. It would be the last thing I should imagine.

I suppose it's the sort of thing which happens to women on their own. "Fair game": the phrase came pat, I must have heard it so often. You should be here, so that it wouldn't happen to *me*. I should be *there*. I still haven't accepted, I still can't believe, that I never will be again.

It's silent in the flat, the silence is deafening, roaring in my ears. I have to remind myself that I told you to leave me absolutely alone.

Hilary

CHAPTER 4

He came home late and tired and disgruntled from a busy day which had got him nowhere. To his other ailments was added reluctance at the thought of a party with no possibility of excuse; on the contrary, having to be prompt because of his undertaking to look after the drinks.

He did at least have time for a bath.

During it his emotions underwent a gradual and soothing transformation, so that by the time he stepped out again on to the landing his prevailing sensation was one of curiosity, primarily (he was aware of vague secondary stirrings) as to how Cathy would strike him when she answered her door.

In the range of reactions he was idly balancing in his imagination he had not included bewilderment and annoyance. But the door was opened by a large red-faced young man with enormous red hands and a lot of roughly cut brown hair.

Neil knew, to his increased annoyance, that his expression had not been immediately under control.

"Good evening," he said politely. "I too am early."

"Is it Neil?" came the breathless call, improving his mood again.

"It is." Neil felt the rough jacket against his hand as he went past, towards the kitchen.

"I'm Don," offered the following voice. "Don Everett."

"Hello, Don. Hello, Cathy."

Neil stopped in the kitchen doorway, swinging on the frame. Cathy, in a loose gown printed with myriad tiny flowers, was neither so mysterious as she had once briefly been at her front door, nor quite so familiar as her daily wont. She stood still when she saw Neil, suspending a spoon over a saucepan.

"Oh, Neil, I'm glad you're here. Thanks for coming so early. Was it a rush?"

"Not really. Everything all right?"

"I think so. Come and taste this."

He crossed the kitchen and was aware of his place at the door being taken by the young man. He nibbled from the spoon Cathy held out to him.

"Delicious," he said truthfully. "Where's the drink?"

"Down there." She indicated two stacked crates. "All wine. Red, white and rosé. Whisky, I suppose, for those who just don't under any circumstances drink wine, but let's not suggest it." Like Neil, she became aware of the large hovering figure. "Oh, this is Don, by the way. I told him you were going to help me but he still came early, to see if there were any extras. Wasn't that kind?"

"Very kind," automatically responded Neil, smiling at the good-natured red face and wondering how Cathy had made its acquaintance.

"I'll take a crate through," volunteered Don, returning the smile. "Cathy tells me you're a detective," he said as he and Neil dumped their burdens side by side on the sitting-room carpet.

"I never know," said Neil, standing up and subduing his slight shortness of breath, "what to respond to that statement once I've agreed to it." He smiled again as he spoke, to show he was being friendly, and the young man reciprocated through his deepening colour.

"Of course you don't, it was a stupid thing to say."

"I didn't mean that, I suppose I should be flattered. I don't imagine you'd say 'Cathy tells me you're a sales manager' quite so early in our acquaintance." Suddenly aware that his companion might be aspiring to become just that, Neil forced himself to think about what he was saying. "No, I only meant that it really is rather difficult to know what to reply."

"Of course. Yes." Don Everett was copying Neil in ranging the pale bottles along the side table, and the dark ones against the long radiator on the adjoining wall. "I work with Cathy," he said.

"Art?"

"Maths."

It seemed absurd, but this was the first time Neil had seen Cathy in any context beyond the solitude of her flat, painting and cooking, or in a classroom with a cluster of children and no adults. Now all at once there was a third picture, a room full of motionless men and women with Cathy their kinetic centre, whirling about looking for her vast squashy bag, accepting it with breathless thanks out of a pair of large red hands. . . .

"Don's very clever," said Cathy, coming in with a tray of little dishes containing nuts and crisps.

"Nonsense," mumbled Don.

"He is, Neil. And I'm not just saying that because of giving up maths so early, on account of not being able to do them." She was darting about the room plumping cushions, manoeuvring pouffes and chairs comfortably adjacent to where glasses could stand. The mathematician's eyes were cast down, but Neil thought they followed her.

"There!" said Cathy, at last standing still and starting to count on her fingers. Neil saw she was wearing her grandmother's pearl ring. "Glasses, drinks, bits, dishes in the oven, plates warming, salad on the side, cutlery. . . . I'm going to serve supper in the kitchen and people can come out and get it and then carry it where they like. Oh yes, paper serviettes, two packets of green ones in that cupboard, Don, could you . . . Just put them on the kitchen top beside the other things and I'll . . . And some music, don't you think; Neil, you find something and put it on."

Don went out to the kitchen with the green serviettes and Neil strolled over to the record-player.

"How many are coming?" He unwrapped one of Cathy's offbeat alliances of classic and modern and put it on the turntable.

"Oh, not many. Hilary, of course, and Winnie, and Mike and Rosemary—I think you met them—"

"Yes."

"And Roger and Sally and Tim and Judy and—and, how silly, I just can't think . . . Oh yes, I asked one of the older teachers from school, Betty Lumsden, and her husband, she's super. I asked Hilary if there was anyone she'd like to bring but she said no. I didn't somehow think there would be, I think I was just being nosey."

"I expect you were." The music was drawing the preparations into an anticipatory whole. Neil felt slightly sorry he had only just noticed the three small leaf and twig arrangements, each starred with a primrose. He indicated them. "Very nice."

"Thank you. Another two couples may come, they weren't sure, but there's plenty of food." Cathy paused, straightening a cushion without looking at it. "I forgot John Underwood. He's the school heart-throb, and much nicer than heart-throbs usually are. Teaches French and Spanish and still a bachelor at thirty-plus—"

"There are a few of us about." He said it, really, to ease her unaccountable embarrassment.

"Well, yes, of course, I didn't mean . . ." As she trailed off Neil heard the lavatory flush, and ceased to wonder why Don Everett was taking so long to deposit the serviettes.

The doorbell rang.

"Stand by the bottles!" Cathy shook her hair back and almost ran out of the room. She came back more slowly, followed by a pleasant-looking middle-aged couple and Don.

"Neil, this is Mr. and Mrs. Lumsden—"

"Betty and Edward," said the woman, advancing towards Neil. "I think Cathy sometimes forgets she's crossed the line between students and staff."

"I have felt a bit ridiculous, telling people things," said Cathy, thrusting out little dishes, it seemed to Neil in all directions, "but I'm getting used to it." The bell rang again. "Neil will look after you."

Two of the young couples had met while waiting for the lift, along with Cathy's particular friend Winnie, and for a few moments Neil was too busy to notice anything beyond the exigencies of his corner. Winnie, to his vague irritation, with the flattened hair she hadn't bothered to comb up and a heavy, unbecoming cardigan, was still reflecting her arrival by motor-bike.

"Thank you, policeman," she said as she accepted her drink from him, laughing uproariously. Neil had already decided that Winnie was appropriately named. But Cathy wasn't the sort of person who would ever cultivate anyone as a foil, so Winnie must have qualities he had not yet been able to discover. "Oh yes," he said, suddenly remembering, "you live near Cathy in the country, don't you?"

"That's right." Winnie, still laughing immoderately, took a gulp of her drink. "Known each other all our lives." So it must be loyalty. "And when Cathy came up to town, I thought—"

"Here's Edward to talk to you, Neil," said Cathy. "Come along, Winnie, I want you to meet Don Everett." With a brief dazzle of smile at the two men, she took Winnie by the arm and led her away.

"Nice little girl," said Edward Lumsden, not needing to be more precise. "Betty talks a lot about her."

"Cathy is nice, yes. . . ."

Beside Edward Lumsden's head Neil could see Hilary Fielding in the doorway. She was standing still, surveying the room without expression. He blessed the ability, which he had fostered in his work, to observe without in the least appearing to, keeping enough attention back to be able to maintain a conversation which had nothing to do with his real concern. It stood him in as good, if different, stead in his social life as it did when he was on duty.

"Yes, it's an upside-down world, all right," Edward Lumsden was saying.

"Never more so," responded Neil on his perfected reflex. "But I imagine that's always how it appears at any given time."

He saw Cathy start over towards the door, then stop as a tall dark man appeared in the hall behind Hilary. Cathy as well as Neil watched as Hilary moved aside for him and he, when he saw her face, stayed still, regarding her. It was Hilary, then, who moved on into the room, and the man followed. Before going forward to greet them Cathy glanced towards Neil and swiftly away.

Edward Lumsden was talking about the Stock Market.

"Excuse me," said Neil, as Hilary Fielding, the dark man close behind her, arrived in his corner.

"Good evening."

"Mr. Carter."

Neil had the ability to raise one eyebrow, and did so.

"What can I offer you, Miss Fielding?"

"A glass of white wine, please." There was no answering gesture. "And for you?" His eyes met the dark man's on the precise level.

"Red wine for me, please."

"Hello, Hilary!" exclaimed Cathy, suddenly in the midst of them. "And John! Hilary, you've met Neil Carter, obviously, but not John Underwood, I don't think. John, this is Hilary Fielding, my neighbour. And Neil Carter, my other neighbour. Oh, and Mr. . . . Edward Lumsden." She gulped for breath. "You've met Edward, I expect, haven't you, John?"

"I have, Cathy."

In the brief pause Neil heard Winnie laughing across the room. Another couple were approaching.

"Perhaps you'll give place to the thirsty," said Cathy. She spread her arms, and the long droop of flower-sprigged cotton excluded both Hilary and John from Neil's corner, leaving Edward Lumsden behind.

Neil had the impression that John Underwood was moving away willingly enough, Hilary possibly not, unless he was interpreting her slow step through the expectation of his vanity—it was hard to imagine her doing anything with vigour. He felt stirring, faintly, as he had felt it already on the landing, the challenge of such languor. . . .

been there for a long time, beside Winnie. Winnie was no longer wearing a cardigan, and had gone from very covered up to very bare. She had shoulders like a boxer and a dress or jersey like a boxer's vest. . . .

"Here you are." John Underwood was back with drinks for himself and Hilary. He smiled at Neil, perhaps quizzically. Hilary picked his plate up off the sofa so that he could sit down, and returned it to his lap. The three of them sat in silence out of which the music drained any embarrassment, rendering it almost sensuous. Hilary didn't turn round, but Neil knew she was aware of exactly where he was in relation to her. She proved it eventually, by the smallest turn of the head necessary to be heard as she softly spoke.

"Neil Carter. You're obviously schooled for long static silences."

"Yes, but not usually with a knife and fork. Can you hear them?"

"I can't hear even your knife and fork."

"Without the music you might have done. Modesty demands the qualification." It was something in the pleasantness of John Underwood's face which brought him to his feet. "Cathy's mousse is very good," he said. "John?"

"Thank you."

Cathy was still on the floor, beside Winnie and Don, and he put his hand on her shoulder as he passed her on his way out to the kitchen.

"Lovely party, child." The shoulder surged resentfully under his hand before he released it. Winnie neighed. Suppressing a strong instinct to kick her glass of wine up over her nose, Neil left the room. When he came back, juggling three bowls of mousse, the record was finishing. It made Hilary's silence against John's resumed narrative flow rather too obvious, and before repossessing himself of his perch Neil put another record on.

The next scene was two of the young couples dancing slowly in the centre of the room, entwined, and Cathy dodging about collecting plates. Neil got up and helped her.

"Why doesn't Winnie come to the aid of the party," he muttered, when they were both crouched in the same corner, retrieving shreds of carpet-bound salad as well as plates. "She's neither use nor ornament."

"She's having a good time," said Cathy. "I don't think she often does."

"You're too kind."

"Ah, Neil, am I?"

Both on their knees, they turned to regard one another, and Neil tucked away the discomfort of Cathy's grave glance for consideration at another time or, with luck, forgetfulness. At least, now, he didn't stop working until the sitting-room was clear of food, and then he asked Cathy to dance with him.

Despite his attempt to draw her close to fit his belief of what dancing should be, there was no point at which her body touched his, and the pressure of her hands was light.

"It's a nice party," he said, his smile failing, for the first time he could remember, to rally a light in her eyes.

"Oh yes, I think it is. But our main objective . . . D'you think Hilary's enjoying herself?"

"I don't imagine anyone would ever be able to be sure with Hilary. Certainly she's spent her time so far almost exclusively with your heart-throb."

"I've been lucky to find three unattached men," she said, when they had shuffled a few steps in silence. Neil had had time to notice they were the only couple whose faces and bodies were not in contact.

"Cathy, sweet, you will always be able to find as many more—if you so wish."

"If I so wish." There was something new in her mood, something less than utterly confiding. "Neil, do you think they would like coffee?"

"I don't know that they haven't gone past it, but why don't you be less than perfectionist this evening, put your big jar of instant out in the kitchen beside the sugar and the cups, and let those who are interested look after themselves."

"That's a good idea!" The more usual Cathy beamed her enthusiasm.

The next thing, he was in the kitchen alone, making coffee. He had followed Hilary Fielding out to the hall, seen her go into the bathroom, known once again that she was aware he was behind her. With a confidence even he rather wondered at, he had spooned instant coffee into two cups. He was pouring boiling water into one of them when Hilary came in.

"Coffee," he said.

"Thank you."

He noticed, now, under the fluorescent strip, that she was paler than ever and that a tiny pulse was fluttering in the corner of her eye.

"How are you?" he asked, quite gently.

He saw only her eyes over the cup, misted in the steam from the coffee.

"Pregnant," she said, "that's how I am. I'm pregnant."

The only definable part of his reaction was surprise that such a woman should have made such an announcement, in such circumstances.

"Do I congratulate you?"

There was a large dress ring on her marriage finger, but that, now, was not necessarily any sort of an indication.

"Perhaps."

The sudden light in her eyes as she set her cup down made him realize how green they were.

"You didn't have to tell me," he said at last. "It isn't a criminal offence."

"I'm aware of that, actually. I told you—because I don't know you."

"Simply because of that?"

"Partly because of that."

For the first time he was aware of her unnatural and unnaturally controlled tension.

"Come and dance."

In the next scene they were dancing, cocooned from the rest of the room, except for brief gaps in the enmeshing fabric through which Neil glimpsed other entwined couples, saw the Lumsdens leaving, remarked Cathy's lugubrious countenance on the far, unfeeling side of the present, and, finally, her Art Deco clock pointing to midnight.

"Shall we go?" His lips were already against Hilary Fielding's ear.

She murmured, "I think I'm ready to go. My bag's in the bedroom."

"I'll get it. What's it like?"

"Black patent with a diagonal red stripe. On the bed somewhere."

In Cathy's bedroom a couple were lying on her not very wide bed, so that most of the coats had fallen off on to the floor, and Neil had to stoop and rummage. Coming out with the bag in his hand, he met Cathy. She must have seen the bag instantly, because of the way she kept her eyes so carefully above the level where he was carrying it.

"I must go," he said, "I've got a day and a half tomorrow."

"Don't work too hard."

"I won't. Cathy, it's been a lovely party."

"I'm glad you enjoyed it." She was smiling diamanté rather than diamonds. Neil had an idea she had had more than usual to drink.

"Not just me."

"Yes, Hilary was the one we were mainly concerned with."

"I was meaning everyone."

"Thank you. Hilary, though, d'you think she's enjoyed herself?"

The unnatural sparkle in Cathy's eyes enabled her to look at him as she spoke without having to meet his gaze.

"Hilary will never be a hostess's dream, she's so unenthusiastic, but I should think she has."

"She couldn't be less like me, could she?"

"Probably not. But that's just to read the surface. And you're not invariably enthusiastic yourself."

"No, Neil, I'm not, you're quite right there."

There seemed to be several firsts that evening: it was the first time he had heard her weary, and he was caught unawares by a wave of compassion which sorted ill with his prevailing mood.

"Remind Hilary, will you," she said, staring at the bag he was holding, "that she's promised to come in in the morning."

"Remind her yourself." Hilary was standing beside Cathy, and Neil put her bag into her hand.

"I'll see you in the morning, Cathy," said Hilary languidly. "Not too early. All right? Thanks for a really super evening."

"I'm glad you enjoyed it," said Cathy lightly. "See yourselves out?"

They stood and looked after her as she went back into the sitting-room, to be claimed for dancing by John Underwood, the man she had invited in the hope that he would protect Neil from their mutual neighbour.

CHAPTER 5

Peter,

I was at my first party last night without you. That is, not to count the little affairs Clara and Arthur have devised for me a couple of times, both of which sent me away in a hysterical fury.

It wasn't like that last night, although I missed you so badly. But I'm not alone after all, I'm not alone, and even now it's because of you.

I don't know whether it was just that I wanted to deny you your right to be told first—which is absurd when you would rather not be told at all, rather not be horrified, disgusted . . . as I'm disgusted. . . . Oh, Peter, we've become monsters to one another, you and I. Anyway, I did something very odd and perverse. I told a stranger. Not even an acquaintance like Cathy. In Cathy's kitchen, over a cup of instant coffee, I told a stranger.

Oh, I still haven't told you, have I? I went to my new doctor on Thursday evening, and he confirmed that I'm pregnant. You talked me out of having children for seven years and then, when you'd reached the stage where you really knew why you didn't want them, when you'd reached that terrible last night, terrible for you, ridiculously wonderful for me, punishing yourself, sorry for me, you took me unawares. In every sense.

And now . . . that relationship you're trying to wipe out of your mind, to pretend never existed, an extra life will be lived because of it.

Yes, that's right, I'm not going to get rid of the baby. There were moments before I was certain I was going to have it, another moment when I woke up in the night after seeing the doctor, when I thought, better to get rid, break utterly free of someone who has broken so utterly free of me. But I think it was only that I had to look the possibility full on, to be able to dismiss it. I haven't any doubts now.

Peter, I'm still alive. And I'm not seeing the baby as something to alter the fact of the break between you and me. In fact I dislike the idea of you being associated with it after it's born as much as you'll dislike it yourself. It's the baby of our years together, not of now.

I had a letter from Mummy this morning, asking me to go home and see her. I probably will, now. I'll probably tell her what's going to happen and her pleasure will be stronger than her loathing for you. After all, it will still be a real baby, made in the usual way! So there'll be no fear of being on my own, trying to work and bring up a small child, I shall be able either to work and let the child spend the week with Mummy and Daddy, or give up the job for a time to look after it myself, because I shall make all of us happy by letting them help me out. I shan't be applying to you.

Happy. I just stopped to examine the word, it seemed so unfamiliar. No, I'm not happy, of course. But I have some hope.

I've just come back from helping Cathy clear up after last night's party. I felt a bit uncomfortable when I went in. It feels almost miraculous to be able to say "I felt" anything, even if only uncomfortable—but I think even without the baby I'd have felt something this morning, a rare unselfish something, because of Cathy being so nice and so single-mindedly concentrated on Detective-Inspector Carter.

I suppose I knew, in some vague far-off way, the first time I saw Neil Carter on the landing here, that there was something sort of waiting between him and me. Well, that's not unusual, the unusual thing is to have the situation going on being available—one sees people and gets that feeling and then, if nothing is done about it, the opportunity has gone. Another unusual thing is that I still have that objective sunset/picture attitude even while I'm aware of him in this other way of feeling that certain developments are quite simple and natural—irrespective of any social checks such as not really knowing him at all.

Not, Peter (and not that you care), that anything has in fact "happened" between Neil Carter and me. Not because Neil is any kind of a slouch—in fact I slapped him mildly down after the party. He asked me at midnight if I was ready to go and I said yes because I'd had enough and wanted to be alone with my new knowledge (but never alone now, Peter, impossible to be alone). I hardly thought he'd suggest anything, not with our actually leaving Cathy's flat together under Cathy's disjointed nose. (No, she's not quite so naïve: she was in fact rather airy and bright, which made me feel worse.) However, on the landing he actually offered me the choice of his flat or mine and I said we'd take both, he the one and I the other, and went in and shut my door before I saw his reaction.

This morning when I went in to Cathy she was like a bubbly drink which has been left with the stopper off. She was very sweet in a wan sort of a way, as well as looking as though she hadn't slept, and I made a point of getting it across that I'd gone straight home alone, and without any encouragement from Neil to do otherwise. It was absurd really, it wasn't so much that I didn't want Cathy to think that I'd "been with" her beloved—after all, she has no more claim to him than I have—but I didn't want her to think I could be guilty of such gross bad taste as to go with him straight out of her house. Only an accident of geography, of course—if we'd lived in different buildings the evening might well have ended differently, but there it was, although not apparently for Neil. I implied in an earlier letter, didn't I, that I feel there's something unscrupulous about him.

Cathy became almost herself again when I'd got my message over, and by the time I left we seemed to be pretty well restored, although with Cathy now facing her fear, I fancy, which is all to the good. I could almost have smiled at the sort of hopeless way she asked me what I thought of John Underwood, if I hadn't hated to see her like that. She asked me the odd other question, which she wouldn't have done if she'd been absolutely herself, and I did just about let her know that as far as "love" is concerned I have had it. It's the truth, which no doubt one should always tell if one possibly can.

I didn't tell her about the baby, I suppose because I want her good opinion, and if she thought I was carrying one man's baby, and looking at another, I would probably lose it. Oh dear.

All traces of Mr. Sz. have been wiped out, and the thin brilliance of my work surroundings has now changed to a sort of brooding sludge. "The Environment of Modern Man" reigns supreme. It's rather surprised me how, with the same walls and curtains and furniture, the whole place feels so different because of the different pictures. The new series may be representational, but for me it gives off a strong abstract flavour—of acute pessimism and depression. The palette-knife shapes of greens and browns are the same for the countryside and the factories, flat and dingy, all the skies are unfeatured grey, and the general gloom is absolutely unrelieved. One Julius Spender would be a permanent dark spot in the home, but a whole gallery of them . . . I find I preferred Mr. Sz., there was at least a sort of tinkly gaiety about his pictures, but Mr. Spender has antique colours without any antique grace.

Stephen was defensive even before I'd said anything, and I didn't say all that much. It's funny, I can't ever pin him down to saying anything as basic as whether he *likes* this modern thing, or that. Perhaps liking is an irrelevant concept with modern art, which would make the whole business more understandable. Perhaps it simply *is* business. I may get some idea if I ever see the inside of Stephen's home, and find out what he's chosen to live with, artwise. (No, he hasn't asked me yet. And no, if and when he does, it will be simply a gesture of our working friendship, there's nothing unspoken between Stephen and me. Yet I already know I like him better than I like Neil Carter. Curious.)

The other morning, sitting eating some toast, I suddenly had to dash over to the sink as if I'd just swallowed a tumblerful of salt water. I don't suppose it will happen again very often, if at all, as the three months are about up. So I suppose I've been lucky. And in a way I feel as well as I've ever felt, without yet feeling at all heavy or ungainly. But that stage won't last for long.

I wonder how well you are. Whether you're being as careful with food and exercise as the doctor and I insisted you should be. Probably not, as Anthony's no housewife—oh, God, I wish I hadn't written that, why did I write that?

No, I can't of course entirely prevent myself from exercising my imagination, although fortunately I nearly always scare myself off in the early stages. Sometimes it's as bad to think of the house and Anthony as to think of you and Anthony. When I've visited some women in their houses, I've had the feeling that really they were hardly more at home there than I was, the visitor. I was always very much at home in my house, which is probably why it's such bloody agony to be away from it, and to think of Anthony in the kitchen. (I've just remembered that evening when the three of us had been out and Anthony decided he was going to help me do bacon and eggs—we were in stitches all over the place, all over nothing. Peter, I liked him, I liked the three of us, I never felt so secure.)

Well, I can only hope Dr. French keeps up his warnings about you and too much food and drink. (And, just now and then, hope that he doesn't.)

Perhaps it's my worries about your health which keep giving me this dream. It's strange, I suppose by now I must know what I'm going to find before I wake up, but each time, I sense the evil on the landing with the same absolutely indescribable shock of horror, and get the same punch when I see what you look like in your chair. I thought I tried, last night, to move a bit nearer to you, get a better idea of what had happened, but I was rooted to the spot, and when I tried to move I just got an appalling ache in my leg—and woke up to that awful itchy pain of pins and needles coming round. In the dream I keep trying to exercise some kind of choice, to break out of the awful inevitable progress of it, but I can't. Last night I noticed the spot of rust beginning on the lamp bracket by the front door—no bigger, of course, than when I last saw it—but that was the only variation I could manage, and it even sort of hurt, physically, to register it. I think I've been hoping that with the start of the baby I wouldn't have the dream any more, but I still have it just about as often. There really are nights, now, when I hold off from falling asleep. The only "good" result is that, of course, I *do* sleep, far better than I did in the weeks after I left. Obviously a cure for insomnia is to find some reason for staying awake!

I rang Clara yesterday and asked her to come and see me. It was easy to tell how pleased she was—although I sensed she was a bit on edge. In a way the telephone can tell you more about someone's morale than seeing them face to face. I suppose that's because the voice is so reflective of how one feels, and when there's no distraction in the way of sight you hear every nuance. There was a strain in Clara's voice, but she didn't need urging to come over. I expect I shall tell her about the baby. I think I'd like dear Arthur to know, too (I expect, among his rigid little series of what one does and one doesn't, there's a clause that says pregnant women must be left alone). But not you, Peter. Well, Clara won't tell you if I ask her not to. And I'm sure there's another of Arthur's clauses which says that promises are to be kept.

Arthur hasn't been back, thank heaven. I find myself on edge for the half-hour or so after I'm home from work, because he may be ringing the bell at any minute. Oh, Peter, you shouldn't have left me to this, you shouldn't.

I've no idea what my reaction will be next time I see Neil Carter, or how I'll behave. I'll probably take my cue from him. Because it doesn't matter.

I've just realized that one reason I'm not feeling quite so bothered about Arthur is the thought of Neil Carter across the landing. Silly, and I think he's almost always out. But he does live there, Arthur's living antithesis as much as you are. I think I shall tell him about Arthur if I get the opportunity.

I know, actually, I shall get the opportunity.

Hilary

CHAPTER 6

There was a minor breakthrough on Saturday in the case he was working on, and his tiredness as he drove home in the late evening was braced by a mild glow of achievement. He paused on his landing as the lift gates closed behind him, looking from one door to another, aware of a dual reaction of amusement and rue. It was the third door, the one not under scrutiny, which opened. Miss Prince emerged, smiling eagerly.

"Ah, Mr. Carter! I heard the lift and wondered . . . One so rarely manages . . . Mr. Carter, I wanted to have a word with you about the persistent disappearance of my polyanthus. You know the management committee agreed that I should look after the strip of flower-bed under my window. A long way under, yes"—as if he had made the point—"but no one on the lower floors was interested. . . . First I lost my winter-flowering aconites, and now the polyanthus. It could be someone in the building. Or it could be anyone from outside. I keep as much of a lookout as I can, but I haven't been able to catch anybody either coming or going, much less *in flagrante delicto*." Miss Prince gave a nervous laugh, pulling at pieces of pale hair which looked as if they had been killed by continual drastic perming. She was wearing bedroom slippers of a classic type. "So I thought, I'll try to get a word with Detective-Inspector Carter. He's just the man to—oh, but forgive me, Mr. Carter, where are my manners, I was so excited to have managed . . . You must come in and have a coffee while I'm telling you, you really must excuse—"

"I'm afraid you really must excuse *me*, Miss Prince." Neil seized on the opportunity, offering the kind but firm smile he found so useful. "I have a telephone call to make at precisely"—he consulted his watch—"eight o'clock. You'll appreciate . . . Anyway," he went on rapidly, as Miss Prince's small thin features failed to register appreciation, "all I could do would be to relay your complaint to the local station, which you can do far better yourself with your exact knowledge of all the facts. Tell them that you come at my recommendation," he added, so that a gratified reaction at last became evident, "of course. It's very annoying for you," he now allowed himself, "I'd be furious, and I only hope the local people can help. Don't be too optimistic, and you might also have a word with the management secretary. Thank you for suggesting coffee, but I really must . . ." He held up his wrist to display his watch to her, allowing his smile to brighten. It brought its usual response.

"Well, thank you very much, Mr. Carter, you're very kind. I'll go round in the morning. And I'll certainly have a word with Mr. Rigby if you really think—"

"I do, Miss Prince, I do. Excuse me now."

Miss Prince's door closed before he had his open, but he didn't resume his contemplation of the other two brass-studded ciphers. He shut himself briskly into his flat, relaxing only when he had assembled some pâté, toast, and a large gin and tonic on a tray and placed them on a small table by the sitting-room window.

Sipping his drink, looking out on the fine fading evening and the few visible branches of Cathy's plane tree, he considered the events of the night before. He had gone to bed in a whipped-up anger at Hilary Fielding for saying good night to him so abruptly on the landing—as much because he resented his acknowledgement that her behaviour had been better than his, as from any sort of frustration.

But it was still more agreeable to think of Hilary than of Cathy—Cathy one moment so attentively still, the next so unnaturally bright, particularly as the picture was superimposed on the familiar one of Cathy when she was giving him a snack, or coffee, her cheerfulness and enthusiasm reaching out and enheartening him, whatever the mood in which he had come to her door. . . .

The heady coolness of Hilary Fielding's announcement, what it could indicate of her reactions generally . . .

At half past nine, Neil rang Cathy's bell.

"Hello, Neil." She was herself, if underextended. "Come in?"

"If I may."

"Of course."

He followed her first, as always, across the hall into the sitting-room, aware of the unaccustomed quietness of her step.

"Coffee, Neil?"

"If it's no trouble." He winced at his unnatural politeness. And it would have been natural for Cathy to react against it, but she merely answered, "It never is," and went slowly out to the kitchen. Neil followed her, leaning in the doorway in his customary style. Like the sitting-room, the kitchen was restored to order. Under the fluorescent brilliance, thinking of Hilary Fielding, he saw that Cathy was paler than he had yet seen her, and dark under the eyes.

"Are you all right?" he asked, before he could counsel himself against a question which might possibly be misunderstood. "You don't look very well," he added, defining the range of his concern.

"Oh, I'm all right. Just a bit tired. Can you reach that tin down for me? Thanks."

"Well, it's a tiredness fairly earned. That was a good party."

"I'm glad you enjoyed it."

He thought that she really was listless, not putting it on.

"I did. Everyone did. I have a slight sense of achievement tonight, myself." She made her first quick movement since his arrival, turning her head towards him, where she was bent over the kettle. Chastising himself for an even more unwise ambiguity, Neil went on swiftly, "We had a breakthrough today on the case. Not the major one, but important."

"I'm glad for you. Must you work tomorrow?"

"I must regularly phone in. I don't somehow think there'll be anything else so soon."

"You can have a lazy Sunday, then."

She picked up the tray, and as usual he took it out of her hands and followed her, *lento* rather than *allegro*, back into the sitting-room.

"Yes. Would you like a walk in a park, or something? We could go to Kew for instance. Just so long as I can telephone."

Now, he thought, she was concealing her reaction.

"That sounds a super idea, Neil." Before the party, the idea would have had her coursing about the room, straightening this, ferreting for that. She sat forward on the sofa. "I really should have liked to come," she said calmly. He had always known she was generous, but hardly suspected the sophistication. "However—I've promised to go over to Winnie for the day."

"Winnie! Must you?" All at once his mental picture of Cathy dancing among the trees of Kew was for his own delectation.

"Oh, Neil, of course I must. I haven't been over to see her for ages, and she'll be making a great lunch and everything. I'll have to go."

"I'm sorry," he said truthfully, while aware of one source of uneasiness disappearing. "Another Sunday."

"Another Sunday, yes."

"Have you seen your parents recently?"

"Not all that recently, no. I think I may go home next weekend."

"Remember me to them. But of course I'll see you before you go."

"Of course, yes."

There was no doubt of the constraint between them; the new quietness of Cathy was pushing Neil, too, into a new role—an initiatory, almost cajoling role. He found himself glad, albeit a little sorry that he should be, when he had been there long enough to suggest leaving. Cathy made no attempt to detain him.

"I expect we're both tired," she observed when they were standing in the open front doorway. It was as near as she had got to any acknowledgement of the change between them.

"I expect so." Very briefly he hesitated, while he denied his instinct to kiss her cheek. "Good night, child."

It was probably the most honest comment he could make, and he had another pang when he saw that it failed to elicit any reaction.

"Good night, Neil. Thanks for looking in."

"When are you off tomorrow, then?"

"Oh, about ten. Good night."

"Good night."

He rang Hilary Fielding's bell at a quarter past eleven the next morning, after a luxurious natural awakening, late enough to find sunshine across his bed, a slow breakfast by the window, and a telephone call which sanctioned his liberty for at least another three hours.

Neil heard footsteps and then silence, wherein he knew that a human eye was being applied to the Cyclopean spy-hole in the door before him. It made him realize that there was never any time between Cathy's quick step and her pulling open of the front door, and he made a mental note to exact a promise that in the future she would look before offering access.

He was not pleased, though, that Hilary was enabled to prepare her reaction.

"Good morning, Neil."

She stood, tall and still, in her doorway, wearing a gilt-edged kaftan and no expression.

"Our private eyes," said Neil, "were put in for purposes of safety, but they also fulfil a social role. Has it ever struck you?"

"Actually, yes." She moved slowly back from the doorway, and Neil walked into an immediate impression of calm and space, derived perhaps from the walls and carpet and prints, which gave a theme of oatmeal and sepia.

"It didn't strike me," said Neil cheerfully, "until just now."

She said merely, ironically, "Come in," and preceded him into the sitting-room. If Cathy hadn't changed, the contrast between the mood and pace of the two women, leading him across their halls, would have been almost ludicrous.

"This isn't a bad time?" he asked, realizing he now felt as easy and cheerful as he was sounding. The sun drenched the room, confirming his first reaction to the flat. "Your place feels bigger than mine," he said, looking round, "although I was assured when I bought that I was at no disadvantage."

"I'm certain you aren't. If I'd had an edge, the estate agent would surely have let me know. It's rather fascinating, the differences people make with the same basic shape. Have you had any coffee?"

"Yes. That's why I came at this sort of between-time. Not for coffee, but to ask you—"

The doorbell rang and he saw her freeze, was pleased to find he was getting, after all, her instinctive reaction to it. Unless with him in the flat it was different from what it had been when she was alone and (his vanity in this area was so natural he gave it the most cursory internal grimace) wondering if it was Neil Carter at the door.

She went slowly out of the room and Neil, moving about it to examine the pale, airy watercolours on each wall, heard unfamiliar male and female voices in the hall. When Hilary came back he thought she deliberately sought his eyes and that there was a baffled look in hers, despite a half-smile which he had not seen on her face before. She was followed by a woman of about thirty-five, overweight and untidy, yet attractive and radiating immediate warmth and energy, and a tall thin man who contradicted her in every way, from his short straight brown hair, through his neat spring Sunday gear of cravat, pastel shirt and thin expensive trousers, to his flawless suede shoes. The contrast was sharp between the faces, too, the woman's features generous and vaguely defined, her mouth mobile, her colour high, the man's small and sharp in a white face, the mouth under a tiny pale moustache scarcely moving as it briefly and tightly smiled.

"My neighbour, Neil Carter," Hilary told them. "Neil, this is . . ." He was aware of hesitation, as if she was considering more than one possible mode of introduction. ". . . Clara and Arthur Shaw."

Neil's training made him watch the other two faces as Hilary made her choice. The man showed no reaction beyond the minute movement which was the retraction of his smile, the woman looked as if she might be waiting, and then, when it was clear Hilary had no more to say about them, she gazed affectionately at Hilary with her large expressive eyes, shrugging her shoulders so that her heavy bosom visibly shook behind its feebly protective blouse. Neil decided it was merely the low angle of Mrs. Shaw's bosom which had made him doubtful about her age—if she wasn't thirty-five, she was younger.

"Hello, Neil Carter." Clara Shaw gave him a comradely smile, throwing herself down on the sofa. There was a dual impression of energy and repose which he found pleasing. Arthur Shaw said, "How do you do?" and went to stare sternly out of the window.

"What are you doing in St. John's Wood, on a Sunday morning?" Hilary actually looked at Neil as she asked the question, the smile growing in her eyes while on her lips it remained ambiguous. Neil thought she was glad he was there.

"A fine spring morning!" said Clara Shaw, throwing one leg over the other in a large gesture. She had the full calves and fine ankles of a physical type which had never appealed to Neil. Her smile, which was attractively crooked over uneven teeth, was on her husband, and Neil suspected she was quoting him. "We thought we'd have lunch Hampstead way, walking on the Heath before and after."

"We hoped you'd feel like joining us." Neil jumped inwardly; Arthur Shaw had somehow given no warning that he was going to speak, and had in fact scarcely turned his head away from the window.

Neil looked at Hilary. Her eyes were still on him.

"To her that hath shall be given," said Neil. "Hilary had just consented to have lunch with me. However . . ."

"Oh, heavens!" said Clara Shaw. Another extravagant gesture reversed the order of her knees. "So long as everyone has some company, that's all that matters."

"Anyway." This time Arthur Shaw turned round to face the room. "We could all move off together." He was looking at his wife as he spoke, then at Hilary. He coughed into his hand.

Clara Shaw gazed round the three expressionless faces.

"That would be nice," she said. Even when she wasn't smiling her face was amiable. "But I think, another time." Her eyes on Neil, she smiled again. He sensed scrutiny. "Today, I think, we'll go our ways. Where does yours lie, Neil Carter?"

"We were just discussing it when you arrived. I was about to mention Richmond."

Mentioning it now, he was aware of a general reaction which he couldn't define, but it made him certain Hilary knew the couple well.

"How nice," said Clara Shaw, after a few seconds' silence. Hilary was walking across the room.

"You won't go," she said, "without a drink. It's almost noon."

Arthur Shaw came away from the window, rubbing his hands.

"Very kind of you, my dear." The conformation of his mouth perhaps made it difficult for a smile to show. Certainly his general demeanour gave the impression that he was feeling well-disposed. "Let me help you." He followed Hilary to the corner cupboard.

"What will you have, Clara?" asked Hilary.

"I'd better have sherry, I shall want to drink lots of wine at lunch. What do you do, Neil Carter?"

Neil found himself sitting down beside her on the sofa. Her brown hair had a sort of careless smattering of gold, as if she had been distracted by something more important to her while in the process of lightening it. It was surprising that features so imprecise could be so sensitive. And Neil sensed in Clara Shaw someone who would not need to have things spelled out.

"I'm a policeman."

"Now, that wouldn't have been one of the possibilities I should have imagined."

"You imagine things about people, then, while you're waiting to find out?"

"Yes. Don't you?"

"I must. Perhaps, it would be more accurate to say that I try to read signs."

"Of course. You couldn't do your job if you weren't super-observant, could you?"

Arthur Shaw handed his wife a glass. "For you?" he asked Neil.

"Oh, sherry, please."

Hilary took her drink to the window, to where there was only one small chair. Neil saw that Shaw was watching her sit down and that only then did he lower himself slowly to the edge of a chair which faced the window.

Clara Shaw gave a heavy, contented sigh. "Weeks of walkable Sundays ahead. I love the thought of it. It might even do my shape some good, if I ate less." She laughed, an agreeable sound. "You must walk some time today, you two."

"What do you do during the week?" Neil asked her.

"Arthur would say I play." Her glance at her husband appeared to satisfy her, although there was no visible response. "I would say I'm a business woman. I have a flower shop. Well, half of one."

"You're lucky if your work feels like play."

"It does, really. Yes, I am lucky." Portrait of a happy woman, thought Neil, as Clara Shaw offered him another warm smile. Arthur Shaw hardly struck him as a happy man, but that could be as much because of his nature as the pattern of his life. It was Clara Shaw who struggled to her feet from the deep sofa, saying it was time to go if everyone was to get the most out of the fine day.

"I'll hope to see you again, Neil Carter." Her hand was rough and dry. She put her cheek against Hilary's until Hilary drew away. "Can I come over for lunch on Wednesday half-day? Here or Mr. Sz.'s?"

"Come here. I'll arrange with Mrs. Tilsley to take a proper lunch-hour. And it isn't Mr. Sz. any more. You can come back with me if you've nothing else on and see who's taken Mr. Sz.'s place."

"Just what I should like."

"I'll call by one evening, Hilary," said Arthur Shaw. His voice was deeper and stronger than his appearance suggested.

"That's very kind of you, Arthur." Neil thought her voice was flatter than usual. She led the way to the front door, turning round as she opened it. "Especially as you may have a fruitless journey. Some evenings now I hang on at the gallery. We tend to get people coming in late, and there's always work I can't get on with when we're open."

"Right. I'll take the risk." Again the brief stretch of the mouth which must be a smile. "Your boss being reasonable, I hope?"

"Stephen?" She seemed surprised. "Oh, heavens, yes. He must be the most reasonable boss in North London. I've been—very fortunate." She said the last two words with an emphasis lost on Neil, which he noticed had an uncomfortable effect on both the Shaws. Clara Shaw blinked and half put out her hand. Arthur Shaw lifted his and coughed behind it. When the door was closed on them Hilary and Neil went back into the sitting-room in silence, and in silence Hilary poured them more sherry.

When they were standing beside the window, Neil said, "Forgive me if I went too far. My instinct isn't infallible."

"I didn't particularly want to have lunch with Clara and Arthur,

with or without you. And thank you for the invitation." They turned
to smile briefly at one another.

"I really was about to issue it when the bell rang. Do you know
the Shaws well?"

"Yes. Arthur is Peter's brother." He waited. "And Peter and I
were together for seven years. So I do know them. Clara, in fact, has
been my best friend."

"Has been?"

"Hasn't stopped being. It's just—one talks about a friend in need,
but since Peter and I split up I somehow haven't wanted even Clara
as much. Maybe it's the connection."

"You haven't any other friends."

She didn't stop to consider. "Not really. Peter and I were rather
mutually exclusive."

"So what went wrong?" In all the circumstances, he didn't offer
any qualifying apology to his question.

"Peter decided he was homosexual." She gave one of her rare full
smiles, indulgent of the look of distaste he had been shocked into
displaying. "Oh, there had been signs, I read them with hindsight.
But it had been good. He never attempted to deny that. Poor Peter.
The change was so drastic, so sort of involuntary, he couldn't really
even go on liking me."

"So the baby?"

"Peter's baby. He'd always managed to talk me out of having one.
I understood that too, of course, in the end. The last night we spent
together he managed—to be sorry for me. Oh, he didn't intend it to
be to *that* extent, of course, but when you force yourself to something, you can overdo it. . . ."

The only emotion he had seen in her at all was this triumph. The
very lack of other response seemed to Neil to point to how much
there had been.

"So, again," he asked her, "why are you telling me?"

"Because I haven't told anyone else. And because I don't know
you."

"As you said the other night. Well, I can understand that, and
you must know by instinct that I'm the last person to feel flattered. I
was merely there at the psychological moment."

"That's probably right, but you can be a little flattered, perhaps,
because I wouldn't have said anything to anyone I so much as suspected of being wrong."

"Cathy would have been wrong?"

"Not wrong or right. It had to be a male, but I don't know why, so don't ask me. I have been called a man's woman."

"Tell me something more, then, and yes, you will be satisfying my curiosity. Is there—one particular man?"

She said steadily, "So far as I know." In the tiny pause he felt her gathering her forces. "Living in. Peter's junior partner Anthony Carey. I liked him. Oh, I knew his propensities, his being the feminine part, everyone knew. He was clever and amusing, the three of us did things together, we were always laughing. . . ."

She stopped again, and in the longer silence Neil was compelled to look at her. She gazed back without expression, motionless but for a twitch at the corner of her mouth. He was unable to break the silence and eventually she said, even more softly, "Clever and cosy, that's what he was, a good friend for a woman. I have to put everything about him into the past tense, of course, because for me now he is the devil incarnate."

There was no reply to this. "Is there something about Richmond?"

"Only that the business is there and we—Peter—lives at Kew." He could tell her shudder was involuntary. But after it, he felt her eyes were once more seeing him. "Although I was the only one who walked in either the Park or the Gardens, unless Peter particularly wanted to please me."

"He didn't like exercise?"

"Not the least little bit. And he was—I presume is—somewhat overweight and not very healthy."

"Is Arthur Shaw in the business?"

"No! Arthur's a solicitor. Not mine. Neil—"

"I know. Enough. Last question. Will you have lunch with me in town, then walk in a Royal Park?"

He liked driving in London on a Sunday. There was an exhilaration in being able to move steadily through streets where on weekdays he must jerk along in low gear and lose all sense of that dramatic change of ambience which comes with no more than the turning of a corner and which for him was the most exciting thing about London. He felt it now, moving smoothly from the Edgware Road into Park Lane, as he felt also a tension in Hilary, aware that she was staring past him up the Bayswater Road, and that she relaxed as they completed the transition, passing Marble Arch on their right. He tucked his question away for the time being, but he probably had his answer, because the Bayswater Road led, eventually, to Kew.

They had lunch at a restaurant in Knightsbridge, English to accord with the Sunday lunch associations which persisted from his childhood. Neil found Hilary an easy person to eat with, she was relaxed during both speech and silence, and he had no need to veil his approving glance, falling now on the gestures of her hands, now on the curve of her cheek or shoulder; plainly it did not disconcert her. When they spoke it was of Neil's life rather than hers, then of the building whose roof they shared, and their respective anecdotes concerning Miss Prince. This led naturally to Cathy, and the only uncomfortable part of the meal for Neil.

"She's exceedingly fond of you," said Hilary.

From any other woman Neil would probably have interpreted the statement as a question, but from Hilary Fielding he took it as no more than an expression of her opinion. He had a funny sort of reaction to it, not all guilty reluctance.

"I know. And I'm very fond of her. A sort of favourite uncle."

"She's not *that* young. Nor you quite that old."

"In her ways she's very young," he said firmly, refusing to accept the complicity of Hilary's look. But some sense of loyalty, vaguely surprising him, made him add, "It's one of the nice things about her."

"Her painting isn't particularly young."

"What do you think of it?"

"I think it's good. I'd like Stephen to see it."

They began to talk, then, about Hilary's work, and their mutual reactions to painting and furniture and buildings and this, with appreciative comments on the weather and their surroundings, was the subject of their sparse conversation during the afternoon, as they roamed the acres of Kensington Gardens.

"I like parks because one just *is* in them, one doesn't have to *do*," murmured Hilary, during one of their umpteen tacitly agreed stops to stand and stare. They were beside the Round Pond, its sun-dazzled surface broken into faceted gleams by birds and small boats, the edge deep in people. A tiny boy stumbled against their legs, and Hilary stooped to steady him, then to direct him towards the right pair of outstretched arms. As she straightened up she drew a noticeable breath and laced her fingers with Neil's. Once or twice during the afternoon he had taken her hand as they walked or stood still, and met neither recoil nor response. He had always been affected by the least physical initiative from a cool woman whom he found attractive, but now, beside the Round Pond, he almost disregarded his reaction, concentrating on the real reason for the gesture, which he knew was Hilary's sudden recall of her condition.

"Are you actually fond of children? I wouldn't somehow have thought you particularly were."

"I don't think I am. I mean, simply because that's what they are. This child—mine—it's not because it's a child, it's because it's—well, another person who's connected with me and not with anyone else. Depending on me. Built-in togetherness."

Hilary laughed, a warm attractive sound, and Neil was shocked that he had never heard it before that moment, at the thought that once she must have laughed regularly, and now scarcely at all. Yet she was not a person he could feel sorry for, she had too much in her favour.

An uneasiness settled on him as he drove home, shot through with annoyance when he realized it was connected with his calculation that Cathy would almost certainly be back from Winnie's.

"I do have one more question for you today," he said, in the moment where he observed the lightning change from town to suburb. "Is it over?"

"Is what over?"

"The day." He didn't really want to be devious or whimsical, and he went on quickly, "Will you come in for a snack supper? Or offer me one?"

"I've plenty of salad stuff. You can come to me."

She answered without hesitation, if without enthusiasm. He knew his relief was as much because there would now be no necessity for delay on the landing, as for the invitation.

A lot later, as he walked the few steps home, he had lost all sense of discomfort. He thought he had renewed his glad acceptance of the pattern of his life.

CHAPTER 7

Peter.

Sitting in the window again, watching people walking in the road below, envying the simplicity and lightness of their progress. (Arrogant assumption, and Neil Carter says my special thing is the ease of my carriage and my walk. So when you're all heavy and bent and hugging yourself against flying apart it needn't show, and I suppose the road could be full of walking wounded.)

Neil Carter. We had lunch on Sunday in town and then walked all afternoon in Kensington Gardens. Lots of people, but still lots of space. I kept thinking of that picture we liked which we had in the shop for a while, of park and trees and man and dog. I think I really did like that picture enough to have kept it, and so I should have kept it. I find I mourn errors of omission far more than errors of commission in the long run. Opportunities lost rather than opportunities rashly seized. One may end up bruised by those, but not diminished.

It's bad today, the baby isn't helping, I've never missed you so savagely. But next time Neil Carter comes to the flat, I'll probably let him stay again.

I suppose I'm dismayed, somewhere, to find myself sleeping with a man and scarcely giving it a thought. But it's all the far side of you and the loss of you, it's as if only a part of me is available to react and the essential me isn't affected at all. This must be the sort of schizoid thing, I suppose, which turns some women into drabs after they've lost the person who counted. I'm thinking of the nice little girl in Maugham's *The Razor's Edge*, who went down and down and down. Not that I've ever been a nice little girl, and I think (I hope!) I'm too anchored by things like pictures and furniture ever to go completely off. Also too indolent.

And it was the baby I thought of when Neil was with me, or at least soon afterwards. I did feel ashamed then, as if I'd let someone burst into his room where he was quietly and innocently sleeping.

The dream's no less frequent, although I didn't (a point) have it while Neil Carter was beside me. I really do find myself, now, in the dream, trying to observe. Not with much success, although the last time, last night, I was aware of various landmarks along the Bayswater Road I haven't noticed for a long time. But that could be simply because I looked down the real Bayswater Road when I was in town with Neil on Sunday. I seemed to remember a whole host of details from that one quick glance. Otherwise the dream was as it always is, and I had that feeling again of actual physical pain as I tried to make my legs move me nearer to your chair when I'd made the sitting-room.

Perhaps I'm just being melodramatic and silly, feeling the dream means something, feeling it points to the future instead of the past. And seeing you as I do, well, I did see you once, when you had what the doctor called that warning attack, your face went slack and you were redder than usual and for a few awful moments I couldn't get through to you. Well, that's the climax of the dream, that's all.

But my terror, and the sense of evil . . . that doesn't come from anything that's happened. Oh, I was scared blind, of course, when you had that attack. But not this *terror*.

I spend all day, in a way, being afraid that I'm going to have the dream again that night.

I still feel well, but I don't see myself reconciling to the dreariness of the Environment of Modern Man as I did, somewhat to my astonishment, to Mr. Sz. And I didn't take to Mr. Julius Spender one bit when Stephen introduced us yesterday morning. He takes himself with extreme seriousness and was even more full of explanations than Mr. Sz., without being so spontaneously enthusiastic. Mr. Sz. was obviously carried away, but Mr. Spender is all posture and deliberate effect.

Stephen and I lunched today at Stephen's favourite trattoria, nice and comfortable and stimulating on the aesthetic level. I do hope he'll ask me to his house eventually, because I become more and more curious to find out what he has chosen to live with in the way of pictures and furniture and décor. I'm trying to decide in my mind, for the amusement of comparing my imaginary Stephen surroundings with the real thing—if ever I get the opportunity! But I suppose I shall reach the sort of easy point with him where I can invite myself. Perhaps I've reached it already, but I'd prefer the invitation to come from him. But he's so retiring! I expect I'll tell him about the baby quite soon.

I told Clara when she came over yesterday. (She and Arthur arrived unheralded at the flat together on Sunday, to my amazement;
somehow I never expected them to visit me as a pair any more. Luckily Neil Carter had just come over—also unheralded—and I still had
this feeling of relief that he was around. I think he tried to read my
reaction before telling them, untruthfully, when they asked me to
lunch, that he had already done so. He read it right—I really didn't
want to have lunch with them. Arthur suggested—naturally—that we
all lunch together, and it was Clara who vetoed that one.) Clara surprised me a bit by hiding any reaction to my news about the baby.
But then, I've hardly been my usual self with her of late. I spent all
our lunch-time in the flat trying, and failing, to tell her, which I suppose was the first uncharacteristic thing, and then eventually I said it
when we were in the gallery, in fact when Clara had followed me
into the back room and we were in semi-darkness while I was rooting
for something. I had my back to her and I certainly *heard* her reaction, unless it was coincidence, she moved suddenly and slipped into
a heap of brown paper which is waiting for me to tidy it, and there
was a fusillade of crackling as she went down. I hauled her up and
when she'd thanked me a bit exaggeratedly I saw there really wasn't
any reaction at all, at least not showing, except for a bit of—well, embarrassment, which is hardly Clara. (It's disconcerting how you can
find yourself in a situation changed for the worse, with no real idea
of how it got that way.) We'd sat down again on our respective upright chairs before she held out her hands to me and said that, judging by the way I'd told her, she thought she had to be glad for me. I
confirmed that she had, and then she smiled, and hugged me, and
obviously *was*. I suppose there are a whole host of things which
could have checked her—the necessity of thinking of you, for a start,
in the old way, when the times she'll have seen you since I left she
will have started thinking of you in your new way. And then (I
should have put this first), the fact that she hasn't any children herself.

We never did get round, did we, to tactfully trying to find out why
Clara and Arthur haven't had any children? It still surprises me that
Clara has never offered me so much as a hint, she's so open about absolutely everything else. She asked me if she was to tell Arthur, and I
hope I didn't hesitate before saying yes, of course. I think until she
arrived I had still been playing with the idea of telling her "about
Arthur" (just saying that makes something to tell, hateful). But

when the opportunity came, I couldn't. Anyway, it would have been pure self-indulgence.

So whatever her first reaction had been, her last was the affectionate old Clara, glad because I was glad. By that stage, I was feeling rather regretful that I'd turned to her so little since you and I parted. I don't want to lose Clara, or even to feel the least bit estranged from her. And by the time she left, I felt we were back as close as we've ever been. She had nothing to say about the work of our precious environmentalist Julius, and I deplored her cheerful lack of taste as much as you and I ever did, but not this time to her face, so perhaps I am still being a bit more "careful" than usual. But really, I think darling Clara would hardly notice any difference between being surrounded by Mr. Spender, or by all the marvellous things in the shop. It certainly wouldn't affect her spirits, which if you think about it is rather to her credit!

Neil Carter, albeit untutored by your standards, likes "nice things." I've just realized I haven't been in his flat as yet. I'm a little curious, but not so curious as I am about Stephen. That sounds so perverse, it can only say something about my real priorities.

Arthur hasn't called again, but learning about the baby will be an opportunity he surely won't miss. Neil's going away for a couple of nights tomorrow, and I feel worse about Arthur right away, at the thought of Neil not being there. It's all the more a stupid feeling because Arthur's only likely to call on his way home (oh, I hope that's the only time he's likely to call), and Neil isn't often here at that time, anyway. I think that when I see him next I'll tell him about Arthur.

I've asked Cathy in tonight for coffee, she'll be arriving any moment. I made a point—apparently in passing—of letting Neil know she was coming, so that he wouldn't ring while she was here. Without it having been put into words, he will now ring my doorbell at any time he feels like it, unless warned off.

Why, I wonder, did I warn him this time? I'm not ashamed of myself with Neil. I'm afraid it was simply to spare everybody embarrassment—which is as potent as anything in the destruction of friendships. I don't want to lose Cathy's friendship—and I'm even less happy at the prospect of Neil losing it. Strange. Also, I hope, I am a little anxious to spare Cathy pain. But I shan't worry about it when she's actually here, I shall just be glad to see her. You once said I had terrific nerve.

It's a beautiful evening, tiny little clouds against the most delicate

blue sky. The sun's gone round the building now, but it's still shin-
ing down on the road and everything's glowing, sort of extra itself.
And I learned from Stephen today that Mr. Spender will be exhibit-
ing with us for only one week longer. I can't imagine that the devil I
don't know can be any more dehumanizing. . . .

Peter. I had to wait then for a cold wave to go over. Kew is in this
world, in this city. Hundreds of people go there every day. In the
summer, thousands. But I must not, and I probably want to go more
than every single one of them. As I said before, that's being civ-
ilized. Well, we must hold on to our civilization. Yes, I really believe
that. But sometimes I think the effort's going to break me in two.
Baby and all.

Hilary

CHAPTER 8

*The familiar smooth steady progress. The lights each side of her
streaming ahead in a golden spear whose point was always in the distance. The sodium glow giving to the emptiness, the straightness, the
sudden item, a sombre clarity. A parked car, two figures turning
down an entry, the glimpsed menace of a blank, blanched face. None
of them impeding her disembodied, inevitable advance.*

*Marble Arch. Did she remember being there with Neil Carter,
going straight on along Park Lane in a world which now seemed
impossibly bright and safe?*

*The car floating round the well-known island, dreamy awareness to
right and left of the solid buildings of the Bayswater Road. Of
sodium orange refracted through branches, railings, the mystery of a
park by night. Aware, but not distracted, as if on a laid-down track.*

*Notting Hill. Shops. A dozen in darkness for one alight. Old ter-
races going off to either hand. So familiar, and in the lighted dark so
strange. Impressions. Figures standing in groups, motionless. Then
moving as the film unfroze. Figures coming out of buildings in thin
shafts of light.*

Holland Park. Breathing trees and green, or imagining it. To her right the triangular wedge of Shepherd's Bush.

The Goldhawk Road, everything all at once smaller-scale, closer, less solid, less certain among the shadows.

Then a widening street, houses, on her left the narrow entrance to Ravenscourt Park, she the only constant in the changing landscape, advancing so steadily while inside herself going faster and faster. . . .

Stamford Brook tube station on her right, right into the Chiswick High Road, no traffic to wait for, on towards the bridge. Starting now, as always, to try and look for something different. Something extra. Failing.

The mass of motorway engineering, above and around, remembering how it grew, and in what chaos. Drifting south, crossing Kew Bridge, into Kew Road, the Garden wall going along beside her, punctuated by its closed gates. Past Newens Café, past brief sharp thoughts of eating maids of honour with Peter, turning left . . . right . . . the pineapple posts ahead. Turning in, trying as always to see if the broken bit of carved name on the open gate had been repaired, and as always failing because of being unable to stop. Aware of the rhododendron branches to the left tapping acknowledgement on the windscreen, turning again, at last slowing down, stopping.

Not wanting to get out but having to, moving as inevitably on foot as at the wheel. Not being able to pause to look for anything, however hard she tried. Recording as new only the patter of bird splash on one of the bulbous wooden pillars supporting the porch, feeling the deep splits in the wood before using the key which was in her hand without her being aware of looking for it.

The familiar movement of the key in the lock, shutting the door behind her as always, as always hoping its fastening click wouldn't disturb, wouldn't summon up—what?

On the stairs now, more wood under her right hand, the broad carved balustrade, her foot finding the hole in the carpet. The turn of the stair, apprehension rising and growing steadily into terror. Terror mounting across the landing, the sitting-room door half-open as always, wanting nothing less than to go in, but going in, seeing the pale arc of the drawn curtains, the table with the vase and the lamp close to the chair. Wanting to delay, trying to look round the room and see other things but her eyes being forced to the centre, to the chair, to the man lolling in it, his face distorted, it could be by shad-

*ows, but his eyes showing white, something between his lips, his
tongue. . . .*

*Her feet clamped to the carpet, leaning forward, trying to see
clearly, trying to hold in the voice which was already shouting inside
her, the shout forcing its way up. Into her chest. Her throat. Burst-
ing out in his name, over and over, louder and louder.*

*And then sobbing, staring at what wasn't moving, not even the
thing between the lips, straining to move forward, feet chained, until
suddenly they were tumbling her backwards, out and out, down and
down, movement, distance, light, dark, not one after the other but
all at the same time, whirling round in a circle which went faster and
faster until it was just a coloured thread.*

*Lying in bed, still hearing her voice, trembling, crying, saying
aloud that it couldn't go on, shouting it indignantly, then mercifully
losing everything except blackness, until a gradual awakening to soft
steady light, bird-song, the grateful recollection of not being alone.*

CHAPTER 9

"Westcote Gardens," murmured the Chief thoughtfully. "Number
Thirty-five." He leaned his great bulk eagerly across his desk, in the
gesture which still caused Neil to feel uncomfortably alert. The sun,
streaming through the slats of the venetian blind, defined the cluster
of hairs just inside the Chief's large red ear. "And you, Carter, live at
Number Thirty-seven."

"Governor?"

And Hilary Fielding lived at No. 35. The Chief's comment was so
extraordinary Neil could have no reaction to it beyond apprehension.
Feeling the apprehension spread over him like a physical coating, he
simply waited.

Before the Chief could continue there was a tap on the door. Sergeant Dobie to deliver a non-urgent and potentially time-consuming
verbal report. Neil read the Chief's few seconds of hesitation, then
Sergeant Dobie was asked to come back later and meanwhile see to

the deflection of any further callers or calls. While welcoming the indication that enlightenment was at hand, Neil's apprehension deepened with the realization that the Chief was giving him absolute priority.

"Governor?" he queried again when they were alone, in restrained response to the Chief's hard stare.

"Ever go to Richmond?" asked the Chief amiably.

It was a not unfamiliar ploy, this touching of a nerve, darting off to some far periphery, working steadily back in towards the nerve centre. But this periphery was already within Neil's vision.

"Well, yes, I have been, naturally, but living where I do . . . If I want air and exercise . . ." *Richmond. We—he—lives at Kew.*

"Hampstead Heath, of course." But the Chief's thoughts were not in North London. "Antique dealer by the name of Peter Shaw," he said conversationally. "In one of those lanes that come through to the Green. Richmond Green. Good stuff. Highly thought of, it appears, among those who know. Found dead this morning. You won't have seen it."

Neil's stiff lips managed to agree no, on a photographic memory of that morning's stop press, empty of print. "In the shop?" came out also, a trifle huskily. Even in his own intense apprehension, he remembered the lesson of experience that he must comment only on that part of the treatise which the Chief was currently expounding.

"Not in the shop. At home." The Chief paused to blow his nose, with the invariable foghorn accompaniment. *Kew.* "Kew. One of those enormous early Victorian houses."

"Governor?"

"A strange business," said the Chief dreamily. "Very strange. The man had suffered a coronary thrombosis. History of heart trouble. Could have killed him. May have done. But his throat had been compressed by human hands." He stared expectantly at Neil, who cleared his own throat in angry anticipation of sounding still huskier.

"Could that have brought on the coronary?" His voice, to himself at least, was almost normal.

"They say not. But obviously it could have killed the man before the natural attack did. Natural attack, and unnatural. Very strange. The coronary on the killer scale. So, two killers. Well, two potential killers."

"But which one was it in fact?" Neil was out of all proportion furious to find the veil once more across his throat. But if he wasn't furious he thought he could go so far as to pass out.

Something in the Chief's eye announced that he had reached what he considered to be the first high point of his discourse.

"They don't know yet, Neil. You see, the physical circumstances of a coronary make so much local blood that even after death—that is, immediately after—the bruising process which follows strangling could happen as it does in life. Especially with bruising occurring so much more quickly than the inflammation which follows wounding. With bruising there's none of that clear-cut business—oh, Lord, I'm sorry—where you see a wound with an abrupt edge and know it's postmortem. Or see the inflamed surround and know it was done to living flesh. Bruises are different." There was another tap at the door, which immediately opened. "Thought I told—" Sergeant Dobie was carrying a mug of coffee. "Bring Inspector Carter's in here, will you?" asked the Chief. He and Neil kept silence until Sergeant Dobie had come and gone again. Neil had never found it so agonizing to adhere to the Chief's timetable. The coffee, to which he added an extra spoonful of sugar, made him feel a bit better physically, to the extent of being able to break the silence according to the rules.

"Will they know eventually, Governor?"

"They say so. But in the meantime, Neil, what *is* certain is that murder was attempted, and so we shall have to treat the death as a murder case unless and until it's proved otherwise. And as far as the press and the public go, it's death with foul play not ruled out. Preliminary estimates, by the way, put the time of it between ten forty-five P.M. and a quarter past midnight." Neil was shocked, the way his mind was swooping about the building where he lived. And it was useless, anyway, he hadn't been there. "The body was discovered by Shaw's friend and partner Anthony Carey on his return by car about midnight."

"Did they live together? Share the house?" Neil amended quickly.

"They did. Share the house," responded the Chief. "We gather it's a fairly new arrangement. Just a few months' standing."

The Chief stared even more hopefully at Neil, who thought of calling it a fair cop and putting his head down between his knees. But somehow he didn't.

"So which seems to be the main mystery, Governor—the cause of death, or the identity of the human assailant?" He had asked the question before he realized it was at last the one he wanted to ask.

The Chief was still staring at him, and then was suddenly flopping back in his chair so that it groaned.

"I was trying to get something out of you, Neil, war of nerves and all that." The Chief did occasionally have these bursts of candour. "I congratulate you on not having given."

"Well, I hardly could," said Neil swiftly.

The Chief sat up straight.

"How well d'you know the wife?" he zoomed.

"The wife?"

For an absurd moment Neil thought that the Chief, who was an entirely self-made man, was referring to his own Amelia Larkin.

"Shaw's wife. Thirty-five Westcote Gardens. Calls herself by her maiden name of Fielding. You must—know her."

He heard his voice, a credit title rolling serenely across the image of a battlefield. "Well, yes, of course, I know who you mean." He was already engaged in a mental search for anyone who might know more about him and Hilary than that he had once taken her out to lunch in Knightsbridge—or even as much as that—but he could come up only with Cathy, and her awareness wasn't knowledge, it wasn't any more than a pessimistic fear. Unless . . . the Cyclopean eye . . . somewhere far off he found himself not wanting to imagine that she might use it for such a purpose.

Although his search was frantic, it was bathed in the relief of discovering why the Chief was connecting Peter Shaw's death so immediately with Hilary Fielding. Hilary Shaw. There was another distant sensation. That of personal affront.

"Neil, you disappoint me. Inspector Ryan reports that your front doors oppose one another, and that Mrs. Shaw is an exceedingly attractive lady."

"Inspector Ryan?" The postponement of a direct reply for even a moment seemed to give him aeons in which to decide on his policy.

"It's to be his case. Which I think is probably the best thing. You can probably do more unofficially. . . ."

"Governor?"

"It's going to be quite a case," said the Chief heavily, sighing as he contemplated it. "Not that there was any choice, but I rather feel that for you to have been on it officially would not have been to make the best use of the extraordinary coincidence of your living where you do."

"If I knew the woman, I suppose . . ."

"Get to know her."

"Now? Suddenly? After what's just happened?"

"Would it be now, suddenly? Would it, Neil?"

The candour had not, of course, marked the end of the war of nerves. But it was the thought of Cathy being manipulated by Bob Ryan or by the Chief himself which made Neil say, "All right, not entirely. We *have* been introduced. And I suppose I *could* go across and sympathize, while assuring her I was nothing to do with the investigation. I should hate to do it," he added fiercely, but the Chief ignored this last remark, and its tone.

"There you are, you see. You don't have to do anything underhand. Say of course you know what's happened, no one better, and how sorry you are—"

"Yes, I am sorry. Is Mrs. Shaw the chief suspect?"

He thought he had managed to throw it in as conversationally as the Chief managed to lob his more lethal shots.

"We can't say as yet that there is one. She lines up, I suppose, with Carey himself, who on preliminary hearing doesn't seem to have much of an alibi. And with Shaw's brother and sister-in-law and the cleaning woman and the part-time gardener and everybody else in London. Not, at least, that there's any sign of a forced entry or any disturbance inside the house."

"Motives?"

The Chief sighed again. "Carey says Mrs. Shaw left her husband three months ago, and hasn't been back since he moved in. Inspector Ryan suspects a *ménage*."

"Why?"

"I gather it was something about Carey himself. Mrs. Shaw didn't merely leave, by the way. She did the best she could short of divorce to restore herself to the unmarried state. The deceased seemed on good enough terms with his brother and sister-in-law. At least, they apparently saw a lot of one another. Pity you weren't at home last night, Neil. Something occur to you?"

Neil had noticeably shivered, as he tied up what Hilary had told him of her dream with what the Chief had told him about Peter Shaw's death. Yet she had insisted the details of her dream on to him, and she was the least naïve of women. . . .

"Not as yet, Governor. Give me a few days."

In a few days, with the charm which was the one quality the Chief ungrudgingly allowed him, he could have found out the things about Clara and Arthur Shaw and Anthony Carey which he already knew. And about Hilary herself, but those he would be unlikely to divulge unless he learned more things to make him more uneasy. . . . And there was that boss of hers. He hadn't liked it at the time she told him, the way he had appeared to be waiting. . . .

"I think I remember hearing that Miss Fielding—Mrs. Shaw— works in an art gallery?"

"She does, Neil, and quite near your joint abode. Got the job soon after moving in. Did you know she was really Mrs. Shaw?"

The Chief was leaning across his desk, without Neil having noticed him getting there. He had the stealth of certain very large men.

Absurdly, Neil's sexual vanity was vying with the relief and advantage of being able to tell the truth.

"I'd no idea," he said, concealing the effort of the admission. "But I gather from what you've told me that one would have to know the lady very well, or have known her before, to know that."

There was another keen look.

"You're probably right. Incidentally, I'd suggest that any association you form should be confined to the shared landing at Westcote Gardens. And to you and me and Mrs. Shaw and any close circle of hers if it can't be avoided, and if not, at the expense of your being casually around."

"Of course, Governor."

Even as he spoke Neil excepted Cathy. She was to be trusted, and she might be helpful.

"How's the Bayswater job coming along?"

Neil grimaced.

"Frustrated lull. Just keeping the pot stirred, really."

"Which Sergeant Hislop can do, much of the time. I'm not suggesting any dereliction of your existing commitments, Neil, but so far as I'm concerned, if it's a question of trying to look busy, you can slope off."

Neil had to protest. "Thank you very much, Governor, but I'm not engaged merely in Bayswater."

"I know, I know. But you know, too. What I'm saying." The Chief got slowly to his feet. His legs were too short for his upper torso, and he never rose quite so high as Neil always found himself expecting.

"Mrs. Shaw," said Neil, making himself bite on the title, "has she simply been told a coronary, perhaps plus?"

"Perhaps plus the unspecified intervention of another person."

"So she's bound to ask me what on earth you mean."

"And you'll tell her it's so complicated only the experts understand it. Well, they don't understand it, of course. Tell her they just think there could be an extra factor involving another person, unfavourably."

"Governor!"

"I'm sorry, Neil. You can see for yourself what a confounded situation it is."

"Couldn't Anthony Carey have seen the marks of the strangulation when he found the body? That is, of course, if he hadn't—"

"He could have done. Well, he must have done, but to a layman they would just seem to be part of the general distortion that the coronary would cause. I gather he didn't make any sort of comment on those lines."

"So that part is our secret."

"For the moment, yes. I know it's difficult."

"For me, in the circumstances which you've just imposed on me, I should say that it's rather more difficult than it is for anyone else. However . . ." Neil knew the Chief always took it in when he made his occasional points.

"One thing, Neil." The Chief was fiddling with some papers on his desk. "At least *you* have a watertight alibi."

"Governor!" It was a genuine expression of shock.

"I only meant," said the Chief, raising his eyes innocently to Neil's face, "that we don't have to waste time, or get embarrassed, clearing it out of the way. Now get back to work."

CHAPTER 10

Bob Ryan might suspect that Neil was to be made unofficial use of regarding the events on his landing, but not that he was already in a position to ring Mrs. Shaw's front-door bell and be silently admitted. He got home at six, at the end of his shortest day for some time which felt like his longest, and telephoned her.

She answered quickly, sharply, with her number. He had never telephoned her before.

"Hilary. Are you alone?"

"I am now. I haven't been."

"I know. Shall I come over?"

"Please."

The Cyclopean eyes were now a gauntlet. He had to make himself run them with his normal stance, not bend to avoid them. She let him in at once, and he put his arm across her shoulders and urged her into the sitting-room without doing more than glance towards her, reluctant to look at the inevitable disorder of her face.

"Neil . . ."

He had not thought it would suit her to be so devastated, and he was right. The face seemed a different and less pleasing shape than when he had studied it by lamplight three nights ago, clumsily angled, the area beneath the eyes disproportionately prominent as two livid arcs, the creaminess of the skin ebbed to grey. It made him remember the baby.

"Sit down," he said, alarmed, and she did so, with uncharacteristic heaviness, on the nearest chair arm.

"Look." He leaned back into the chair seat and pulled her against him by an arm round her waist, so that his cheek touched the soft edge of her hair and there was no chance of seeing her face. "I know what's happened and who you are."

The hair stirred, tickling his skin.

"I'm sorry about that, Neil. But I haven't been able to think . . . Even to myself . . ."

"It's all right. It's nothing." His personal reaction to that part of the Chief's revelations already seemed ancient and absurd. "But listen. I'm not going to be involved in the investigation." He had spoken before he realized that his last word would be a painful corroboration of what Bob Ryan had told her. She jerked impatiently against him.

"You know about it, though."

"Well, I know—"

"You just said. You just told me." He could feel the mutual tension, in his cheekbone and her neck. He preferred her impatience to the controlled hysteria which abruptly succeeded it. "All right, he had a coronary, they told me that. That's—easy. Dear God. But they said—they said they thought someone else might have had something to do with it. Neil, what did they mean? Something to do with the fact that he died? That he had a coronary? I kept asking them and they just kept saying he'd had a coronary but that there were other factors—yes, that was what they said, other factors—which made it seem that someone else might have been involved. *Neil*. It's awful, having to keep going over and over the dream and how he looked to try and find out what they could possibly mean when they wouldn't tell me . . ."

Going over and over a dream?

"They couldn't tell you. Yet." His longing to tell her at least what he knew himself concentrated itself in a strong feeling of hostility towards the Chief. "It really is all highly complex forensic stuff. I gather there's something in the appearance of—the body—which makes the backroom boys think that another person—"

"Christ, Neil!"

"I'm sorry, love, I'm sorry. But this sort of gobbledygook must make you see that we honestly don't know yet. We don't know whether he—your husband"—the word was a sort of penance on himself for having to let her suffer that bit more than she really need— "died from coronary thrombosis or—"

"Murder? Do they mean murder?"

"Where there's this sort of doubt," said Neil gratefully, "the investigation has to be treated as a murder investigation." He awaited a response but there was none, she was motionless and silent against him, even when he parted her hair with his lips so that he could chastely kiss her neck. On an unfamiliar impulse of pity and concern he put both his arms round her and drew her across him, cradling her, setting her head on his shoulder, trying to prepare the way for the tears which now came.

Not that they were tears so much as sobs, her body convulsed almost soundlessly, and when at last she lifted her face it was still pale and dry. Not the good cry he had hoped to give her. But hardly surprising when even he couldn't bring himself to think head-on about how she was bound to be feeling.

He tried to intercept her staring eyes.

"I know it's as much hell as anything could be."

"Thanks." She saw him. "I'm sorry."

"For heaven's sake!"

"No, I am. It wasn't like me."

"Nor like me." He smiled warily enough for it not to insult her situation, and had a fleeting response. "And the whole thing isn't like anything anyone should have to suffer. And I know it didn't begin today."

"No. . . . Neil, do you know just where and how he was found?"

"I don't. I'm sorry, I should have—"

"No, I'm not asking you, I asked them. He was in the first-floor sitting-room, in his chair up to the centre table."

"Yes?"

"As *he is in my dream*. They told me that, but they didn't tell me whether or not his tongue was sticking out."

Neil coughed, to hide the involuntary jerk of his head. And he was astonished as well as dismayed. By this least naïve of women.

"Did you ask them?"

"Yes. But they managed not to answer me."

Neil thought in momentary terror of his Chief. "So it's sticking out in your dream?"

To his further surprise she was suddenly bewildered, passing a hand over her forehead, leaving the short front hair spiked stiffly up. "I think so. . . . And then when I try to remember exactly, I'm not sure . . . it's like the vase. . . ."

He heard her say "It's like the vase," and registered his non-comprehension, but he wanted to ask her something urgent. "Did you tell the police about your dream?"

She was looking through him again. Staring at her interior picture. "No. All I did was try and find out . . . and ask and ask. . . ." Again he cradled her unresisting to him, guided her head out of sight on his shoulder. Her voice went on. "I remembered after they'd gone. I'll tell them next time. They said there'd be a next time."

He would have advised her, as casually as he could, not to tell them, on the grounds that dreams were no sort of evidence, but she had asked Bob Ryan if her husband's tongue was in the position of someone who had been strangled.

"When you tell them, tell them that's why you asked about the tongue, I mean"—as her body stiffened—"it seems an odd question, otherwise, and policemen don't leave odd questions alone."

She pulled herself away, to sit up and glare at him. "So they'll ask me what I meant, and I'll tell them. If by that time I haven't told them already." Her face softened, heralding another abrupt change of mood, a returning awareness that he was there, with her. "Neil, I can't help being glad I haven't been near the place since I left. It makes it sort of easier than having to say 'Well, I was there last week.' As it is, I was there all the time. And then suddenly none of the time."

"Of course," he responded automatically, studying her face. Its planes now were almost restored, his presence, his arms, were bringing back its colour. She was almost her elegant, sophisticated self. Sophisticated, not naïve. The least naïve of women . . .

"I hope you've talked to your parents."

"I rang them as soon as the police had gone. The police asked me for their address, Neil. *Their* address! But I got hold of them first. You know, if the police hadn't asked me for their address, I might have forgotten . . . I'm in a different world, you see. Actually, I don't feel as if I'm in any world. . . ."

"Why don't you go to your parents?"

"They wanted me to. I suppose I had a bit of a job with my mother. But I told her the police rather wanted me to stay in London."

"Did they?"

"They said it would make it easier for them to keep me informed of developments. It's funny, those sort of official phrases stick in the mind—"

"Have you told your mother about the baby?"

"No. Oh, I will, Neil, I was intending to. But not just yet, not now. I'd never be able to stop my mother coming up, if I did."

"And you don't want her to?"

"Do you?"

He was pleased that she could be even so feebly provocative.

"I mustn't come into it."

"I don't want them now, Neil. Later. I've told them I'm much more with Clara and Arthur than I am. My mother approves of Clara and finds Arthur reliable, so that calmed her down. I'll go and see them when . . . I'll go eventually."

"You should keep in touch with them."

"I will, I will. I'm not a monster."

"Sorry." Propitiatory, he leaned forward and nuzzled her ear. "One thing. Don't mention your dream to the Press. Don't, in fact," he hurried on, "offer the Press anything at all. Just answer their questions as briefly as possible. Ideally with a yes or a no."

"The Press?" She was bolt upright. "Oh no!"

He cursed himself.

"It's all right. But any death which—isn't quite straightforward, the Press want to know. If you really *were* Miss Fielding, then it would be extreme bad luck if they got on to you. As it is . . ."

"But how do they get on to *anything*? I mean, at this stage, when even the police—"

"Because there are crime reporters all ready to pounce. Looking for a job all the time. And when they know your husband's dead and the sort of—"

"Anthony. That will be enough. He'll have told them everything he can and some things he can't. He's got a great sense of drama."

She didn't look or sound as if she was being spiteful, merely as if she was stating facts.

"Won't he be—upset?" asked Neil in pure curiosity.

"Actually, I don't know." She was, he thought, intrigued by her inability to answer his question, briefly distracted from her dreadful task of trying to imagine how her husband had looked when he was discovered dead. "I've always somehow assumed that with Anthony it was the main chance and being provided for, but I don't know. I knew with Peter." She was staring through him again, in the way which made him feel so uncomfortable. "I keep reminding myself about Peter, that he can't possibly be anything to do with me now because of how he felt about someone else. But Anthony . . ." With her return to Anthony she was looking at him in her usual cool way. A *light touch*, he had thought once, about the way she looked at him.

"Did the police come to the gallery?"

"Oh yes." As she recovered her poise, it was less and less productive to study her face. If she had been like Cathy, he would have had a far better chance of learning things from looking at her. Although at the moment, of course, Cathy . . . "I thought I was on my own, and enough was said to show why they were there, and then as I was leading the way into the back, there was that wretched Mrs. Tilsley suddenly busy with a duster. The damage was done, but I asked the police if we could come back to the flat to talk, and they drove me."

"Stephen wasn't there?"

"No. But I had to ask Mrs. Tilsley to hold the fort and she'd tell him why, and then she'd tell him what she'd heard, and what she made of it. To be fair, she's just as likely to talk to the Press as Anthony. More likely, perhaps. He just could be too wretched."

"Yes, you are fair. When was this?"

"This morning. Ten o'clock. And I thought you said you weren't anything to do with the investigation."

She was enough pulled together for him not to be able to tell whether she was teasing him, or really suspicious.

"I'm not. Sorry, love. It's a reflex. And I'll tell you frankly that I intend to keep my eyes and ears open among your husband's family

and your friends." Not quite frankly, because he would not tell her
that he was an appointed copper's nark, nor that her husband's family must include her—although that, of course, she should see for herself, particularly if she had been at home alone the night before. . . .

"Oh, Neil, no!"

He appeared to have bulldozed her yet again. He said gently, "I
don't suppose you've thought about it yet. But there was no sign of a
break-in. And although it will be the least uncomfortable thing to
think of Anthony, you mustn't. All on his own, I mean."

"I don't want to think of anyone. God. *God*."

"My Chief remarked," said Neil, forcing a grin, "that seeing I
lived where I did, it was convenient I had an alibi."

"You!" She was diverted again, by astonishment, as he had hoped.

"It was part of an attempt to make me admit that I knew you."

"But how could he know you do?"

"He doesn't. He was only hoping. That if I did, he could trick me
into revealing it."

"And did he?"

"He didn't." His grin this time was spontaneous, pleasurably rem-
iniscent. "Only into the acknowledgement that I knew who he was
talking about."

"That wasn't bad."

She gave him an approvingly appraising look, and he saw her face
change as she remembered what for a few seconds she had forgotten.

"I thought it was pretty good," he said quickly. "You know, in
some odd way I think my Chief felt it was my fault that I should
have been on the geographical edge of your husband's death."

"What an unreasonable Chief." Her voice was light again, cool
and unconcerned, but her hand trembled as she held it up to look at
her watch. "Arthur," she murmured. "I should think almost certainly tonight."

"Arthur. Your brother-in-law, I now see. And by the way, my
Chief isn't unreasonable in the least unreasonable way."

"I'm sure not," she said absently. "Neil . . ."

"Yes?"

"Arthur's—a nuisance."

"A nuisance?"

"Well, not actually. But I fear about to be."

"You mean . . ." He remembered Arthur Shaw staring at Hilary and not sitting down until he had seen there was no possibility of a seat beside her.

She looked disgusted. "Yes."

"For how long?"

"Only since I left Peter. And he started coming here—Arthur, I mean—to see how I was. It was a beastly shock. Just to recognize suddenly how he was feeling. He was here the first evening you were away—the night before last—it was the first time I'd seen him since Clara had told him about the baby, and I just couldn't think whether it would bring him on or—"

"Did it?"

"No, thank heaven. But it gave him the excuse to fuss about and keep saying that now I needed a man more than ever and hadn't got one, he would drop in more often to make sure I was all right. So that whether he does or not I get a bit jumpy about half past six in case—"

"Did you tell the police about the baby?"

"No. I don't know why, really. Probably because it seems such an odd note on which to leave a husband." She was still cool. "Do you think I ought to have told them?"

"I don't think it matters, really. I think you certainly oughtn't to tell the Press. You've got to gamble on the strong probability that it'll all be cleared up before there's any involuntary evidence of the baby's existence."

"'Strong probability.'" Her laugh was a bit tremulous. "Neil, are you trying to cheer me up?"

"Of course. But not with false encouragements. You must know by now that they're not my style. Incidentally"—he was reminding himself of the way he and the Chief tried to sound casual with one another when they were at their most serious—"I suppose they asked you what you were doing last night?"

"Yes. I could only tell them, sitting reading and then going to bed. Not even being able to say what I thought about this or that TV programme, because of not having had it on."

She laughed again, but he found his reaction was to the receipt of bad news.

"And they asked you if there was anyone who could corroborate your story?" He put a sort of mock-legal emphasis on the last words. "They always do. I should say, we always do."

"And they did. And I said, no, there wasn't. I didn't even see

Cathy last night, or coincide with anyone on the landing when I went out with my rubbish."

"You know," observed Neil, with a cheerfulness he could only hope sounded less hollow to Hilary than it did to him, "it's much more usual to find people without alibis than with them. I suppose because the majority of people do simply spend the evening—"

The front-door bell shrilled, and her body leaped against him. Neil hugged it as if it was a child's, for an instant felt his pressure returned. Cheek to cheek he whispered, "Go and answer it. And, I'd better just say it quickly"—heavens, he should have said it at the start—"I'm just a neighbour. A policeman, if you like, but not involved, and not a particular friend. I'll tell you why—"

"Oh, I can see all the whys for myself. Thank you for being a neighbour."

As always with Hilary, as he watched her move gracefully away from him, he wondered at once if she had ever been near. There was a brief break in her steady step across the hall (he remembered the mirror), then the uninterpretable murmur of voices. Neil was on his feet when she came back into the room closely followed by a tall youngish man with a lot of brown hair and high broad shoulders. The face was broad too, brown-skinned and with generous features, pleasantly lived-in. But it was Hilary who struck him the more, on the momentarily objective view made possible by their brief separation: she looked again as she had always looked and yet less positively so, as if he was seeing her on television with the colour turned just lower than was natural.

"Neil, this is Stephen. Stephen Elliott, my boss. Stephen—Neil Carter, my neighbour. A policeman, actually, but not connected. With this awful affair." Again the one betrayal, in her laugh.

The two men murmured. Neil found himself regretful of the agreeable impression which Stephen Elliott had immediately made on him. But it was easily enough submerged in his dislike of the way the man was standing so close to Hilary, watching her so keenly and so anxiously and placing his hand from time to time on her arm. Either she was unaware of it, or she didn't mind. Or was simply used to . . . For a start, it didn't accord with what she had told him about her boss and her job.

Neil had advised her not to cast Anthony Carey in the role of villain. Was he himself so casting Stephen Elliott?

Whether or no, he knew there was already something he would suggest to the Chief.

CHAPTER 11

The front-door bell rang again.

"The lift shot down as soon as I got out of it," observed Stephen Elliott amiably. There was a hesitation in his voice which made Neil think he might once have stammered.

"I'll go."

Neil was into the hall as he spoke. He realized as he approached the front door that his interest was in the spy-hole. Not for its distorting properties, although these he always found intriguing, tending from his experience of his own door to believe that they emphasized the salient features of a face, bringing it to honest caricature. Of more interest now was the possibility of the current face being off its guard.

But the distortion worked against what this time he wanted. Arthur Shaw, as Neil peered through upon his tiny figure at the far end of the telescopic process, had no observable facial expression, merely an enormous forehead. At the expense, fancied Neil (as if there was only so much material available), of his small mouth, which had to be searched for and then was only a line beneath the beige blob of the moustache. A clever man? Devious, he had thought at once, the only time they had met. But—clever?

Arthur Shaw's fidgeting was taking the form of pulling at his tie, then lifting both hands together and stroking them over the sides of the smooth hair which looked no more than a slightly darker skin. As Neil watched, a comb flashed up and was passed rapidly and without visible effect over that flat surface. It was a gesture which he found so distasteful when carried out other than in private that he read it as an indication of extreme self-distrust. Then conceded that to know one might be under surveillance was probably less persuasive than the inhumanity of that minute unblinking eye. Self-distrust, yes, but not necessarily extreme.

Pushing away the temptation to start pondering on front-door spyholes as new media for the psychiatrist, he let Hilary's brother-in-law into her flat just as a gigantic finger was raised to ring again.

"Come in, do." The necessity of saying something made him realize he had also wanted to establish his own position.

"Mrs. Shaw?"

Yes, this man would act as if they had never met.

"She's all right. Come in and see."

But the neat figure stepped no further than across the threshold. The small mouth was still a line, narrower by the second.

"I'm not official," said Neil, bringing his official charm to bear. "But I *am* a neighbour, as you know."

Arthur Shaw continued to stare at him, as if rooted just inside the front door.

"I'm so very sorry," persisted Neil, finding it an increasing effort to speak politely. "I know what's happened, you see, because of being in the Metropolitan force, but I've nothing to do with the investigation. I came over just to say I was sorry. And to reassure your sister-in-law that policemen are human."

The little joke, which Neil himself didn't think much of, had no noticeable effect on Arthur Shaw, although he did at last move. Ignoring Neil, he set off with quick, rather short strides towards the sitting-room. Neil followed at the same pace, so as to be able to witness the second check. It came in the doorway, so abruptly he almost ran into the dark-suited back.

"Oh, Arthur. Good of you to come." Hilary's voice was flat, and she didn't move from beside the window, where she stood with her third visitor. "This is Stephen Elliott, my boss. Stephen, my brother-in-law Arthur Shaw. Neil Carter you've met."

"Ah, Mr. Elliott." A far more suitable person to have about the house, interpreted Neil. Shaw was even shaking Elliott by the hand. Then moving closer to Hilary so that she took a quick and, Neil thought, instinctive step backwards. Arthur Shaw searched for and picked up her hand where it hung at her side.

"My dear. Oh, my dear. You must come back with me."

"That's very kind of you, Arthur, but no. I'd rather stay—at home."

Something in the way she said the word "home" made Neil wonder if she had ever used it before about No. 35 Westcote Gardens.

"Hilary . . . dear . . . you can't stay alone here—now."

"Why can't I, Arthur?" For the first time that day Neil heard genuine amusement in her voice. She withdrew her hand.

"Well . . . it hardly seems . . . Clara is expecting you. The guest-room will be all ready."

"Clara isn't expecting me. She's been here and I've told her that I'm staying put. I want to stay here, Arthur. Actually, I want to be alone. No!"—in response to the general shuffling of feet—"not this exact moment. But I feel the need to be where I'm used to. In my burrow. Like all animals when they're sick." Neil disliked this laugh even more than her earlier ones. "Help yourself to a drink, Arthur. And give the others what they want."

"Not for me, thanks, I must go." Neil had glanced at Stephen Elliott and seen no prospect of his refusing hospitality. He started towards the door. "Let me know, Hilary, if you want anything. And of course I'll look in again." She took a step after him. "I'll see myself out."

In the doorway he turned for a brief acknowledgement of the two men, reciprocated respectively with a smile and a stare. Neil thought he had seen just enough of Stephen Elliott to assume that his habitual expression was one of friendly amusement. His instinct approved it, even while his suspicions rekindled as Elliott also took a step forward and was again standing beside Hilary, again putting his hand on her arm. A second later Shaw came level on her other side, putting his hand on her shoulder. From between them she stared expressionlessly at Neil, who saw how they might find the scene funny, particularly if he encouraged certain memories of himself and Hilary alone. . . .

In the hall, and until he shut the front door, he heard Arthur Shaw's deep voice.

"I identified Peter, my dear, I took care of that. Carey wouldn't do it, of course. It's only a formality, but a rather unpleasant one. Anyway, it's taken care of."

Swearing under his breath, Neil rang Cathy's bell.

"Hello, Neil."

The new, subdued Cathy, holding her door half-open instead of letting it bang back against the wall. He had forgotten, had been anticipating the familiar ease of flopping in her most comfortable armchair while she enthusiastically refreshed him. His disappointment was so keen he tried to dismiss it as childish.

"Hello, Cathy. May I come in?"

"Of course."

She opened the door a bit wider, still controlling its movement.

He waited while she slowly closed it and set off at her reduced pace towards the sitting-room.

"It's a quarter to seven. Would you like some sherry?"

"Yes, please." The chair seemed slightly less comfortable. "Are you having one?"

She was facing the cupboard. "Actually, I don't think I will, I've had my bit of supper."

"I'm sorry, this was an awkward time to call."

"Don't be silly!" She turned round with the glass of sherry in her hand, smiling at him, and he wondered if she had really been talking to herself.

He smiled back as he took the glass.

"Sit down," he said. "Have you seen Hilary today?"

The sooner he could put the name into its new context, the better.

"Not today."

She was looking at him steadily as she snuggled back into the sofa. "Why, Neil?"

"Because something awful has happened which involves her. I know about it through work, and I'm going to tell you."

She interrupted him early on, with the suggestion that she ought to go over to Hilary, but he explained that Stephen Elliott and Arthur Shaw were probably still there. He explained most things, including the fact that he was going against his Chief's injunction by telling her anything at all.

"So why, Neil?"

Cathy leaned forward, so intent she let herself topple on to her knees on the carpet, almost at his feet, and stayed down there while she pulled a funny face at him.

He felt briefly happy. "When the clown has removed his round red nose, I shall tell him."

"He has." She scrambled back on to the sofa. "Go on."

"Because you can help me."

"I can?"

He saw pleasure as well as surprise.

"Yes. I don't necessarily mean by doing things, I mean just as much by—well, by being there for me to talk my ideas out, and to make suggestions, and of course by watching and listening—look, Cathy, I'm asking you really to be two-faced."

There was, after all, a relief in being back at Cathy's, in being able to be entirely honest, not trying to find things out and pretending he

wasn't, feeling worried and making hearty remarks implying he was without a care in the world.

"How, Neil? Will you have some more sherry?"

"Yes, please." He had just decided that if she asked him he would say yes, and next time he came bring her the present of a bottle. He was glad to see her fling herself to her feet. "Has Hilary told you about her dream?"

"No." As she turned back to him her face above the brimming glass was wary again.

"I thought perhaps not," he said, lightly and truthfully. "She's the sort of woman who finds it easier to confide in a man than another woman."

"One man? Or several?"

He was tempted then, really tempted, to tell her everything, to say, "I think only one man, and yes, I have become that man, because I have become her lover, and I am no jot less fond of you, you sweet thing, than I was before"—but that last part would certainly not do because of its implication that even if it had not been Hilary there was no chance that it would have been Cathy.

No, although he knew it must come out at last, and although he wanted it to come out because he told her rather than because she discovered it for herself, he also knew it was not yet the right time— which would present itself not as tempting but as inevitable.

"I hadn't thought." He paused, as if considering the matter for the first time, aware of regret that after all he was still being deceitful. "I don't really know," he said. "But the point is that it's man rather than woman, however many or few."

"And the even more relevant point is that it doesn't exactly matter which it is, so far as you and I are concerned at this moment. Go on, Neil."

She looked away from him, overcome, he thought, by her mild outburst. He began without comment to recount Hilary's dream.

"Did she tell you this *before* last night?" asked Cathy as he finished.

"Yes. And I'm justified already in deciding you'd be helpful, that's an important point."

"Well, it does make it honest." He was glad to see how she betrayed her pleasure at his praise—in the old way by ignoring it, and blushing scarlet. "But it's so extraordinary. I mean, a dream . . ."

He knew what she meant. "She has a history of second sight," he

said quickly. Hilary might have told him that this afternoon, if Cathy asked, but she didn't, she was pondering.

"I don't know . . . It's weird." She shook her head violently, so that her cap of hair took several seconds to swirl back into place.

"What worries me," said Neil, "is the way she doesn't seem to appreciate that the police aren't simply going to take her word for it. That they're going to have to line her up with all the other people who have a place in the story and even that she may be the only one of them without an alibi. She seems almost to be offering her dream as a substitute for one, in conjunction with her apparent certainty that she didn't stir last night. It isn't—well, it isn't like her."

"No, I should say it isn't."

Already, thought Neil, shifting in his chair, Hilary had come to mean something new between him and Cathy, important yet impersonal.

"What did *you* do last night?" he asked, grinning. "And I'm asking you with Hilary's alibi in mind rather than your own, which I think I can categorically pronounce will not be required."

To his surprise she seemed embarrassed, looking down to pick at the fringe of a cushion.

"Actually, I went out last night, which is turning out to have been a bit of a pity."

"I don't know, at least it means you were on the landing a couple of times, and in the lift. What were the times?"

"It must have been about seven, I suppose, when I left the flat. I had a meal out with Don Everett." She followed the information with a restored steady glance. "I didn't see anyone except Miss Prince and of course she made us move off especially quickly."

"It isn't really the going-out time which is so significant." Neil had registered some sensation at the news of how Cathy had spent the previous evening, but didn't wait to find out what it was. "My Chief tells me the time of death was probably between ten forty-five P.M. and a quarter after midnight. What time did you get home?"

"I remember exactly, as it happens," she said slowly. She looked down again at the cushion. "My clock had stopped and I put it on from my watch. Nearly a quarter to twelve."

"A long dinner," said Neil. He hated the heartiness of manner he seemed of late to be adopting.

"No, not actually, I went back to listen to some records with Don, and he ran me home. He didn't come up." She was looking at him again.

"And did you see or hear anything then?"

"Not a thing, Neil. Funnily enough I *did* think of looking in on Hilary, but then I thought it was probably a bit late." He wondered if the very slight extra colour in her face was for having had these thoughts because he, Neil, was away, and there would have been no possibility of embarrassment.

"And you didn't hear anything?"

"Absolutely nothing."

"She didn't scream in her sleep?"

"No. Not that she has done lately. I didn't even see her this morning, which I quite often do."

"That's a pity, but it can't be helped. As far as the earlier part of the night's concerned, though—I mean, you must have been quite late to bed. Crossing the hall and so on . . . you're awfully keen-eared."

"I know, but I was tired and I wasn't really listening. . . ." Cathy jumped to her feet and swung round to the drinks cupboard, not in time to hide her confusion. "I think I'll have a ginger beer." Of course, he had been away and she would have relaxed her vigilance.

"Well," said Neil, not irritated this time, "I'm afraid that what would have been your easiest job is no-go. For the rest of it—will you talk to her, Cathy, listen to her? Ask her questions, if you can possibly reach that stage, about her husband and the brother-in-law and sister-in-law and so on, and about what she thinks must have happened. More information of *any* kind." He paused. Cathy was sitting forward intently again, cradling her glass in two hands. He noticed that her twined feet were wearing socks but no shoes. "Ask her about her boss, even. It seemed sort of pat, how her job happened."

"Yes, if it really was like that," commented Cathy reasonably.

"If it really was," he responded, having to disguise a moment of inner giddiness. He had after all, in regard to what Hilary had told him, nothing more to go on than his instincts and experience. "Do you think you could make a Welsh rarebit?"

"Neil!" She leaped to her feet and he got up too, even though the chair had grown more comfortable. In the hall they both turned on an instant away from the kitchen, towards the front door, from beyond which the sounds were coming—feet and voices. Cathy applied her eye to her spy-hole, quickly yielding him place. The distant, tiny tableau showed Hilary in her open doorway and the four men on the landing beside it, two of them carrying things which he made out after a moment to be cameras and photographic equipment.

"All or nothing." It was a man's voice. "And I wouldn't advise you to make it nothing, Mrs. Shaw." The tone was one of friendly advice. Evidently there was a conjunction of rival interests. Did she glance across at Neil's front door? She said, "Come in, then, will you?" and everyone disappeared. Neil turned round to Cathy, told her.

"Poor thing!" said Cathy passionately.

"I know." He couldn't echo her actual words, not about Hilary, but he was aware, as he and Cathy stared uneasily at one another, that they now shared something which in its way was as exclusive as the thing he shared with Hilary. A conspiracy. He would certainly, now, feel even less honest when he was with his mistress than when he was with his friend.

He didn't ring Hilary until almost eleven, then apologized for the truth that it hadn't occurred to him she might be asleep until he had finished dialling.

"I thought you were more realistic, Neil."

"The doctor must have given you something."

"I haven't taken it."

"Shall I come over?"

"Yes. I'll leave the door on the latch."

Her door was opposite his, and Miss Prince and Cathy formed the other sides of the square. If he moved immediately right he could lean forward and put his hand over Cathy's gilded eye and then swing himself past her threshold before releasing it. He could, but he never would, of course, it was just a thought which was inevitable in the circumstances. He wouldn't even cross the landing with particular stealth. He was grateful, though, that he didn't have to linger outside Hilary's flat. He shut her door from the inside, sliding in the chain.

She was standing in the centre of the sitting-room, her arms hanging at her sides, staring ahead of her. The room around her was even tidier than usual, but there was a rough smell, compounded of smoke and accumulated masculinity, which reminded him of the Press.

He ran the last few steps, with the same sense of unfamiliarity as when he had earlier drawn her onto his lap. She was motionless even when he put his arms round her, not lifting hers.

"I've put the chain on. But do you want me to stay?"

Her head inclined against his.

"You're sure?"

He just heard the whisper. "I think I'd like you to stay longer. And do less."

She raised her head, but even as her smile began her face broke up in brief, ugly preliminary to the gushing tears. Amazed at almost everything which had happened that day, and finally at his own strength, Neil picked her up and carried her out of the room.

CHAPTER 12

It was in the very early morning that he remembered. The four words he had registered and tucked away. *It's like the vase. . . .*

He had been awake for only a few seconds, but he was restless already in his eagerness to ask her what she had meant. Light was filtering into the room through the thin curtains, as yet frail and grey but enough to show him that she was dreamlessly sleeping, on her back with her head towards him, so that he could see a tear beside her eyelid. His hand slid towards her in automatic response to the sight of her rather than to his curiosity, but he drew it back. To deprive her of a moment of vacant sleep, knowing what she would waken to, would be an act of cruelty. And as his impatience grew he saw her eyes were wide open, staring at him, the knowledge of what she had learned the day before flooding back into them like a change of colour. He took her in his arms, hugging her with the fierce strength of an adult for a child.

"Neil . . ."

"It's all right. Hold on."

Slowly and in silence she relaxed from awareness of his comfort to awareness of him, a gradually returning awareness which he matched and found intoxicating, only with a vague sense of shame, because she could not really be finding it so, she could only be finding it a postponement of her thoughts, a ludicrous substitution for the man she would rather be lying with, who was now dead as well as gone. . . .

"*Neil!*"

"Hush!"

It was the only sort of moment in which there was a danger of being overheard by Cathy, although neither of them had ever put the horrific possibility into words.

She swung away from him. "I'm not really . . . Please don't think . . ."

"I don't think anything. You don't have to explain anything. Well, you do, but not about that. Tell me"—he put his arm round her and she turned slowly back to him—"what did you mean when you said, 'It's like the vase'?"

"It's strange." They had perfected an audible, non-straining whisper in this room. "I seem to have said so much lately, things I've never said before. But I haven't said anything about the vase. Not to you or to the police. And I suppose it could be a clue."

"Tell! For the love of Allah, tell!"

In their short time they had even learned to laugh *sotto voce*.

"Yes, I will." Yet she was silent. He couldn't see her, but he read the brief stiffening of her body as a moment of acute pain.

"Come on," he said softly, having to curb his impatience.

"Yes. Have you ever heard of the Portland Vase?"

"The phrase sounds familiar. But that's all I can say."

"It's a navy-blue glass jar cameo'd in white, made by Roman craftsmen in Alexandria somewhere about the time B.C. became A.D. Sir William Hamilton, husband of the renowned Emma, bought it in the early 1780s in Italy, when he was British Ambassador to the court of Naples. 'The person I bought it of at Rome' "—even from her whisper he could tell she was quoting—" 'will do me the justice to say that the superior excellence of this exquisite masterpiece of ancient art struck me so much at first sight that I eagerly asked, "Is it yours? Will you sell it?" He answered, "Yes, but not under a thousand pounds." "I will give you a thousand pounds." And so I did, though God knows it was not very convenient for me at that moment.' He bought it from a Scotsman who bought it from the Barberini family who had had it for centuries."

"You seem to know a lot about it." He had found her little lesson poignant, in its rare glimpse of her outside her hurt.

"You'll see why. Sir William brought the vase back to London and sold it to the Duchess of Portland. Horace Walpole described her as 'a simple woman, but perfectly sober, and intoxicated only by *empty* vases.' " She chuckled softly, and he had to rub his head against her cheek. "She died soon after installing the vase in her private museum, and it was sold. But her son, the third Duke, soon bought it back, and lent it to Josiah Wedgwood to model in the jasper ware he'd recently invented. Am I boring you, Neil?"

"For heaven's sake!"

"You can imagine how difficult it was, even for a genius like Josiah, to reproduce dark blue glass in black stone. But he worked at it, and produced about forty what are now called early copies. Twenty-two of them are still officially in existence."

"And the original?"

"In the British Museum. The fourth Duke of Portland deposited it there in 1810. I suppose he thought of it as the safest place, but in 1845 a young man in drink picked up a nearby antiquity and smashed the glass case the vase was in, and the vase itself into little pieces. 'I was suffering at the time from a kind of nervous excitement —a continual fear of everything I saw—and it was under this impression, strange as it may seem, that I committed the act for which I was deservedly taken into custody at the Museum.'"

"But Wedgwood had made his copies?"

"Oh, yes. In the early 1790s. But anyway, the vase was mended and put back on display. Where it still is. It was mended again in 1949, and it looks marvellous."

"And the copies?"

"You can see number four of those early copies in the BM. And there's another in the V & A. And a later one at the BM in blue. It's odd, but the black is far more like the original, I suppose because the original is such a dark blue it looks black unless there's light behind it. Sir Joshua Reynolds said he couldn't tell the black Wedgwood copy from the original. They've been making them ever since, of course. Victorian taste even draped the naked figures. In the 1880s Wedgwood started putting out what are known as 'ordinary jasper portland' in all the jasper colours. It's quite common and of very varying quality. . . ."

He felt her muscles tighten as she paused, and he whispered quickly, "And did you come by one of the twenty-two, or an undiscovered twenty-third?"

She relaxed on a snort of laughter.

"Neil, you're too clever by half. The highest-quality extant copies nearly all have a number in manganese pencil on the inside lip. The manganese pencil mark on Peter's copy says sixteen."

The light in the room had warmed to orange-yellow. The tear glinted more strongly beside her half-open eye. He smoothed it away.

"How did he come by it?"

"I don't know. I only know he got it for very little, from someone who didn't know what he was selling. It used to worry him sometimes, to think that in a way he'd swindled a man out of a fortune. I'm absolutely certain he and I were the only people in the world who realized what the vase was."

"And now?"

"And now, I can't believe that Anthony doesn't know as well." Even her whisper was stony. He stroked the hair on her forehead, and she lay silent and unresponsive under his hand.

"You're absolutely certain," he whispered at last, "that the vase is *the* number sixteen?"

"Absolutely certain. You see"—she twisted round and sat up, and he lay back in turn, under her intent gaze—"I met Peter because of the Portland Vase. I was working on all this material when I was at Ruskin, and Peter came to give a lecture in an occasional series—I think it was on furniture fakes—and was introduced to me afterwards, because he said he was interested in the vase." She paused, and he made himself wait in silence and immobility. "We were married," she went on slowly, "before I knew what he had enshrined in the little wall cupboard in the upstairs sitting-room. At least he didn't marry me for my information—he picked my brains dry before he even proposed. Before . . ."

"Hold on!" He took her hand and pressed it to his side. She sat very straight, staring sternly at the wall above his head. The light was brighter behind her by the minute, fuzzing the outline of her tumbled hair. "I ought to go. Isn't it inconvenient, living so close?"

She saw him again, and briefly smiled.

"Yes." Neither of them had ever mentioned Cathy by name in this connection, although they had mentioned Miss Prince, and giggled.

He held her hand even more tightly. "And the vase is in the dream?"

"Yes." The bewildered look he had seen before was back in her face. "It's on the table by his chair. Just where he used to put it when he looked at it. He never actually brought it out when I was there, but if I came in when he was looking at it he'd ask me to join him, and then he'd point out its particular beauties. Neil, you can imagine—how I felt about it, too."

"Yes, of course." His sombre thoughts were shot through with the thrill of danger. "When did you last have the dream?"

"Last night. I mean, the night before. The night he died."

They stared solemnly at one another. Eventually he said, spurred by the gathering day, "And the vase was there?"

"I'm sure I'd have noticed if it wasn't."

"Take me to the British Museum?"

"Yes, of course. This afternoon, if you like. If you can."

"I can. I'm playing a bit of a waiting game at the moment. But can you? It's only Friday."

"Stephen said he was going to be at the gallery today and he wouldn't expect me if I didn't feel like going, or—or if I was wanted for anything. I will go in this morning, I'd rather, but I needn't go this afternoon. Stephen's being—awfully nice. Somewhat unhimself, though. I mean, I wouldn't have expected him to be so concerned."

"No, well, I don't know him. He seems a nice enough chap." He tried not to tense, not to let her notice his interest.

"Oh, he is, but I've never thought he was the sort of person who was very much aware of other people. That's why he surprised me a bit yesterday."

"I must go." Neil sat up, put his hands on her shoulders and pushed her gently back on to the pillow. He moved his hands down her body. Between the still sharp pelvic bones her stomach was slightly rounded. "Do you feel any different?"

"Yes. Fuller. And aware of my top half. It was exciting."

"It still is," he said glibly, "it's life." He kissed her forehead. As he crossed the landing he recalled how Cathy looked when at her spyhole, from watching her when she had leaned up to peer out at Hilary and the Press. The possibility of being seen by her at such an hour was nothing like so disagreeable as the idea that she might be looking. He was grateful, as he let himself into his flat, to realize he was unable to believe that she could be.

He didn't really know why he rang her bell as soon as he had finished his breakfast. Cathy came to the door with one of her home-thrown coffee cups in her hand and still wearing her conspiratorial smile. His relief at seeing it might explain his presence on her doorstep.

"Come in, Neil! Coffee?"

"Quickly, then."

He wasn't sure yet whether he was going to keep the fact of the

vase from Cathy as well as from the Chief, so he merely asked her if
he could see her later.

"I asked Hilary to supper and she said she'd come. But I don't
suppose she'll want to stay very late. Shall I give you a ring when
she's gone?"

"Yes, I suppose that's the best thing."

And Hilary, ringing to tell him she was at home and awaiting him,
would find the line engaged or else no reply. It could now be as
difficult to keep his conspiracy hidden from Hilary as to keep his liai-
son hidden from Cathy.

He had an impulse to book into a hotel.

CHAPTER 13

Aphrodite was crouched beside a mosaic the size of a goldfish pond,
her blank eyes on its medallioned bacchantes. Behind her a flight of
steps led up to a curtain before which stood Apollo, caught in the
serpentine twists of a lute which suggested to Neil nothing so much
as a Victorian heating system.

"Nineteenth-century?" he suggested.

"First!" It was her one ghost of a smile since the lunch table,
when she had begged to see the worst of the newspaper pieces and
he, who had seen them all in the office, had gone out and bought it
for her. "Roman copy of the Greek. The vase is behind the curtain."

"It's got quite a setting."

He stopped abruptly at the foot of the steps. *Marble portrait
statue of a woman found in the temple of Aphrodite at Cyrene.
Roman* A.D. *130–150.*

"You're here already!"

The surprise of the encounter tingled in his scalp and spine. Same
height, same carriage. Same bones and nose. Same elegant small ears.
He put his hand up to push back Hilary's hair and confirm his impression, then held her to the spot by her warm brown arm. The cor-

responding marble arm was missing, the other held up the enveloping robe, eternally revealing the skirt beneath.

"What do you mean?" She shook her hair back into place.

"Look in the mirror."

"What mirror?"

"The ancient one in front of you. For instance, the toes."

She put a foot forward, brown sandalled foot against white one, each long second toe breaking the slanting line. He was aware that she shivered as she drew back.

"That's how I've felt, too. Cold as marble."

"But you found you weren't." He had to regret his indulgence. "As E. B. Browning pointed out, 'Touch it' "—he laid a finger on a sightless eye—" 'the marble eyelids are not wet. If it could weep, it could arise and go.' " But he had wished she would weep again, when he had watched her face at lunch-time. He pressed her arm against his side. "You should be flattered that I have your feet and ears by heart."

"Come on."

Behind the curtain was a small bright room with a few sparsely occupied display cases round its edges and in the centre, on a pedestal, a black vase with a white frieze of near-nude classical figures and foliage. As they drew nearer, it appeared both more imperfect and more impressive. The white was just translucent, hinting at the dark body of the vase beneath, and Neil saw for himself that the body was a very dark blue. The fine network of breakage was unimportant.

"What's it all about?"

"Nobody really knows." Her whisper formed a curious continuity with their conversation of the early morning. "The front runner is the betrothal of the sea goddess Thetis to the mortal Peleus, which I dare say doesn't tell you much."

"Well, no." A disc with the relief image of a fully clad man under a tree was propped up in the case. "What's that?" He pointed, glancing at her rapt face.

"It was pinned to the bottom of the vase until the attack, but it doesn't belong. The original base would have been blown with the body, and must have been broken off. This one is old enough, but the work is quite different. 'Alien but ancient,' as the guide rather nicely puts it. Oh, Neil. It's tremendous, isn't it?"

"Yes." He meant it, although he wasn't swallowing hard as she was, and suspected the impact on him to be as much from her reaction as from the vase itself. "I don't really know why, though."

"Josiah explained it." She prowled a circle round the case and began to quote softly when she was once more standing beside him. " 'It is apparent, that the artist has availed himself very ably of the dark ground, in producing the perspective and distance required, by cutting the white away, nearer to the ground as the shades were wanted deeper, so that the white is often cut to the thinness of paper.' You see . . . 'The blue glass, when formed and still red hot, was coated over, as far as the bas-reliefs were intended to reach, with the white glass. . . . The figures were afterwards produced in this coat by cutting it down to the blue ground in the manner of real cameos—by which means he has given to his work the effect of painting as well as sculpture; and it will be found that a bas-relief with all the figures of one uniform white colour upon a dark ground, will be a very faint resemblance of what this artist has had the address to produce by calling in the aid of colour to assist his relief. That hollowness of the rocks, and depth of shade in other parts, produced by cutting down to the dark ground, and to which it owes no small part of its beauty, would all be wanting, and a disgusting flatness appear in their stead. It is here that I am most sensible of my weakness. . . .' You can see that weakness in later copies." Hilary turned away from the case and smiled at Neil. "Figures in icing sugar. But in his own first work—Josiah got it right."

"It must have been fantastic for you—when you suddenly found yourself able to touch and hold."

He had never seen her flushed like this, her lips apart, her face open. But it closed as he spoke, and her eyes went cold. He felt again the brief thrill of danger.

"Yes, well, I can't show you Peter's treasure, but I can show you the nearest thing to it."

They had to come back into the main hall and mount the long shallow flight of stone stairs. The effect of sumptuous artifice in the upper galleries made him aware, now he had lost it, of the sense of golden age simplicity and innocence he had felt below.

"In here," said Hilary, but even as her hand took his arm to lead him forward, it grasped him painfully to drag him back.

"Hell's teeth, what is it?"

They were in the corner of the cabinet-lined corridor which led to the gallery they had almost entered. She was pressed back into the angle, and held him in front of her, close.

"It's Anthony. Looking at the vase. Standing staring at it."

He heard himself suggesting there was no reason why he shouldn't go in alone. "And I'd like to see Anthony as well as the vase. I'm rather good at not being noticeable, I won't lose my advantage. Look, love, hold on." Her grey face and staring eyes had pierced his professional excitement. "I'll get you to the ladies first, or—"

"No, I'm all right. It's a chance, you ought to take it." She dropped her hands. He saw her will-power at work in the tightening of her mouth. "Go on, Neil. I'll wait for you on those seats that go round the building outside, where it says not to feed the birds. Just cover me along here."

He stood at the entrance to the gallery, looking in on the slight intent figure beside one of the lighted cases, until a backward glance showed him the corridor was empty. Then he moved forward, making his way stealthily but slowly towards the only other person in the room. By the time he had passed Carey, Neil had the externals by heart. A small man, graceful in his stance and movements, dark hair curling in tendrils towards a face whose pallor could only be guessed at in the distorting gloom. The eyes had to be large, judging by the size of the dual shadows which hid them, the hands were small, as Neil saw when they came out towards the glass, again and then again, in a movement which made him think of the forward flickering of a snake's tongue—but of course, the build-up and the eventual setting for the encounter would encourage extravagant reactions. Neil would have been prepared, without any build-up at all, for a meeting of eyes with this man to evoke an interested response, and so he must not let it happen. He walked slowly round the gallery, not risking a proper look at the Wedgwood Portland, but keeping within his oblique glance the small figure circling and recircling the same showcase. When he left, Anthony Carey was still absorbed.

The seat she had chosen was well away from the entrance. Disconsolate pigeons round her feet were pecking at litter and their own droppings.

"It's all right, he shows no signs of coming away and I don't think he even noticed anyone else was there. But let's move." He glanced at her as they walked rapidly to the gates. "You look a bit better."

"I'm all right. It was just the shock."

"You're seeing the doctor?"

"Of course." They were in Great Russell Street, and slightly relaxing their pace. "Could you—tell anything about him?"

"Oh, yes. I could tell that if he had noticed me at all, he would really have noticed me."

"But you're sure . . ."

"He didn't. He was totally taken up with the vase. I wonder what it means?"

"I should think he's simply making sure that his treasure is really what he hopes it is."

He should have thought about it before. "Hilary—what about Peter's estate? The house and contents?"

She stopped to stare at him. A small fat woman who had been walking behind them cannoned into her and edged past with an irritated glare. She didn't notice.

"I don't know. We both made wills ages ago leaving everything to each other. Anthony must have seen to it by now that Peter made another. Anyway, I don't want anything, I took the few things that counted when I furnished the flat."

"Don't be silly. If Peter made a new will and didn't leave you anything, you'll have to contest it. Anyway, the law today says a wife must get something." She had begun to look through him again, at one of her ugly pictures. He took her arm and urged her on. "Don't think about it now, and even when you have to, it'll be done at a distance. Have you got a good solicitor?"

"Yes. Yes." A fat man with a red face went past them lingeringly, staring at Hilary. She saw him, jerked her head exaggeratedly away. "Neil, he's seen that photograph. I didn't want them to take it, but they said there'd be bound to be one, some way, and better to have a dignified one. As if there was any dignity in any of this! And that man is just one of the people who've seen it."

"He's seen a beautiful woman in the street. A damsel far too evidently in distress. Let's get home and have tea. It's not often we can have afternoon tea on a weekday."

She said listlessly, "I'm having supper with Cathy. She'll be so careful not to upset me she'll probably make me angry."

"Plenty of time first for tea."

He knew she would be unlikely to eat them, but he bought some scones on the way from the tube. When they came out of the lift they went to their own front doors, but Neil strolled back across the landing as Miss Prince emerged from hers and started speaking to Hilary.

"Oh, Miss Fielding, your assistant rang my bell this morning and gave me your note authorizing me to let her into your flat. I'm afraid she must have thought me quite senile, I just stared at her at first, but I'd been reading the paper, and—I'm so very sorry, Miss Fielding —I mean Mrs. Sharp, isn't it, no, Shaw—and I somehow hadn't

imagined you would have gone to your business today. . . . But any-
how I pulled my silly self together and let her in. It's no wonder you
forgot your key, what with . . . I'd have been a bit nervous without
the note, but—"

"She gave you the note?" Hilary's name would most appropriately
have been steel.

"Well." Miss Prince blinked and smiled at them uncertainly. "I
said that, and of course I held it in my hand while I read it, and
then somehow she must have taken it back, because when she had
gone I looked round to tidy it up, and it wasn't there. Not that it
mattered, I'd let her in and told her to let herself out. . . . When I
heard her leaving I came out and locked the mortice. I hope she
managed to find the references you asked her to look up. *Such* a nice
girl, Miss Fielding, Mrs. Sharp, such a refreshing change to see a
young girl these days wearing a *skirt*. And she even wore *gloves*, clean
white cotton gloves."

Neil was close enough to feel her shudder, but her voice was still
calm.

"How long was she there, Miss Prince? How long did it take her?"

"Well, I did hear the latch click, as I said; I suppose it was about
twenty minutes to half an hour, about half past ten, and I saw her
through my little spy-hole, going towards the lift. She'd put her
gloves on again, so refreshing—"

"Thank you," said Hilary, so faintly that Miss Prince's kindly face
clouded over. She took a step forward.

"If there's anything I can do, Mrs. . . ."

"Call me Hilary. No, thank you very much, I'm all right."

"I don't know, dear, you don't look . . ." Miss Prince's vague yet
penetrating gaze turned on Neil. "But of course, Mr. Carter being a
detective . . . such a sad business . . ."

"I'm not concerned professionally," said Neil, "but I can at least
advise Mrs. Shaw on what to expect in the way of police formalities."

"Formalities, yes," took up Miss Prince eagerly, "and it did say the
police weren't . . . oh dear"—she blinked from one to the other—"I
must let you go and rest. I hope your young assistant—I don't think
she told me her name though it must have been in the letter—I hope
she found what she was looking for?"

"She didn't, actually," said Hilary. Her door, with her and Neil
behind it, shut before Miss Prince's. "She didn't, she didn't, she
didn't."

She leaned against the wall with her eyes shut, banging her head back with each repetition, beside the open cupboard door. The bottles inside tottered as if a seeking hand had struck from edge to edge, a couple of small boxes lay open on the carpet beneath, their contents scattered.

"Go and look in the other rooms, Neil"—she didn't open her eyes —"and come and tell me. *Go on.*"

In the sitting-room the desk top was down, the deep bottom drawer half out. Sofa and armchairs were not quite in their usual places, a low deep cupboard was gaping, a scatter of assorted objects half in and half out. In the two bedrooms and the kitchen the invading presence had left a stronger trail, because there were more enclosed spaces to investigate.

"No damage," said Neil, coming back to where she still leaned against the wall with closed eyes. "Nothing that won't respond to tidying up. It was a search, I should say, for something which could have been standing in a cupboard or a deep drawer. Little drawers aren't open."

"Of course it was. It was a search for the Portland vase. You know as well as I do now the size of it."

"I don't know the size of all this." He laid his hand against her cheek, without response. "Come and sit down. Either let me carry you or open your eyes. It's not going to be too upsetting. You haven't got an assistant, have you?"

"Of course not." She opened her eyes and walked slowly, with her usual step and stance, into the sitting-room. "Oh, I knew exactly what you'd find, I knew as soon as that silly old woman . . . But I can't blame her. . . . Neil, he hasn't got it!"

"Who hasn't got what?" She had sat down on the sofa and he swung her legs up on to the neighbouring cushions and squatted on the floor beside her, holding her limp hand. To his relief he saw that her colour was almost normal and that she had focused her eyes. There was a sort of triumph in them.

"Anthony! He hasn't got the vase! But he knows it exists, he's looking for it, or why would he go through all that business to get in here? Neil, Peter must have done something with it—and Anthony's afraid of *me!*"

He could only stare at her, as he worked to keep his thoughts out of his face. The least naïve of women . . . yet apparently unable to think of any way the vase might have come into her possession except by the intention of her husband . . . of any other reason why Anthony might be afraid . . . Anthony . . .

"What do you mean, Anthony? Miss Prince said it was a young girl."

"Oh yes," she said impatiently. "Anthony makes a most convincing young girl. I've seen him at parties. And anyway, even real men are fantastic in drag, you must know that."

"Yes. I am myself. But it seems—"

"The vase is priceless. But how he knew about Miss Prince . . ."

"That would be the easiest bit. The local electoral roll. Miss Prince is a near-numbered flat—Number Thirty-eight."

"Or easier still. Peter found the flat for me, he must have seen Miss Prince, she's bound to have been hovering."

"And being a retired lady, at home most of the time, was likely to have been entrusted with a second key. And Peter could have brought Anthony with him, or at least mentioned the setup. Anyway, it could only have been a try-on. If it was Anthony."

"It was."

"Even if it hadn't come off, he was safe in his disguise, he only had to take his leave. And—can you see into the gallery from the street?"

"Pretty well, yes."

"And you?"

"When I'm at my table, and I suppose I mostly am."

"Well, then, the young girl had only to look in your window to find out if it was worth going on to Westcote Gardens. Now, I'm afraid you must ring the Yard and ask them to send someone over so that they can see what's been done here, and hear the story."

"You don't count, then?"

"No."

"But you can telephone for me? Please, if you can."

"Oh, I can do that."

"In the bedroom, as you well know. Neil, do they have to be told about the vase?"

He leaned forward and put his face against hers. "What do you think?"

She gave a long sigh. "Yes, of course they do. It was just . . . I've just realized how much I enjoyed the secret."

"It stopped being one when Anthony was let into it."

"Of course. Neil, you're so nice sometimes."

"I'll leave you to tell them about the vase. And your theory. Don't move. I'll put the kettle on on my way back."

He asked for the Chief, got him, and told him the facts deadpan.

"Right you are, Neil, it's quite unexpected. Are you with the lady now?"

"Yes. I thought I'd better make her a cup of hot sweet tea."

She sat up to take the cup from him.

"No sugar, thanks. I feel a bit sick, thinking about Anthony being in here. Thumbing through my things. Just being here."

"And then on to the British Museum."

"To refresh his memory. Neil, I can't even make it to Cathy tonight. And I've got to be here anyway when the police come. Will it be soon?"

"I should think so. I'll go and tell Cathy for you. Even eat your supper if she'll have me." This evening, at least, would be easier vis-à-vis the two women than he had feared.

"Thank you. Leave me the scones, I'll have a try at them later. I think I'll be quite glad for you to go now. And come back . . ."

He got up. "Don't touch anything. And tell the other policemen everything you've told this one. Tomorrow I'll go to your husband's shop. See Mr. Carey again. Can you give me a handle?"

"Long-case clocks," she said listlessly. "Grandfathers. He owns a very good William and Mary walnut. It's at the house."

"That will do."

"You'll lose your anonymity."

"But I may gain something else."

Although he no longer expected Cathy to be exuberant, he fancied she seemed worried rather than glad when he invited himself to supper. But it was still a relief to be able to talk without reserve. He tried not to be conscious of an increasing nervousness in her manner, the way she made eager rushes at conversation, then lapsed into preoccupied silence. The big theme of Peter Shaw's death just got them through the meal.

Silence took over as Cathy served the coffee and snuggled into her corner of the sofa. Usually, realized Neil, a companionable thing between them, and he watched with interest as she struggled to break it—too much interest to try and help her out.

"The fact that Anthony was looking for the vase," she managed with relieved enthusiasm, after a long restless minute, "if it is a fact" —briefly she dropped her eyes again—"doesn't really tell us anything, does it, about whether he killed Peter—meant to kill him—or not. I mean, Peter might have hidden the vase, or disposed of it, or someone else could have killed him and taken it. Or Anthony could have killed him for it—and then found it wasn't there."

"Yes." It was a string of good points. He said slowly, "Hilary seemed—*triumphant* at the thought that Anthony apparently hadn't got it."

"Which could be a very natural reaction, or . . ."

"Or mean that she herself had put it out of his reach," finished Neil steadily. "And yet—I'm certain she's telling the truth when she says she hasn't been back to that house since she left it more than three months ago."

"Of course!" said Cathy. The unconvincing heartiness of her tone would have bothered him, if he'd thought her mind had really been on what he was saying.

"Don't worry," he said. "You are worrying, aren't you? Is that what it is?"

She took a gulping breath, her face flooding scarlet.

"No. I couldn't think you'd notice . . . Neil, I wouldn't say this if it wasn't that you asked me to help you."

"Wouldn't say what?" She was so unlike herself, twisting her hands together, not looking at him while she spoke. "What is it, Cathy?"

She looked up then, imploringly. "Neil, Hilary writes a diary, the book lives in a drawer of the desk in her sitting-room. She's often said that's what she's doing when I've gone to see her, and I've seen her slip it into the drawer. You know how we don't always lock our balconies. If you got me one of those little cameras they have in films for photographing the pages of books—well, I could photograph pages of that for you, if that isn't going beyond what you feel you ought to do."

He thought about it for a brief moment from Hilary's point of view, then with alarm from his own. He had never in his life been at such a miserable loss to respond to a suggestion.

"I wouldn't look at it," said Cathy, staring him now in the eyes. "It wouldn't be for me to look at it and I wouldn't want to. But even so, Neil, I'm going to tell you now what I know, so that you'll be absolutely sure I didn't look at it—that is, if it says anything . . ." She faltered again, then looked away. "I just want to tell you," she told the chair arm, "and this may make things easier for you too, now that we're working together and you'll perhaps be seeing more of me than you normally would, to save you at least from having to explain to *me*, if not to Hilary—"

"Come on, Cathy."

"I know you and Hilary are lovers," she said firmly, to him. "So you don't have to cover things up. And I'm awfully sorry for you."

"Thank you, Cathy." There was absolutely nothing else to say. And for the moment, nothing to feel.

"Do you love her very much?" Cathy asked lightly.

He opened his mouth to say that that didn't come into it, but suddenly thought she might be more shocked than pleased. He found himself hoping she wouldn't find out about the baby before—when? What was he thinking of?

"No," he said. "Did Hilary tell you? Or have you seen me come or go at a revealing time?"

"No!" She was angry. "And Hilary hasn't told me, hasn't hinted. . . . I just happen to know you both and—be fond of you both. And not an utter fool."

"I'm sorry," he said humbly.

"It's all right." She leaned forward to pour him more coffee. He was unable to prevent himself from putting his hand on her wrist. She drew back neither more quickly nor more slowly than usual. "So don't worry," she said, pouring coffee for herself, "if you can't see me because of—that. Just tell me Hilary, and I'll understand. Don't make up a story."

"I won't. And I'd far rather not." The only tribute his gratitude could pay was in not protesting itself.

"Shall I photograph the diary, then?" She shook hair out of her eyes. "As I said, you'd have to get me the right sort of camera."

"I don't know. I'll tell you tomorrow, when I've thought about it. I'm going to see Anthony Carey tomorrow, too. Incognito, of course."

"And the brother-in-law? And big Clara?"

"Clara, like Carey, is open to the public. I shall see her again."

"I met her at Hilary's, I liked her. Warm, and lots of energy which she seemed to be handing round."

"Uncle Arthur?"

"Him I haven't met. I don't think Hilary likes him much."

"He's a cold fish. A complete contrast to his wife. He hates my guts. I don't know why," he added quickly. He thought he did know, that it was an instinct of the rival male, but he remembered he wasn't telling Cathy of this extra among Hilary's troubles.

He was glad to stay with Cathy until their new and uncomfortable understanding seemed to have been absorbed in the atmosphere of their conspiracy.

He went, now, from one door to the other. When she had let him in Hilary turned away without a word and he followed her into the bedroom. She sat down on the edge of the bed and stared at the carpet. He stood beside her.

"Was it very awful?" he asked at last.

She didn't look up. "No. Not at all. I told them everything as you said I should."

"Good. But you're tired. Do you want me to stay?"

"I don't want it, and I don't not want it. The truth is, Neil, I don't seem to have any views on anything. Except the baby. So don't worry, I'll look after myself." She raised her head then, trying to smile, but her drained pallor seemed to strike him physically.

She didn't say anything else until they were in bed and he had begun to doze, despite feeling that it would be kind to stay awake. She said very softly, "They took away a pair of my shoes. The flatties. They said they might as well take them while they were here. They needed them for a routine check. Routine check, they said. Good night."

It was a long time then before he dozed again, and he couldn't be sure whether Hilary, silent beside him, her back turned, slept or kept vigil, she slept always so quietly. One moment awake, the next he was jerking up from unconsciousness, from the red head of maths master Don Everett, rising over the horizon of a dream. Trying to keep still in the darkness, he realized he had lost the one point of relief which while he had it he had failed to recognize: the thought of Cathy knowing where he would be in the night, and of how she had taken it.

CHAPTER 14

He had looked at a map, and he knew which road to take off the long straight highway bounded by Kew Gardens wall. He didn't intend to stop at the house, but the lucky coincidence of a woman with a pram waiting to cross allowed him a glimpse of the curving drive and the Gothic eaves among the treetops.

Holly Lodge . . . The gateposts were surmounted by hospitable stone pineapples, but as he accelerated away Neil shivered in the heat of his sun-drenched car, thinking of a dream become a nightmare. Thinking, too, that a car drawn up to the front door would not be visible from the roadway. . . .

Kew was still a village, radiating from its Victorian Norman station, which precisely faced Victoria Gate, the length of a plane-lined street. He managed to park at the hub, and before he had locked his door he could see what from Hilary's description must be Clara's shop—bow-window set with random bottle glass, white wrought-iron troughs on the pavement, one in a line of variegated small premises with only charm in common.

Neil sauntered along the road. It must be his unofficial status making him feel relaxed, despite his constant awareness of his own oblique role in the crime he was stalking. But his long habit of official investigation still made him move in such a way that he would be hidden from the interior of his objective until the last possible moment.

The caution paid off as handsomely as it had ever done. While still safe from discovery he was able to see that there were two people in the shop, to see Clara Shaw at close enough quarters to read the expression of her face, masked intermittently by the shoulders of the man she was talking to. Or listening to. Or simply looking at. Idling in his shaded angle, glancing at the newspaper in his hands, at his watch, at the newspaper, Neil was registering the naked desire in Clara's gaze. It was an astonishing, an unhinted-at thing, and yet he found that it was not really a surprise to him, as if that Sunday morning on Hilary's sofa she had somehow signalled its potential. But for a moment, hardened as he was to a range of unsocial reactions, it made him feel uncomfortable, as if he was looking into a bedroom rather than a shop window.

And then the man moved into his full view, and Clara Shaw was glancing aside, smiling, as Neil remembered her. She walked to the door and opened it and the man hurried out, passing Neil at a rapid pace, heading for the station. A tall good-looking man, younger than Mrs. Shaw.

She now was in the sunshine, rearranging the pots in one of the troughs, biting her lower lip, expressionless. Slowly Neil moved the few steps necessary for her to be aware of him.

"Neil Carter! What fun on a Saturday morning! Your work falls in quite pleasant places."

She had known him instantly, and was there a wariness preceding her warm response? He could have imagined it. She held out a hand to him. It was hot, slightly moist.

"Sometimes." Absurdly she made him think of Cathy, but her slightly breathless spontaneity might not be what it seemed, surely couldn't be, in the family circumstances. She also wore a quizzical look.

"You're at work now?"

There were two things she could have meant. "Yes. But not at this moment. Or at this precise spot." Not for the first time, he was grateful to have the kind of work whose current intricacies no one expected to be informed on. "I've come very slightly out of my way to say how sorry I am about what's happened."

Her face didn't change, but he was all at once aware she was tired. "Thank you. You're consoling Hilary?"

He took a gamble. "Very unofficially, as things are."

"You mean—you *are* involved in the investigation?"

"No. But my colleagues are. I don't want to tread on their toes, so my profile is low, to be wildly anatomical in my metaphors." He smiled frankly, knowing the usual effect of it, but doubtful now. Certainly Clara Shaw didn't show any reaction. The reaction he had seen in her face when he first caught sight of her began to appear even more extraordinary.

"I'm very glad you're across the landing, anyway." She was smiling now, but her eyes were keen. He was as sure that she knew what was going on between him and Hilary as he was that Hilary hadn't told her. He realized again how much he was inclined to like her, without finding her in the least attractive sexually.

"Of course. She's feeling terrible."

"She was very much in love with Peter," said Clara Shaw lightly. "And that 'was' goes right up to his death. A bit rum, isn't it, not knowing whether it's murder or natural causes? Won't you come inside?"

"Just for a moment. Thanks." The dazzling dark of the shop told him he had been facing into the sun. "It's all very strange and difficult," he said. She could go on guessing just how much he knew.

"More than rum, really." Through the gloom Neil saw her turn and titivate some carnations in a tall jar. "None of us has an alibi. But I expect you know."

He felt himself reacting to good news.

"I told you, I'm not on the case. But—none of you?"

"Well, none of us was doing anything special. Except dear Anthony." She was being rough, now, with some white flowers in the next container, so that a cluster of petals snowed to the floor. "But it seems rather odd that it should take him an hour to drive home from the City in the middle of the night."

"How do you know?" asked Neil. "I hardly imagined you and he—"

"We don't." She took a shuddery breath and her bosom, no more strongly reined than when he had last seen it, swung in its straining blouse. "But Arthur really thought he should go round. To get some idea, for a start—"

"Yes, of course." He could imagine those cold eyes at work in the rooms of the brother's house, making mental inventories to compare with the ones made inevitably over earlier visits. Had they ever fallen, knowing or unknowing, on that blue-black shape which Neil already felt so deeply familiar?

"And Anthony was blabbing all over the place about being harassed because he couldn't account for all the time spent between leaving his City jamboree and getting home."

"Anyway, Hilary hasn't been around her old home for the last few months," commented Neil, watching.

"No." She looked back at him, as intently, and he was all at once extremely uncomfortable.

"Well, I must go, I'm on the job."

"Thank you for coming." She smiled her crooked smile. It was harder and harder to believe what he had seen. But the shop, perhaps, was like its owner—untidy, packed with flowers and plants preponderantly large and bright, giving an impression of being only just under control. . . .

She was urging him to see as much of Hilary as he could. Evidently her husband, if he had put his angry disdain into words, had failed to influence her.

"Of course." He suspected they were both thinking of the baby. Clara Shaw, though, could not be sure that he knew about it. "And you will too, I hope."

"I have and I will. Not that Hilary gets in touch with me as much as she used to. Well, I suppose I remind her."

"Perhaps you do." She had been standing in her sitting-room window. *Since Peter and I split up I somehow haven't wanted Clara as much. . . .* Nor her husband. . . .

He was lucky she hadn't really responded to his premature intention to leave.

"How has your husband taken it?"

"Badly. Not that he tells me. But I know him so well." There was a sort of power in her smile. He could imagine that neat head against her bosom only if he thought of it there as suppliant rather than lover.

"It's strange," he said, "to be concerned for Hilary, for you and your husband. And not to know what it is that you've lost. Tell me, Mrs. Shaw, I haven't the least real idea—what was your brother-in-law *like?*"

She felt with her hand behind her, transferred part of her weight to the counter. Her heavy body emphasized the slenderness of her ankles and wrists. "It was the overall thing that got you. Charm, I suppose." Her face, briefly, was softened by her memory. Out of his league, no doubt, Neil thought, on a jealous pang which annoyed him. "He was the kind of man who made everyone feel he or she was the only person who mattered. I say everyone because I've seen him do it time and again with women selling flags and people who served him in shops or restaurants. He was witty too, and entertaining—he made you laugh." She stopped, laughing herself, a bit self-consciously.

"Was he," asked Neil, "cruel?"

She stopped laughing. He could see she was considering the question.

She said at last, slowly, "No. I don't think he was. That's what made it worse."

"It?"

"When he had—done with people. I used to think—well, it was Hilary who said it, when they were still together and looking happy —the shopkeepers and women selling flags were the best off, really. He was charming to them, and they hadn't got him to lose."

"He tended to move on?"

"That was it. I'm not talking particularly about sex. He and Hilary had a good marriage. But he had an energetic, inquiring mind, and it was always leading him on. Business. Bees in his ingenious bonnet. So leaving Hilary was eventually part of that, I suppose."

"Was it sudden, do you know?"

"I'm certain it showed itself suddenly. It always did. Oh, we saw a lot of him and Hilary. He and Arthur are—were—very different and not at all close, but they were—aware of being brothers, if you see what I mean."

"I think so."

"I think in a way Arthur was fascinated by Peter, even where he didn't approve of him. Not that I'm saying Peter was exactly a subject for disapproval. More that Arthur has rather strict ideas of right and wrong."

"What did Peter Shaw look like?"

"Tall, large build, adding up to a good-looking man, someone you noticed probably more than the other men in a room. But if you took him feature by feature you wondered why. Except for his voice. It's hardest of all to believe that Peter's voice is dead. Oh, Neil Carter"—her whole weight now was against the fortunately sturdy counter—"I can hardly bear to think of Hilary." She stood upright. "Or that little toad in Holly Lodge!"

"You don't like Carey, then?"

"Neil Carter!"

"What I should have said was, you didn't like him?"

She shrugged. "I didn't like or dislike him. I suppose I never thought of him as very important." Her lips parted, briefly and unattractively, in a self-mocking rictus. "I didn't object to him on principle, as Arthur did."

"Even when he was minding his own business?"

"Well, he was minding Peter's business, actually. And Arthur doesn't approve of the third sex." Was there irony in her voice? There was none in her bland face.

"You think your brother-in-law would have moved on from Carey?"

She nodded vigorously, and he was slightly ashamed as he realized she was unable to speak.

"I do apologize," he said, with instant tenderness, "for asking all these questions and not even being involved—except in being concerned for all of you."

She shook herself, and he thought of a large dog bounding out of the water.

"I'm sorry, too, but it's just that it's—so awful. And oh yes, I'm convinced Mr. Carey was no more than Peter's means of expressing the—the change in his nature. Announcing it."

"A real change, then?"

"It must have been." She shifted her weight.

"I dearly hope," said Neil, "that it will be quickly resolved. If it is to be resolved at all."

"You think it may not be?"

"I think—there are cases where that is the best solution."

She moved past him, picked a long-stemmed rose, broke the stem, and pressed the flower into his buttonhole. Close to, she remained a person to him, strong in her personality, but not a desirable woman. "It's much too bright and open a day for riddles, Neil Carter, and I too am on the job."

There were three people in the open doorway.

"I'll look forward to seeing you the next time," said Neil. Her hand now was cooler and drier.

Richmond Green looked magical, but yielded no parking place. A quarter of an hour had passed when he returned on foot to the lane whose longest façade was headed *Peter Shaw Antiques*.

Again he watched, from an undetectable spot, a proprietor in conversation, but saw only what looked like the routine sale of an alabaster figurine. He passed its buyer in the doorway, a young woman with whom Anthony Carey had appeared formally courteous. Neil defined the response in the moment he saw it assume, on his own entrance, a further dimension. A caution. But an awareness . . .

"Can I help you?" asked Anthony Carey.

"Not specifically," said Neil. "Your windows are so magnetic you must get a number of people just wanting to look around."

"I invite them to look around." Carey waved a hand towards the door, where the white card was affixed. Neil remembered the last time he had seen Carey's hand raised, stretched out. . . . He was certain he was being observed for the first time, and in the daylight which, although tempered with shadows and the glow of artistically poised lamps, was infinitely brighter than the upper gallery of the British Museum where they had first stood together, he felt that he too was studying a man not previously seen.

"Thank you," he said, examining a Chinese vase, absorbing the sober conventionality of Anthony Carey's business costume, grey suit on palest blue shirt and blue tie, the face-framing brown curls, the small features in a pale face, the large, blue and keenly intelligent eyes. The eyes, really, were the only distinguishing features, the rest were so conventionally correct, on their small scale, they could have belonged to a composite picture of a youth or maiden. . . . If Neil had seen Carey first in drag, unknowing, he would probably have made a bit of a fool of himself. And—several times, inevitably, with his own lean grace, he had been approached from the stronger side; once, at school, tempted from the weaker. But that had been before he had discovered women, when all he had known was that he had something. . . .

When Carey smiled, as he did when Neil suddenly looked at him straight, Neil saw one front tooth ahead of the rest and a glint of gold and found himself thinking of Hilary's tall husband.

"There is something, actually," said Neil, rather sooner than he had intended, but to change the direction of his thoughts. Carey was all attention, gliding the few steps which had separated them. There was no sign in the expectant face of any strain or distress but—if Hilary was right—the man was an actor.

"Yes, sir, what is it?"

"Long-case clocks," said Neil, lingeringly to make sure he didn't sound as if he was saying it by heart. "When I was a boy we had a walnut one—turn of the seventeenth/eighteenth centuries—"

"Of course."

"I loved it without appreciating it, and it was sold."

Anthony Carey clicked his tongue in reproachful sympathy.

"And I suppose I've been vaguely looking for it ever since," said Neil, almost believing what he was saying and rather proud of the extempore development of his original story. But then he, too, was an actor. "I only ever seem to see it in museums, but I can never resist asking."

"Ask, and it shall be given unto you!" It was in those few gospel words that Neil first noted the camp timbre and pattern of Anthony Carey's speech, emphasized by excitement.

"You don't mean . . ."

"Not here, not I'm afraid for sale. But I have a very fine example at home. Daniel Quare. Yours, perhaps?" The conventionally lovely features stretched in an impish smile. Neil, aware of the charm, involuntarily shivered.

"Oh, I was too young to register the maker of mine," he said, managing not to sound hasty. "And it wouldn't have meant anything if I had. It still wouldn't, I'm afraid, I'm a furniture fancier, but no expert."

"Appreciation is what comes first in all the arts," said Carey firmly, provoking from Neil at least one willingly approving response. "I should be delighted," he went on, looking briefly down as Cathy might have done, brushing specks off a leather table-top, "to show it to you. Would you—"

The blue eyes swooped up to Neil's face.

"Goodness," said Neil, "that's really awfully kind." He wasn't bothering to try and keep his distance, because he wouldn't be going alone.

"Nothing would give me more pleasure. When could you . . . I'm only in Kew, by the way." A card was in his hand, in Neil's. The face had clouded for the first time. "I'm Anthony Carey. And if you haven't realized why this place is familiar, it'll click when you put everything together, so I'll say it now, don't feel embarrassed, don't feel you have to avoid—"

"Oh dear," said Neil, "yes. Peter Shaw Antiques. Mr. Shaw . . . of course I've seen . . . I'm very sorry."

"We were friends as well as business colleagues," said Anthony Carey softly. "We both lived at Holly Lodge." He said it in such a way that, had Neil not known otherwise, it would have sounded like an immemorial arrangement.

"Then I'm more sorry than I can say. And I'm sure you won't possibly want a stranger coming to look at your clock—"

"But of course I will. Peter wouldn't want me to stop spreading the word because . . ."

Carey faltered, the blue eyes took on an additional sparkle. For the first time Neil felt the reaction could be involuntary.

"All right, then," he said. "Thank you. Of course I'd like to see it."

"When would you like to come, Mr. . . . ?"

"Collins. Well, if you don't want to wait—"

"I shall be glad of company. It's a large house and an empty one. Monday? Eight o'clock?"

"That really is awfully kind of you."

"Not at all. You'll be doing me a good turn. . . ." Perhaps there had been a pause there, for a sign which Neil hadn't given. Anthony Carey hurried on. "Is there anything else I can show you?"

"Oh, I could stay all morning," said Neil, all at once unable to stay another minute. "But"—he consulted his major get-out—"I see I'm already late."

Anthony Carey conducted him to the door. Neil wouldn't or couldn't turn round as he walked up the lane, but he felt Carey lingering in the doorway, looking after him, and was conscious again of that thin thrill of danger which had punctuated the last few days. He didn't think it was necessarily for himself, but it was good to get back into the office, even to sit down opposite the Chief.

CHAPTER 15

"Still no joy," said the Chief.

"Bob Ryan been round them all again, then?" asked Neil, merely as a lead-in.

But the Chief fell on the question, dissecting it savagely, hurling the pieces back at Neil in a rain of rhetoric.

"All, Carter, all? The people next door? Opposite? Down the road? Collecting the rubbish? Looking for a doss?" He had to stop then to cough himself from red to purple. Neil, from experience, stayed silent, his eyes on the desk. Fortunately the Chief didn't often lose his cool, and when he did it didn't desert him for long.

"The ones with names," amended Neil, when the attack had subsided sufficiently for him to be heard in his normal voice.

The Chief glared at him on a residual gasp. Neil was relieved to see that the large face was already paling back to crimson. He wondered what had affected his superior so sharply. The Chief was used to unsatisfactory suspects, there were no children involved, the only person who could possibly whip up his compassion had had her shoes taken away. . . .

"Tell me?" he suggested gently.

The Chief boomed his nose through a handkerchief with blue-striped borders. "I went round with Bob this time," he growled. "That's why you've only just found me." He consulted his watch, and a morose satisfaction softened his chunky features. "Five P.M. on a Saturday afternoon," said the Chief, a man who had managed to find one source of light in a dark situation. "Hope you haven't had to cancel anything enticing."

Neil shrugged. It was politic not to make too precise a denial of frustration. "Not to matter, Governor. So, nothing more."

"Nothing. The sister-in-law. Clara Shaw. She had to be at her shop in the late evening, didn't she? Home 'about' eleven."

"What was she doing there?"

"This and that. She didn't try to be exact. A bit of cleaning and

prettying up, I suppose." There was a pause in which the purple
wash flowed in and out of the Chief's face. "The husband," he muttered, "the husband, Arthur Shaw . . ." and brought the handkerchief back into play.

"Yes, Governor?"

"Damned jackanapes. Called me 'my man.' 'My man.' Me. Little
strutting . . ." The coughing fit this time was more prolonged. To
have laughed would have been the equivalent of a messily bungled
act of *auto-da-fé*.

"Clara Shaw's husband," managed the Chief at last, "had gone for
a walk, if you please, home 'about' the same time. He'd looked at his
watch. Just the type that would, of course, strutting little . . . The
Arthur Shaws, as you will no doubt have ascertained, Carter, live in
Kew, about a ten-minute walk from the dead man. Each corrobo-
rates the other's story, such as it is. And they neither of them saw
anybody they knew."

"One might think—if they needed alibis and were manufacturing
them—"

"I know, Neil, I know. Carey at least can be vouched for for part
of the evening. He'd been at an antique dealers' junket in the City.
Left at eleven. So he did, but it apparently took him an hour to get
home. *He* said he had stopped to cool off when he realized his driving performance might be impaired by what he'd had to drink."

"Where?"

"Some vague deserted spot, of course. But no spot in London is totally deserted."

"So he came home," said Neil swiftly, "to find the deed done. Or
nature having taken her course. Whichever—"

"That's his story. Came in and telephoned the police. Mrs. Shaw
—Miss Fielding—tells us she spent the evening at home. Unfortu-
nately you weren't around to confirm or deny. A funny thing," said
the Chief, ceasing to look at Neil for the first time since they had
faced one another, telling Neil he was at last ready for a reaction,
"she volunteered the information—for want of a better term—that
she'd been dreaming what's happened, ever since she left her husband's house. Even asked Bob Ryan if her husband's tongue had
been protruding, without having been told what the human agent
had done to him. Now that, Neil, does make you think."

"She told me about the dream, too," said Neil, "and that she's
supposed to have second sight. If she had—been back," he said with
difficulty, putting the simple, impossible, idea into words for the first

time, inside or outside his head, "would she have talked about a dream? Would she have asked that particular question?"

"Ha!" said the Chief, grim-faced.

"All I can say, Governor"—he had to work to make it sound casual —"is that I feel she's telling the truth when she insists she left the house three months ago and that was it." The Chief was continuing to stare at him, without expression. "She also tells me," went on Neil, glad now to get it mentioned, "that Bob's people took her walking shoes away. Told her it was routine."

"So it was, Neil, so it was. There were usable footprints in front of the house. Turned out to be Carey's." The Chief was watching him.

"I see." Anything immediately further on these lines might begin to menace the advantage of the true and secret situation. "Stephen Elliott," said Neil. "Mrs. Shaw told me how 'kind and attentive' he's been since her husband's death. That is to say, all at once on her husband's death. She also told me the apparently chance way she picked up her job in the first place—Elliott lounging in his doorway as she walked past, inviting her in, recruiting her. Do you know— anything—about Elliott?"

The Chief sighed, shifting his bulk in the protesting chair. "Not a thing. Only that he seems to have a flair for his job. He's opened a second business in the West End, leaving Mrs. Shaw to cope in St. John's Wood. Could be that they both had a piece of luck."

"Of course. It just seems—well, I've met him in her flat and he seemed a diffident sort of a chap. But there again, I suppose if he'd— done anything, he'd hardly change his stance in a way to make the lady comment . . . though my point is that he *has* changed his approach to her. Well, I just thought it was worth watching."

"Of course it is, Neil, and that's where you're so valuable. Elliott was quite disarming, by the way, when he told us nobody could vouch for him being on his own at home on Wednesday night. And, like Mrs. Shaw, he didn't watch television. All these independent-minded people . . ."

"I think I'll call on Elliott. I can get a better feel of a person against the chosen background. I'll just tell him, off the record, how cut up Mrs. Shaw really is and how we appreciate his attention . . ."

"That's it." The Chief sighed again, and was suddenly leaning across the desk towards Neil, who shifted in his turn to ease the lurch of his stomach. "None of them, Neil, admits to being in Holly Lodge at any time during Wednesday. Except for Carey, of course. But he left for his City junket about six o'clock."

"Why didn't Shaw go with him?" asked Neil warily. He had never yet known the Chief lean towards him without some particular reason of blow or revelation, and neither had yet come.

"Only because he wasn't feeling one hundred per cent. We've told that to the Path. boys, but of course it's only Carey's word. But then everything is only somebody else's word. Truth to tell, Neil, I've felt impatient from the start with the generally pussyfooting attitude. While I was with 'em today, I told 'em all the truth."

"The truth?" The Chief had leaned back, so he must have made his point. It hadn't been one of his sharper ones, because it wouldn't have meant all that much extra to Neil, if it hadn't been for Hilary, which the Chief didn't know. Didn't *know*. But would so easily suspect. "You mean—what the human agent did?"

"That's it. Thought it might shock something out of someone, particularly if they were hanging together. Don't really know why we held it back, except we were thinking about the Press. If they get hold of it now, well, they do. But the show interviews with the suspects are over, and, with or without my advice to keep quiet, I can't quite see even Carey ringing the *Daily Horror* simply to pass on this extra titbit about his—about the dead man."

"No. Was there a reaction anywhere?"

"Well, yes, of course there was. Everywhere. Shock, disgust, dismay. The usual. Real or feigned. Thought Mrs. Shaw—Mrs. Peter Shaw—was going to faint."

It was a physical feeling again, remembering the baby. He was cravenly glad he had not been bidden to tell her, or to watch her receipt of the news.

"The turnover at Mrs. Shaw's flat: are you mentioning it to Carey?"

"Not as such. We asked him what he was doing yesterday morning. He said he went to view some sale items at Sotheby's. Which of course he did."

"So you believe Mrs. Shaw's theory?" Yet again he found himself back with Hilary. But he was expected to know her at least better than he knew any of the others.

"We don't know, Neil. It is a theory."

"And somebody did something."

"Even if it was Mrs. Shaw herself."

"Even if that." It was extraordinary, he was learning, how minutes in the head could be lived against seconds in the world outside. In the space of those three words, and the normal pause each side of them, he seemed to be able to face the fact, another first, that Hilary could be crazy or crazily devious, to swirl dizzily, to recover, and to end up thinking, as he had begun, that she was honest and sane. Watching the Chief's attentive but unaffected face, Neil was relieved to realize that he seemed able to endure these internal adventures without giving visible sign of them.

"Was there anything significant about the mess-up as far as you could see, Neil? Any pattern, or anything you wouldn't have expected?"

"There was a pattern," said Neil slowly, wishing it was coffee time, and laced coffee at that, "which the lady interpreted. I said to her that it seemed to have been a search for something with a bit of height—no little drawers or spaces had been disturbed. She said of course it was: whoever it was—well, Carey, she said—was looking for some sort of valuable vase which had belonged to her husband. A vase that always lived in the same cupboard at the house—but you'll know this, and more. . . ."

"Yes." The Chief paused, coughed deeply as introductory fanfare. "According to Mrs. Shaw, Neil, it was a copy of the—er—Portland Vase, one of the famous early copies."

"Governor?" It was a pity he had no one to share his brief enjoyment.

"The original's in the British Museum. Priceless. Early Greek. One of the well-known china men—Worcester—no, Wedgwood—made some copies in the eighteen-hundreds. Limited edition, and some went missing. Mrs. Shaw maintains her husband came upon one of them."

"If it isn't a figment of her imagination." The remark really hurt him to make.

"If it is," said the Chief, "she's sharing part of her dream world with Carey, which one has to admit is unlikely. We shared that part of her story with him, and he bore it out. Also admitted that when he looked for the vase after he'd rung the police on Wednesday night—for which I'm pretty sure we should read 'before'—it wasn't in its place, wasn't in the house."

"And he thought Mrs. Shaw had been back and taken it, with or without attacking her husband."

"He said she must have done, because he was certain only she and he and Peter Shaw knew about it."

"When had Carey last seen it?"

"The very moment he said good night to Shaw and set out."

"Anything else missing?"

"Carey says not. It's a bit of a frustrating business, Neil."

"May I ask you what *you* think, Governor?"

"Not all that much as yet. But I do feel that Carey *could* have dressed up and broken into Mrs. Shaw's flat. Arthur Shaw's a strutting jackanapes and a cold fish but we mustn't let personalities—"

"Of course not." And the Chief was keeping his regular colour.

"Nor must we lose sight, Neil, of the fact that Shaw that night could have let in someone from a wider circle than just his immediate, or immediately ex, family—and Carey."

"But you don't really include the passer-by among your suspects?"

"I'm not inclined to, no."

"And really, your inclination is to limit the field to people called Shaw or Carey?"

"Yes."

"Why, Governor?"

"Well, Neil . . ." The Chief rose and paced slowly to the window, where he made a space in the blind slats with two thick fingers, applying his eye. The glint of gold made Neil wish he would pull the blind up and warm the increasing cool and pallor of the office. But he was more concerned that the Chief's action in fiddling with it invariably heralded an attempt to justify a belief which he was unable to substantiate. "Shaw—the dead Shaw," said the Chief to the window, "had a lot of acquaintances and a reputation as the life of the party, but no one really close to him except his family and his wife and then Carey. I think he presented a sort of a bland front. Trying to broach it was like trying to get a grip on a slippery slope. Couldn't really be done. Carey and the sister-in-law and Mrs. Shaw all said this same thing in their own ways—"

"Arthur Shaw?" prompted Neil warily.

"Didn't say anything." The Chief continued to address the window. "Just spat out the odd expression of outrage and closed his little mouth. I almost expected to hear it snap shut." Neil tried to discourage the rare sensation of oneness with the Chief. "But the other three implied that Peter Shaw didn't know anyone well enough to be a murder victim in any sort of a crime of passion sense."

"Not even as regards his change of sex habits?"

The Chief's square tweed shoulders rose even closer to his ears, slowly subsided.

"They don't know, Neil. And of course neither do I. But I have one of my feelings. Hope it's right. It's a marvellous shortener of the field."

"I'm impressed, Governor." The Chief's feelings, not frequently cited, had been proved worthy of respect. "But there's Shaw's business."

"Of course." The Chief returned to his desk on another gusty exhalation. "Though I gather that for some time Carey has seen to all but the most exclusive."

"The exception which could prove—"

"I know, Neil, I know."

"Business could include Stephen Elliott."

"It could. Elliott told me he'd never so much as heard of the Shaws until the day Mrs. Shaw walked by his gallery. And not even then, of course, because she was Miss Fielding. And Mrs. Shaw herself has never had any indication that her husband and Elliott ever met. She worked closely with him, you know, in the business, until she left."

"Did she, now?" Sensible to profess ignorance where he got the chance.

"She did, Neil. So. You may not have learned that, but you must have learned some things. Got any idea?"

"Already, Governor?"

"Neil! You rang me from the lady's flat, for a start."

"A bit of luck, that." He heard the shameless confidence of his voice. "I came up in the lift with Mrs. Shaw and as soon as we emerged Miss Prince started tackling her and I went with her into her flat in the way of duty."

"Hm. Mrs. Shaw is really cut up, you'd say?"

"I would, yes." Again, the shaft of danger. "And Mrs. Arthur Shaw, whom I called on this morning, thinks so too. Said Mrs. Peter had been very much in love with her husband, and still was."

"So you've called on Mrs. Arthur Shaw, Neil. What pretext?" The Chief had been unable to check a very small outward sign of his interested attention.

"I was near by on a job and just thought I'd express my concern and assure Mrs. Clara I'd keep an eye on her sister-in-law."

"Anything come out of it?"

All at once his mind's eye was devouring Clara Shaw's yearning face, but he told himself that to mention it would be to introduce an irrelevant theme. "She seemed a bit cynical about Carey's alibi, but has obviously grown to dislike him. Just as obviously seems affectionate towards Mrs. Peter, although she said her sister-in-law didn't get in touch with her as much as she used to. Well, I should think that's natural."

"It certainly could be."

"I asked her what the dead man was like, and she said charming and noticeable and ruthless without meaning to be, because his energies were always leading him to the next thing, which meant good-bye to the one before."

"Say anything about wife, boy-friend?"

"Said the marriage had been good, she thought, until suddenly. Said it was thought Peter Shaw really had changed his habits, but that Carey was no more than his—what did she say?—his announcement of it."

"So that Carey really would have been advised to make hay?"

"She didn't say that, but of course it's the deduction. I went on to see Carey."

"Neil—"

"As a seeker after long-case clocks. I told Mrs. Shaw I would, as part of my unofficial interest in the *dramatis personae*, and she told me about the clocks—seems Carey has a thing about them. He's got one at Holly Lodge, offered to show it to me."

"He doesn't know who you are?"

"Governor, do you mind?"

"So?"

"I'm going on Monday night."

"Good lad. Anything you felt out of that first sight?"

He just stopped himself in time from reminding the Chief that it was the second. "That he's clever. And all controlled responses, except that once I suspected a tear—although even that of course can be organized. He was very ready to spell out why the various names might be familiar to me. Sense of the dramatic, with self in interesting role. Shall I ring you at home on Monday night when it's all over?"

"Only if you feel there's something extra for me to know. And if you do—then surely ring me at home. We have Shaw's will, by the way. Made just over a month ago. Everything to Carey." The Chief stared at Neil before grudgingly lowering his eyes to his broad red wrist. "Better go off now, salvage the evening."

"Thank you, Governor."

Neil knew his Chief was due out to dinner at seven.

CHAPTER 16

"Now, you're Hilary's neighbour and a policeman, but I can't for the moment . . ." Stephen Elliott rumpled the back of his hair with an apologetic hand, with the other opening wide his white front door, one in a row of identical doors set at regular intervals along the elegant neo-Georgian terrace.

"Neil Carter. Why should you remember? Thanks."

"Do come in here."

The room had small square panes in its sash window and an outer fringe of wistaria.

"Nice," said Neil as he looked round. Hilary had been curious about this house. Wondering whether over the last few days her curiosity had been satisfied, he noted with reluctant approval the agreeable blend of old and new.

"Do sit down," urged Stephen Elliott, busier still on his hair so that it stood upright on the crown of his head. He flung himself down on a low sofa as Neil took the most formal chair. "Yes, it is quite nice and getting more mellow. I think they got the proportions right although I'm told by some of my friends it's not the thing to reproduce old styles. I can't for the life of me see why." He grinned at Neil. "Sorry I took so long to come to the door, but I'd gone on in the garden longer than I'd intended and I'd just come out of the shower."

"Is there a garden at the back?" It was strange how the thought gave him a moment's pang.

"Yes." Neil tried to find the continuing slight apologetic tinge to Stephen Elliott's manner irritating rather than attractively modest. "Very small but with a high wall so that it's private. Secret, I felt, when I first saw it. I think it was that secret garden which clinched the house for me. But you're not here to listen . . . What can I do for you, Mr. Carter? May I get you a drink, by the way?"

"No, thank you. I only came . . ." He himself could rarely sound apologetic, but at the moment he had to choose his words. "I really wanted to say, off my own personal bat—you know I'm not officially connected with the Shaw inquiry—how glad I am you're keeping a regular eye on Mrs. Shaw. From my experience of crime—of victims as well as agents—I would say she's been pretty badly shocked."

"She doesn't show much, but I'm certain she has," responded Stephen Elliott earnestly. "I mean, anyone—in such a case—and if you're the type who holds it in . . ."

"I know." He was pleased to find that Stephen Elliott, a man of what appeared to be infinitely greater instinctive sympathy than he, Neil, could ever own to, had not overcome Hilary's defences.

"There seems to be a mystery about how her husband died." The honest, open face appealed to Neil behind the words, then through them. "Do they know who was involved? Oh, forgive me, Mr. Carter, of course I shouldn't—"

"They're working on it. But I'm not, as I said, so I may be a step or two behind. And even if I'm keeping pace, you're quite right, you shouldn't ask."

Neil smiled, but Stephen Elliott's wide brow had ridged in a troubled frown. "She doesn't look well. But she promises me her doctor is keeping an eye on her and that she's taking the pills he's prescribed."

"Well, that's something." Neil had insisted that Hilary check in so many words that the pills could in no way harm the baby. Meeting Elliott's anxious gaze, he felt confident the man was not in a position to share that additional anxiety. "It's good, too, that she has her job. That's bound to help."

"Yes!" Elliott leaned eagerly forward. "I told her not to feel she must come in for her usual full day, but I tried at the same time to stress that she is rather needed. Which is true, anyway. Are you sure you won't have a drink?"

"Quite sure, thank you. I'm on my way home. I just wanted to say that as acquaintance and neighbour I appreciate your being around, and that I hope you'll keep her going on her work. What's happened is particularly nasty, even in my experience. Did you ever meet her husband?"

"No. It was after she'd left home that I first met Hilary, when she was looking for a job. I didn't know until—until her husband's death that she was married."

"Nor I," said Neil, forcing an answering rueful grin. "But I just thought you might have come across Shaw in your business."

"I never actually met him, no. The police—I mean the police on the case—asked me that." The gaze was still as clear and direct. "I'd heard of him, but our business interests hardly coincided."

Again Neil looked round the room. "Privately you'd have had interests in common," he said lightly. He had instincts rather than knowledge, but he'd have thought there were a number of old and valuable things close to where he was sitting. He got to his feet.

Stephen Elliott laughed, a pleasant sound. "That's true. And if I'd lived west of London . . ." His length unfolded. "As a matter of fact," he said, "I'm just on my way to your place. I've persuaded Hilary to come out for dinner this evening, and she asked me for a drink first. But come and see my garden."

Neil was so enormously and, he thought, absurdly delighted by the garden that he concealed the strength of his response. Certainly it increased his growing dissatisfaction with flat life. There was nothing to be seen over the rosy brick wall but other people's bushes and other low creeper-shrouded façades. There was an emerald patch of lawn edged unevenly with shrubs, green arms of differing heights, shapes and shades clutching the walls, a small paved area with white furniture and tubs of brightly coloured flowers immediately outside the french window. Most heady of all, he was standing under the sky on one man's private piece of ground.

"It's only a tiddly thing," said Stephen Elliott apologetically, "but mine own."

"I can see the attraction," conceded Neil. He could see, also, that Stephen Elliott was either an unusually gentle and agreeable man, or a consummate villain. "No good my offering you a lift, I suppose?"

"Thanks awfully, but I shall want to take Hilary home eventually and see her in. Not that I'll linger. She wants an eye keeping, as you say, but at such a time one mustn't be intrusive."

"Of course not." Neil was thinking that Elliott according to Hilary was about a hundred per cent more intrusive than he had been a few days earlier, and he had murmured agreement before, on an inward smile, recalling his own role as supreme intruder. He wondered, not for the first time, just how conceited he was.

Elliott's car was at the kerb, beyond his own, and they kept in easy convoy through the evening streets. A third car followed them through the Westcote gates, larger and heavier than the two small saloons. Arthur Shaw got out, returning their dual greeting as if recalled against his will to a more trivial situation.

But they must take the lift together. As they rose, Neil battled with an insane desire to ask Shaw if he came there often, anchoring his irreverence on the thick tufts of Stephen Elliott's ruffled hair, reflected in the dim lift mirror.

Silence and immobility were maintained through the six floors. When the doors opened Arthur Shaw strode out first and pressed Hilary's bell, filled the gap when she opened the door.

"Hilary . . . my dear . . ." His deep voice was at once masterful and tender. Neil, staring at her with veiled anxiety, saw by the renewed pallor, newly etched circles under the eyes, that she was unable to be even briefly amused by the composition of the trio on her step. He took Shaw's arm, experiencing a physical shock at its fleshlessness, and drew the man not quite gently backwards.

"Mr. Shaw," he said, forcing himself to cajole rather than insist. "I shall be delighted if you'll come across the landing and have a drink with me. Mr. Elliott is Mrs. Shaw's invited guest, and I know they have an appointment."

"You *know?*" Arthur Shaw detached his arm with sharp dignity from the circle of Neil's fingers but nevertheless retreated slightly from the threshold.

"We've just been talking," supplied Stephen Elliott.

"You can all come in, of course," said Hilary indifferently. "Although Stephen and I *are* going out, Arthur. In fact, he's a bit late and I'm ready . . ."

Neil said, "So do come over to me, Mr. Shaw, and have a drink."

"I'm sure you'll understand, Arthur," said Hilary, even more mechanically. "It's business." Neil wondered in a trickle of jealousy what she would say to Elliott when they were alone.

"Oh, very well. But—you're all right, my dear? I was worried . . . the further disagreeable news . . . Are you sure you won't come to us at least for a few days?"

"Quite sure, Arthur. I really am all right. I'll—see you."

"You will indeed. Good night, my dear."

"My love to Clara," said Hilary wearily. "We'd better go, Stephen."

"Of course." Stephen Elliott turned a blank face momentarily to Neil, and Hilary disappeared to pick up coat and bag. Neil and Arthur Shaw waited while, to the accompaniment of silence and painful smiles, the lift was resummoned and bore the other two away.

"Come along," said Neil, reflecting that Shaw had probably derived a crumb of comfort from the fact that it was Elliott rather than Carter with whom his sister-in-law was spending the evening. It perhaps explained why he had accepted Neil's invitation. Unless of course, contrary to appearances, he was human enough not to be able to resist the possibility of picking up some information.

He didn't ask for any. He followed Neil into the sitting-room and, after curtly agreeing to be served with scotch and soda, went to stand in the window. Neil took his time, and joined Shaw with the two glasses. Daylong sun was beginning to descend the sky, and the end of its arc, lengthening towards summer, was the centre of Neil's balcony view. He looked down with a new interest on to the varying green patterns below and across the road, which were a line of small private gardens.

"Lovely evening," he suggested.

"Yes," said Arthur Shaw, "yes." The pale eyes were fixed straight ahead, but Neil suspected they were seeing interior views.

"I'm so sorry about this awful business," said Neil. "It's good of you to keep an eye on your sister-in-law."

The neat figure turned, focused slowly upon its host.

"She has a lot of courage," said Shaw, somehow to Neil's surprise. Perhaps he hadn't expected to agree with anything the other might say. "Was there a reason you invited me here, Mr. . . . er . . . ?"

"The name is Carter." Why, really, was this man so intent on keeping him in his place? The best counter-irritant was doubtless to appear unaware of the continuous contempt, although he could think of a more pleasurable response. To a consoling mental picture of Shaw falling back against the table behind him with bloody nose and flying spectacles, Neil went on quietly, "As I said to you the other evening, Mr. Shaw, I'm not connected with the inquiry into your brother's death, I'm merely Mrs. Shaw's neighbour. But even in my fairly wide experience, this ranks as a nasty business. I just wanted to say—"

"It was a nasty business," pronounced Shaw, turning back to the window, "some time before my brother's death." The profile was so spare and colourless Neil couldn't imagine it ever looking any older. Or, for that matter, any younger.

"Of course—"

"The new will was made just a month ago." Shaw turned round to Neil again, this time with an energy which might indicate he had decided to make use of the situation where he found himself. "I knew, I knew . . ."

"New will?" Caught in the corner of his eye was a sparkle of water drops rising and falling in one of the distant green gardens.

"Carey." The name was spat at him so forcefully Neil imagined wiping it off his shirt.

"I'm sorry, I don't quite—"

"Peter had remade his will in Carey's favour," said Arthur Shaw impatiently. "Entirely. Cutting out his wife." The eyes bulged with indignation.

Neil said mildly, "She can, and must, contest it, of course."

"That is scarcely relevant to what Peter did. To what he was made to do!"

"Made to do, Mr. Shaw?"

"By Carey, of course. Peter was—bewitched." Neil had the feeling his visitor had had to search for even this banal metaphor. "Carey got him to change the will and then . . ."

The eyes faltered before the sudden blaze of Neil's.

"I feel I should advise you for your own sake to be careful, Mr. Shaw," murmured Neil. "Until guilt is proved by the due processes of the law, you are all of you equally innocent."

"All of us?"

"You, your wife, your sister-in-law"—he thought Shaw's body jerked—"yes, and Mr. Carey, and persons unknown, all equally innocent."

"Clara . . . Hilary . . ." Neil saw fear, then fury. "Really, Mr. Carter, I think you presume—"

"To tell you to be careful, yes. Oh, I can understand how you must feel." No, he couldn't, never in a million years could he understand the feelings of this man. "And how you must resent your sister-in-law's sufferings—"

"My God I do!" Even in its rage the face remained putty-coloured. "And she has enough suffering to come without being dragged into the squalid events of the home she was forced to leave for ever. For ever," repeated Arthur Shaw sternly. "She has never gone back. Yes." Anger was giving way to a sort of portentousness. "Enough suffering to come."

Neil suddenly recalled the moment on Hilary's threshold, with Arthur Shaw's eyes fixed steadily on her stomach. Summoning back his vision of the aftermath of physical violence on the man beside him, he said calmly, "Yes, I think she will suffer the most of you if anyone is brought to justice."

A shock—perhaps—across the eyes again. But Arthur Shaw said with comparative amiability, "I wish we could persuade her to come and stay with us, at least until the wretched business is sorted out."

It was impossible to know whether the fierce gaze betokened entreaty or continuing outrage.

"She's independent as well as brave, perhaps," said Neil, glad to see Shaw's tumbler was empty. "But you can be sure young Cathy next door will keep a close eye on her. I know Cathy pretty well, she's a sympathetic soul and she tells me your sister-in-law seems glad of her company."

"No need for her to go for company outside the family. And Clara has always been her closest friend."

"Perhaps you, both of you," suggested Neil gently, "just at the moment, remind her . . ."

Arthur Shaw set his glass down sharply on the table beside him, the table which Neil kept seeing in his mind's eye on the other side of the room, a leg broken from the impact of Shaw's reeling body. He stretched out his hand towards the glass. "May I give you another one?"

"Thank you, no. I must go." Arthur Shaw started, without another look at Neil, towards the door.

"It's a blessing your sister-in-law has such an interesting job," observed Neil, following him. "And what seems to be a highly sympathetic employer."

There was no check to the short steps, but he couldn't see the face.

"I should have thought you would be too busy, Mr. Carter," said Arthur Shaw as he stopped at the front door, "with those inquiries you *are* engaged on, to be so concerned about the people involved in this one."

"I expect it's Cathy," said Neil cheerfully, "she really is concerned, being so fond of Mrs. Shaw. I suppose it's rubbing off on me."

"You know her well," stated Arthur Shaw distastefully.

"She's like the sister I never had." Neil opened the door and Shaw walked out, hesitated. "I hope you don't feel your journey tonight was entirely unnecessary," continued Neil. "And I hope for all of you that things will be quickly resolved. Remember me to your wife."

For the only time of their acquaintance Arthur Shaw met Neil's eye without disdain or rancour.

"Thank you for the drink. And for—thank you."

"Good night!"

Neil shut the door before his visitor reached the lift, then looked through his telescopic eye at the tiny distant figure. The best moment of the encounter was once more to see the quick movement of

hand and comb about the head. But he had achieved nothing except
to confirm earlier impressions.

And to put himself in need of an antidote.

At first he thought this might be solitude, but after mooching
through the flat, realizing that it seemed a long time since he had
been charmed in his customary way by his own company and that it
continued to be undesirable, he washed the whisky glasses and went
out on to the landing.

The laughter began almost as soon as he had rung the bell.
Cathy's laughter, mainly, as he hadn't heard it for ages, young and
uninhibited and thoroughly amused. It was backed by a deeper and
more intermittent sound, and there was a scuffling of feet, and a
"Do you mind?" from the female voice, before a sudden short silence
and renewed laughter.

Cathy opened the door, Don Everett at her shoulder.

"Good girl," said Neil at once, before he had time to think about
anything. "You looked before you leaped."

She pulled a face. "How do you know?"

"Simple. I heard feet, and then a pause. How are you, Don?"

"Fine. And you?" Don Everett was grinning cheerfully. It was
something that he hadn't said "sir."

"I too am fine. Cathy . . ."

"Will you come in, Neil?"

"No, thank you, child. I've got paperwork and telephoning and I
can't put them off any longer. But by the end of the evening I shall
probably have the answer to that question you asked me. I was only
going to suggest you popped in, or rang, before you go to bed, and I
can let you have it." In their joint circumstances, this was no doubt
the best way to explain his visit. But he was aware of another, familiar, element—that of preferring not to put himself in the position of
a refusal.

"That *is* good of you, Neil. Yes, I'll do that."

"Don't worry how late it is. Have a nice time."

"Thank you." Cathy's face was almost grave as it disappeared
behind the door. Back at his own door, Neil found himself listening,
and when he heard the renewed laughter, distant and muffled, he
went into his flat.

It was, he supposed, supper-time. He poured another whisky, went
into the kitchen, turned on the stove, and laid three strips of bacon
in the grill pan. He assembled the scrambled egg ingredients, cut two
slices of bread and propped them in the toaster, then went back into

the sitting-room. The sun had disappeared, but a splatter of orange-red up the sky marked its departure, reminding him of Arthur Shaw and his own itchy fist. The memory was disagreeable. He recalled the sensation of standing on Stephen Elliott's patch of ground, under the sky. The memory made him bad-tempered and restless.

He stood beside the open balcony door, moodily sipping. It seemed a long time since he had stood there after Cathy's party, thinking of her and of Hilary. Hilary . . . the uncomfortable cosiness of his growing self-pity dissolved in a rush of concern and alarm. The day's ugly new knowledge . . . a baby in its precarious first months . . . so much unnatural pressure . . . Surely Elliott wouldn't keep her out late, looking as she had looked tonight. He would ring earlier than usual to see if she was home, and alone. But Cathy would take him at his word. . . .

At least this was a better worry than some others. Suddenly brisk, he was on his way back to the kitchen when the bell rang. Cathy's caricature, pointed and kitten-like, as always made him smile. And he was remembering his mother's description of him. The original cake and halfpenny boy.

"I'm sorry, Neil," said Cathy breathlessly, as he opened the door.

"What for?"

"For not being . . ."

"Come in. Have you had supper? Or I should ask, if you haven't, are you free to join me?"

"I haven't and I am."

"Don's gone, then?" He was leading the way to the kitchen.

"Oh yes. He was only here for tea. But you're already having your supper."

"No I'm not, and it isn't even on the way. I switched the oven on but forgot the grill. I've got more bacon."

"Shall I do it?"

"No. Go and look at the sky. It's actually a projection of my sub-conscious. Arthur Shaw was here, and the sky's what I felt like doing to him."

"How did you get Arthur Shaw in here?" asked Cathy, when they were seated in the big window with a tray apiece on their knees. The sky now was marked merely by a blood-red line, low down, with the faintest pink surround. The injury after cleaning up, thought Neil.

"We coincided downstairs. I was with Stephen Elliott, who I'd called on and who was about to come over and take Hilary out to dinner." He might have seen surprise in her eyes at the evenness of his tone. "She looked ghastly when she opened the door—my Chief told them all the whole truth today about what had been done to Peter Shaw."

"Oh, Neil."

"So I said that she and Elliott had an appointment and invited Shaw over here." Just in time he remembered there was one thing he had decided not to tell Cathy. "He really had no choice."

"And?"

"And nothing. Honestly, I'm sick of telling people how good they are keeping an eye on Hilary. The Shaws. Elliott. I seem to spend my life doing it."

"Yes, and as things are . . ." Cathy had her hand over her mouth, but her large eyes seemed to spell out the enormous hypocrisy. But he suddenly had a wild idea that she was trying not to laugh. If this could possibly be so, he would help her.

"Arthur Shaw had his own little scenario worked out," he went on swiftly, "in which Carey, after getting Peter Shaw to alter his will entirely in his, Carey's, favour—that's the truth, by the way—then bumped his friend off before there was any time or chance to alter it again. Taking advantage of the heart attack, I suppose. I reminded him that everyone at the moment is innocent, even he himself, managed to keep my hands off him, and saw him amicably on his way. Well, that *is* an overstatement, I suppose, but he did say thank you on the landing." He was feeling better by the minute. "But there is something else, something to be *done*, thank heaven, however little comes of it. For you too."

"Neil!" She had put her tray aside and was pressing her hand down between her denim knees, hunching her shoulders in excitement.

"I called on Anthony Carey in the shop in Richmond this morning, professing an interest in long-case clocks—Hilary told me they're his passion. He has one at Holly Lodge, and I've been invited to go and see it. Eight o'clock on Monday."

"And—you're going?"

"Oh yes, and I'm going to take you with me, if you'll come."

"Neil! Why, though?"

"Frankly, dear, to make sure there's no misunderstanding. It's a shorthand he'll be able to read. And—I should like your reactions as well as my own."

"Are you thinking about the vase?"

"Among other things. I suppose I—just want to get the feel."

"Hilary's house . . ."

"Yes, but I wasn't—"

"Oh, Neil, I know, I didn't mean . . . I only meant, it's all so peculiar, isn't it?"

"Yes. Will you come?"

"Of course I will. Neil—I wanted to ask you something too. Do you—have you decided whether or not you want me to do anything about the diary? Hilary's diary."

He had decided very quickly after they had discussed it, and then not thought of it again. "Yes. I don't want you to do anything. I don't feel the situation justifies it." In his head he went on a little. *Not yet.*

"I'm glad." She smiled at him, stretching her arms and legs and slopping down in her seat.

"I'm Mr. Collins," he said, "and Oswald at that. It's my middle name, and don't you ever tell anyone else. Think you can call me Oswald without giggling?"

"Oh, I don't suppose I shall feel a bit like giggling. I'll be my mother's maiden name, Johnson. And her first name's Prunella. I always used to wish they were my names."

"So here's your chance. And you're likely to remember them. Carey's clever. And very watchful. And if he's mislaid a fortune as well as losing a protector . . . We'll be careful. And your role is only that of my girl-friend. Not too difficult. Now, would you like to make the coffee?" He hurried on without a pause, suddenly afraid he might have been unkind, or embarrassing.

But Cathy got up smiling, adding to Neil's faintly disagreeable impression that she had begun to be different.

She got up a second time, to take her leave, before he needed to think about prompting her.

Hilary rang him as he was deciding to ring her.

"You're alone?" he asked.

"Yes. Yes. Are you coming over?"

"Of course."

She looked a bit better, but he hoisted her legs up on to the sofa and sat beside her on the floor.

"Did Elliott tell you I'd called on him?"

"Yes. He seems to have appreciated it. He's a nice man, Neil."

"Either a nice man, I should say, or a villain."

"For God's sake!"

"I only want you to be careful. Not to trust anyone just now. Except Cathy and me. And that's only partly my jealousy."

He said it to clear, if only briefly, the painful solemnity of her face. But he hoped it was true.

CHAPTER 17

He couldn't help thinking of the dream as he got into the lift, because that was where it began. She had told him about all at once standing there, no thoughts in her head, nothing but the knowledge of where she was, and where she was going. Her car was always out on the parking ground, as his was now.

But it was daylight, and Cathy was beside him, asking a question.

"Was Hilary's car put away that night, Neil? I thought I saw it, but I told your boss I couldn't be sure."

"Nobody in the building could be sure," said Neil shortly. "Only, apparently, Hilary herself. That it was not put away."

Hilary had insisted the car was out, as in the dream. Insisted, one might say, that it had been easily available. The least naïve of women . . .

"Is this—is this the way she went in the dream?"

"It is."

But it was absurd to be short-tempered with Cathy, especially as teamwork was about to be important. He made an effort, banishing to the back of his mind thoughts of the parallel journey through deserted darkness. "Now, Prue, have another go at getting your tongue round Oswald."

"I think you're just being awkward. It doesn't have to be Oswald."

"Yes, it does. But don't for goodness sake attempt Ossie or I'll put us in lumber."

"I can promise that, Oswald Collins."

"Of?"

"Scarsdale Villas—no, I won't give a number unless pressed—where I'm spending a few days of my spring holiday."

"I promise you it won't affect your Aunt Fiona."

"I'm not bothered. Prue and Oswald . . . Are we a nice couple?"

"Insurance and secretarial? A bit dull, maybe, in Neil and Cathy's opinion."

"Neil, we may not have to use any of this, may we?"

"I don't really expect we'll need to use anything more than names. Isn't that exciting enough for you?"

"Oh, quite."

He felt the snuggling motion of her tension, knew her hand would be driving down into the unaccustomed feminine lap of sprigged cotton, her shoulders hunching under the white cardigan.

"I can hardly believe we're going to the house where—well, where Hilary spent last Christmas. Cards on the mantelpiece. Ordinary. I know that sounds silly, but—"

"I know what you mean."

"Not being married," said Cathy earnestly, "I don't suppose we can imagine what it must be like. But if you're—if you're happy, your new home must come to feel like your old one, mustn't it, and to lose it, to have it become the last place you can go, instead of the first—"

"I have moments when I can understand," said Neil, abrupt again, perhaps because he had had a moment of realizing that neither old home nor new home were phrases for his personal comfort.

They were silent then, until the open gates of Holly Lodge, which made Neil's instinct to leave the car in the road seem stupidly irrational. He suppressed it. The drive was a deep curve, continuously bordered by rhododendrons.

"Abandon hope, all ye who enter here," breathed Cathy.

But Hilary must have driven up, and walked up, countless times, eager to regain the centre of her life. . . .

Pseudo-Tudor, much embellished. A dark house, even on the best of days (in both senses, thought Neil), but the sun would be sinking on the other side, over the garden.

The slight figure, dancer-like in tight black trousers and black wool shirt, was in the porch watching them, intent but expressionless. Neil wished he had seen it before it had seen Cathy, to learn if the face had changed. Anthony Carey came forward as they reached the bottom step, holding out a hand.

"Mr. Collins. How good of you to come." The eyes moved to Cathy, returned to Neil.

"It was good of you to ask me. I hope you don't mind—my young friend Prue is staying with me and I've brought her along."

"Of course. I'm delighted to see you, Prue. Do both please come in."

The smile was charming, but Neil thought the blue eyes remained cold, without animation. He and Cathy had the same impulse on the same instant, and followed their host into the enormous hall hand in hand.

He stepped back to shut the heavy vestibule door behind them.

"We'll go through into the drawing-room."

An impression of oak panelling, panelled doors, elaborately turned posts, to the banister rail curving centrally aloft. One of the doors opening, and a dazzle of evening sky from the floor-length window at the end of the long room.

Anthony Carey, gliding noiseless, led the way to it, and they stood looking out. A grassy slope centred with balustered steps and lichened urns led down to a lawn shaded by one huge beech and thickly surrounded by other mature trees.

"The secret garden!" exclaimed Cathy, but Neil had been more impressed with Stephen Elliott's small portion. And not entirely, he thought, because here he must try not to think of Hilary running up the steps, her dark hair swinging. . . .

He turned to her successor.

"I hope you're beginning to feel better," he said politely.

Anthony Carey shrugged. "I'm feeling rather small, Mr. Collins, in this big place."

"You'll be leaving?"

"Oh, I shan't be in a hurry." Neil was more aware than he had been in the shop of the reedy tone of the voice, its light precision. "It's all too easy to do something unwise when one has lost . . . Mr. Shaw and I were friends as well as business partners. But let me get you something to drink. Miss . . . ?"

"Johnson," said Cathy promptly, smiling with unnatural fierceness because, supposed Neil, she was so little inclined to smile at all. "Prue Johnson. But I don't think—"

"Coffee. Let me get you some coffee."

"Well . . . Oswald?"

Neil looked away from her, at Carey.

"Thank you."

"Good. While I'm getting it you can gloat."

They followed him back along the length of the room. The clock, splendidly orange-gold, aswirl with fine seaweed marquetry, stood in an embrasure.

"What a beautiful thing," said Neil, in honest admiration.

"Yours, Mr. Collins?"

"No, finer than mine, or my memory of it. But like."

"I'll leave you to contemplate."

The room was full of costly and beautiful old things. Neil had started to look for a small wall cupboard before remembering that Hilary always climbed the stairs.

"It must have been super," murmured Cathy. "Neil, I never thought this would be a *sad* sort of an expedition, but I suppose I should have—"

"Look, Prue." He scowled at her. "Look closely at the case . . ."

They sat down in the window to drink the coffee. The shadows in the garden were growing, the area of light flaring and yellowing as it shrank, in last-ditch defiance of the dark. Carey leaned towards Cathy.

"How long are you in London, dear?"

She pulled a face. "I've got to go back tomorrow. The office."

"Too bad. You come up often?"

Prue turned adoring eyes upon Oswald, who thought she might be enjoying herself.

"As often as I possibly can."

"That's nice." The response was automatic.

"This is a splendid house," said Neil. "And, well, of course, full of splendid things."

"I know," said Anthony Carey serenely. But still watchful. There had to have been one occasion when he had found treasure in an attic.

"It must have been rather awful, police swarming all over it. At least, I'm sorry, that's what they do on TV. . . ."

"That's what they did here, Miss Johnson. As you saw in the newspapers you obviously read, Peter's death may not have been a simple case of coronary thrombosis. Some human agent may have been involved."

Anthony Carey swung off his chair and stood very close to the window with his back to them. But Neil had seen the incredulous hatred of his gaze.

"I'm so sorry," said Cathy. "And for a stupid remark." There was a slight concessionary gesture. Anthony Carey might have been too full of feeling to reveal his face. He might be acting, rather well.

"Have you any other particular treasures to show us?" asked Neil after a few seconds.

"No, Mr. Collins, no other particular treasures." Carey had turned back to them. His face was bland, and Neil could have been imagining the penetration of the eyes. "But—let me point out the particular features of the clock."

They all got up. The last gold triangle disappeared from the grass as if someone had shut a door.

"Just a moment." Carey leaned towards the window. A large spider was making its way up a sash rope. Neil arrested his instinctive movement of protection as he saw that Carey was similarly inclined. "I'll put him out." The top sash was already lowered in parallel with the lower. "Now, I just need . . ."

"This should do."

Cathy, who had reached into her bag, proffered an oblong of cardboard. Carey slid it expertly under the advancing legs of the spider, and the velvet dot jerked across lettering as clear and black as itself. Neil was queasy before he understood why he should be, watching Carey carefully raise the card over the upper sash, shake it gently, bring his arm back, and be abruptly motionless when the card was level with his eyes. For a few seconds no one spoke or moved, and then Carey handed the card back to Cathy.

"Thank you, Miss McVeigh," said Carey quietly, "of Thirty-six Westcote Gardens, NW one."

Cathy's contrite face shot round to Neil. Neil could only watch Carey as he slid silently along the room, watch him open a drawer in an exquisite side table, extract something small, return to perch on the arm of his chair and level that something at them.

It was a service revolver, the sort used by British army officers in the Second World War. But looking as if someone had recently cared for it. Carey's eyes, bright blue tempests of hate and fury, contrasted dreadfully with his expressionless face.

"And you," said Carey, still quietly, "are the detective. Number Thirty-seven? Thirty-eight? I don't know your name, but I've had enough of detectives, even those who come honestly. Yes, Mr.—"

"Carter. Neil Carter."

"They did swarm all over my house. It was—rather awful. Like this charade tonight. I could have killed you for it, in the last minute. You were fortunate that life has taught me to control myself."

"I'm sorry."

"You're sorry." Carey laughed, harsh, too rough for his slight frame. But the gun hand remained steady. "Nothing you have done tonight, Mr. Carter, can have been without purpose, so why did you ask me if I had any other—particular treasures? You were thinking of one particular one, weren't you? And now you're here, you can tell me where it is."

A pretence of total ignorance would only intensify the fury, only waste time.

"If I knew where it was," said Neil, "why would I ask that question?"

"You ask no questions of the man with the gun." Carey pointed the weapon even more explicitly. "He asks them. And this particular gunman doesn't like to be made a fool of. Why are you here?"

"I'm here," said Neil slowly, finding the barrel of the gun an easier resting place for his eyes than Carey's glitteringly angry ones, "because Miss McVeigh is a friend of mine, and she is a friend of Hilary Shaw. So I've met Mrs. Shaw, and as I'm not officially on the case I can exercise my instincts of friendship and detection only by stealth."

"And I, of course, am guilty."

"On one charge, I think, yes. You turned Mrs. Shaw's flat over."

He had at last interrupted the other's rage. Anthony Carey looked at him instead of through him, with a flash of contemptuous triumph.

"I did. Why do you think I did?"

"I must suppose you were looking for the elusive vase. Or going through the motions of looking."

Carey said sharply, firming his hand round the gun, "Don't get too complicated, Mr. Carter. I was looking for the vase. Therefore I don't know where it is. It was on the table upstairs when I went out on Wednesday night. When I got home"—the eyes, without closing, seemed briefly to darken—"it was not. It was not anywhere in the house."

"You looked all over the house before contacting the police?"

Just perceptibly the shoulders rose and fell. "Peter was dead. I didn't need the police to tell me that. But *you* are doing the explaining. Where is the vase, Mr. Carter?"

Neil just heard Cathy's sharp intake of breath. "Why should I know?"

"All questions from me, remember? Although I will answer that one, since you appear to be slow in understanding some things. The vase was with Peter. It isn't with me. There is only one other person it can be with. Only one other person—then—who knew of its existence."

"You didn't find it."

"Oh, Mr. Carter!" Anthony Carey smiled. Not charmingly. "You must do better than that. I really wasn't all that surprised that I didn't. There are such things as bank safe deposits and the world is still full of secret places. But I don't really think I have to look any further." He leaned forward behind the gun. "Please tell me."

"I'm just going to have a look at Cathy." Neil moved his head slightly, forced a reassuring smile. She stared back at him with large dry eyes. Not risking the movement of his hand, he turned back to Carey, seemingly relaxed on the arm of the chair opposite, but with feet flexed in the small soft shoes. "Mr. Carey," said Neil softly, out of the few vital seconds of thought, "hasn't it occurred to you that Peter Shaw might have decided to bring someone else into the triangle? To see a dealer while you were out? I believe he was originally going with you to the City dinner, then pleaded ill health."

"He was ill," said Carey between his teeth. For the first time the gun hand trembled. Neil knew he was gambling life or injury. But his own. It was at his heart the gun was pointed. If it switched . . .

"All right, we know he was ill. But you can no more assume he didn't bring somebody else in than you can assume the vase is with Hilary Shaw. You don't know in either case."

"I know Peter didn't bring anyone else in, I know that." The voice trembled now like an instrument in ruthless yet sensitive hands. "More and more," said Carey, "the vase was his passion. He looked at it, handled it, in the last weeks, nearly every day. And he had promised . . ." The eyelids came down, cutting off the remainder of a sentence Neil thought he could guess. "He would never have voluntarily parted with it. So it was stolen. There's another thing. . . ." The gun barrel came nearer. Neil, for a hideous moment, wondered where the hurt would explode in him, and how keenly. "The vase, now, is mine."

"Shaw had altered his will?" At the same time, danger did pour him adrenalin.

"No questions, Mr. Carter. But yes, he altered his will. The police know that, you needn't be concerned with that. What we're talking about now is the whereabouts of the vase. Tell me."

"I don't know."

"I shall shoot you. Not to kill you—not at first—just to hurt you. And then if you still don't tell me, I shall shoot you again."

The fierce eyes were on him, piercing into him. Cathy choked back a shriek. Time passed, marked by the sudden angry chatter of a blackbird among the trees. By a stifled sob from Cathy. By the ticking of the clock. As he stared back, trying to transmit the message of his ignorance, Neil saw in Carey's eyes that sparkle which he had seen once before, in the shop, saw it spill over and gleam its way down each pale cheek. Without relaxing his bright gaze, Carey slowly put the gun on to the chair seat beside him.

"I find I believe you, Mr. Carter." There was no change in the calm voice, but the tears rolled faster. Neil was aware of Cathy shifting in her chair, the harmless report of her ankle bone. "And I find that I couldn't have shot you, anyway, even if the gun had been loaded. It's Peter's old service revolver. It hasn't been loaded for years but I cleaned it up so that it could look dangerous if anyone tried to break in. I'm nervous here, alone." The eyes, incredibly, were still proud and angry. "I think I'm disappointed to learn that I really couldn't hurt a fly. Well, a spider, at least."

There was no antipathy at all in Neil, but a world of it still beaming back at him, even in the little joke. Carey might not hurt a spider, but he hadn't proved that he couldn't kill a man, only that a certain gun wasn't loaded. A man. Or a woman. Neil stood up, drawing Cathy with him.

"I'm sorry. I'm sorry about it all."

"You should be." Carey was on his feet too, with the minimum of gesture.

"And I can understand," said Neil, against the regular nipping pressure of Cathy's fingers, "how badly you must want the vase."

"I do, of course." There was a sort of dignity in Carey, the way he contained his fury. "And yes, Mr. Carter, even without the vase, I have a more settled future than when Peter was alive. I hardly expected, then, to be here indefinitely. No doubt your colleagues are considering these implications."

There was no possible response and they followed him in silence down the room, across the hall. His hand on the latch of the front door, Neil said, "I don't see any purpose being served by a mention of tonight to the police on the case. I mean, you did produce a gun, and there is only your word for it that it wasn't loaded."

The eyes were blue ice, freezing into Neil a shiver of regret.

"I quite agree, Mr. Carter. And it wouldn't look very good, would it, that you had been—detecting—on your own, involving a member of the public in police business in an area where you yourself have no mandate to go."

"I quite agree, Mr. Carey." He had an absurd impulse to pay overt tribute to the man's intelligence. "I'm glad we understand one another. I wish you justice. Good night."

"Good night. By the way, I told your official colleagues today that I was in Hilary's flat."

He stood motionless on the step as they rounded the curve of the drive.

Neil stopped a little way along the road.

"Are you all right? I really am sorry." What was the extra sense of shock he couldn't define? He took hold of the hand lying in Cathy's lap. After one convulsive acknowledgement it withdrew.

"Of course I'm all right, Neil, although I was absolutely terrified."

"So was I. You were brave, do you know?"

"I was an idiot. I'm the sorry one. I never thought I could be such a fool." Her head was bent and through the drooping hair her face was scarlet.

"You're not a detective, child, I should never have asked you. . . ." Heavens, he shouldn't. His sense of incredulous regret was not unfamiliar. This was not the first time he had taken someone too harshly in hand.

"Yes, you should, I'm still glad you did." But he could take no comfort or credit for that, only relief. "What time is it?"

"Just nine."

"Only an hour? It seems like days."

"Time plays tricks when you're . . ."

"In danger? Did you think—did you think he was going to pull the trigger?"

"I didn't think. I mustn't. I suppose in a sort of way I pretend it isn't real. Cathy, I'm sorry."

"It's all *right*, Neil."

They drove home in silence. In her hall she kissed his cheek, disengaged herself from the unpremeditated circle of his arms, promised to go straight to bed.

The telephone was ringing as Neil opened his front door. He was angry at the acrobatics of his heart as he heard the Chief's voice.

"I've just this moment got in, Governor. No joy from Carey." Except that he had admitted to going over Hilary's flat. And saved Neil a headache by admitting it officially. "I looked at the clock and the garden and drank coffee and wasn't propositioned."

"Oh, I'm not ringing you about that, Neil, I'm ringing to ask you to come straight to me, and early, in the morning, I want to see you."

"Will do, Governor."

As he walked across the hall he saw a scrap of paper on the floor inside the front door, bearing the imprint of his heel. It was a note from Hilary to tell him the doctor was giving her a sedative and she would see him next day. He was reassured rather than alarmed; he had been alarmed, increasingly, by the look of her through the wet Sunday they had spent together, trying to do jigsaw puzzles and crosswords, by the sound of her through the night when she had tossed and moaned. He was glad that she would sleep.

The Chief's injunction was the main preoccupation of his own restless night.

CHAPTER 18

He went out at eight in the morning across a silent landing, to an angry red-grey sky which seemed to orchestrate his swelling apprehension. The grey shreds of cloud, against their blood-stained background, were all over London, drawing a baleful response from stone and brick, making glass and concrete look like flimsy stage-sets. He let his anxiety rip inside him, he was so sure it was justified.

The Chief was already at his desk, and Neil thought he would have been surprised if the heavy chest had not immediately leaned towards him across most of its worn surface.

"Morning, Neil. Well, now, we could be getting somewhere."

"Governor?"

There was a small plastic envelope on the desk, and the Chief's large red fingers went to work on it, eventually laying before Neil, from the expansive pads of thumb and index finger, a gold dot on a stem.

"Pick it up," encouraged the Chief.

His thin fingers less dextrous, Neil succeeded on a second attempt. It was a minute earring on a butterfly fastening.

"Recognize it?" asked the Chief, with the deadly amiability of his most effective moments.

"Should I?"

Oh, but the picture was instantly there, not all that recent a picture, maybe not the relevant picture, but clear enough: Hilary in profile against Cathy's window, talking to a good-looking man.

"I don't know. Do you, Carter?"

"It's not exactly distinctive." Neil laid the tiny object carefully down.

"True."

"Where does it come from, Governor?" The blind was up and the sinister sky had pursued him even here.

"It comes from the carpet in the room where Peter Shaw died. Gewgaw in one direction, fastening in the other."

"Perhaps Carey has pierced ears?" suggested Neil, as a thinking device.

"He doesn't. Neither does Mrs. Clara Shaw."

"But the other Mrs. Shaw does." He had thought, and he must not show reluctance to reach the inevitable conclusion.

"Does she, Neil?"

"I can be sure," said Neil. "My other neighbour Cathy McVeigh had her ears pierced recently, because she admired the sort of earrings Mrs. Shaw was able to wear."

"Small earrings?"

Neil shrugged. He didn't have to go that far. "I presume it must be difficult to wear very tiny ones if you have to clip or screw them on."

"Of course. Yes. Neil, I want you to do something for us."

"Governor?" He knew he was about to hear what the sky had been signalling.

"I'm sorry, but it's too useful not to take advantage of. I want you to take this, tell Mrs. Shaw you've found it—lift, landing, anywhere —and see if she lays claim to it."

"And if she does," said Neil through stiff lips, "she's been back to Holly Lodge since she walked out three months ago."

"Just so."

"Although you'd think a microscopic thing like that could have been lying unnoticed for years."

"Maybe in a fringe, under a piece of furniture, if people weren't too fussy. Not in the centre of a fitted carpet."

"No." But he felt himself stumbling on to firmer ground. "When was it found, Governor?"

"When the place was searched, of course."

But the Chief was all at once embarrassed, a condition so rare for him he didn't have much practice in handling it.

"Did they search twice, then, Governor?"

"What d'you mean?" growled the Chief.

"I mean that they searched last Thursday and today is Tuesday and if they'd found this on Thursday you'd have shown it to me then." The Chief was looking down at the desk top. "So if it was found at a later search it could have been planted by Carey, having been taken from Mrs. Shaw's flat when he went through it. Or did he hand it in, for God's sake?"

"You're getting a bit het up, aren't you, Neil? I assure you that small thing was found on the one and only search, and you must take my word for it."

"With respect, Governor, if I'm to do this nasty little job, I can't take your word, I've got to know exactly how and when the earring came to light. You must see that." He was trying to sound relaxed, impassioned only by justice. Insistent, though.

The insistence at least got through. The Chief sighed, dropping back in his long-suffering chair.

"All right, Neil, I suppose that's fair. I was just trying to protect young—well, I won't give you his name, and you'd better not create about that. This earring was gathered up with other potentially interesting objects on Thursday as ever was, since when it has inadvertently remained in this wretched boffin's wretched pocket. At least when he discovered it the second time he brought it to me and owned up. That'll help him a bit."

Although it had been with him only a matter of moments, there was a draining, weakening sensation in the ebbing of his hope. Even more draining, more weakening, was the confirmation of his fear.

"All right, Governor, thank you for telling me. I'll do it."

"Today, Neil."

"Today. Maybe not especially early today, because I should like to do it on home ground, so that the lady can collapse in suitable surroundings."

"Collapse?"

"Governor! You know what she believes."

"Do I, lad? You tell me again."

"She believes that, except in her dream, she hasn't been near Kew, let alone Holly Lodge, since she left her husband."

"And you believe that, Neil?"

"I believe—absolutely—that *she* believes it. But of course I don't believe it myself if she claims this fleck of gold. Not that that means I'll necessarily even then believe she actually put her hands round her husband's throat and squeezed."

He bit deliberately on the ugliest image of them all.

"I don't know what the hell sort of evidence all this dream stuff is meant to be, Neil. We can hardly rely on the logic of a dream—and I can hardly credit what I keep being made to say. Anyway"—there came a note of relieved defiance into the Chief's voice—"we're still bound to consider that the whole rigmarole may be the super-sophistication of someone who never had a dream in her life."

Neil said, following the slightest of pauses, "Of course we are. But all my instincts tell me Hilary Shaw believes what she says and if she —did the murder or attempted murder, then I can't think she knows it."

"I've been talking to our amateur analyst," said the Chief heavily and perhaps sadly, making Neil aware of the injustice of his hostility to his superior immediately the subject was Hilary Shaw, "and he said something I do just find myself able to understand. He said the shock of losing her husband in the way she did could account for her mind refusing to accept the reality of her visit. And he said this would be even more likely if she herself was responsible for what she 'saw' while she was in the house. Truth to tell, Neil, Andy said that her dream, especially a recurrent dream, could even have been a sort of advance planning of what she intended to do, consciously or unconsciously."

He heard a voice which seemed to be coming from a remote corner of the room. "I suppose so, Governor, I hadn't thought of that."

But now he had, now he recognized the most plausible explanation yet for all that had happened. Hilary not just an unwitting traveller. An unwitting killer, too.

"And *that* theory," the Chief was going on, "still has us believing in the dream business. Which apparently suits your view of things. You already seem to have established a point of view."

"I'm bound to have a few ideas, Governor." He was still listening to what someone was saying across the room, but the dreadful flash of logic had passed, leaving it only one possibility among others. "All I was saying, Governor, was that I shan't confront her with the earring in the gallery, I'll wait till she's home. And as Cathy McVeigh tells me she wasn't well last night, I'll quite likely find her at home this morning."

"Think I'd like you to go and see, Neil. And if she isn't—could you suggest lunch or something?"

"I'll do what I can."

The Chief proffered the plastic envelope. Viciously concentrating, Neil was able to pick up the earring on his first attempt, and seal the top of the container with fingers he didn't think were noticeably trembling.

"All right, Neil. What I suggest is: when you've told the lady, and have her reaction, ring me or Bob Ryan. If the identification's positive, or you suspect prevarication, keep with her and we'll come over."

"I don't really think," said Neil coldly, "that I'll meet prevarication. If she's consistent, she'll give a clear yes or no. Governor"—it was his one, unavoidable, luxury—"she asked Bob Ryan if Shaw's tongue was protruding! You can't believe she's done anything knowingly." He could only hope he was not trying to convince himself.

"Perhaps not, Neil, perhaps not. We'll see. You'll go now?"

"I'm on my way." Oh, he was, or he might be on his way across the desk with a fist into the centre of that undisturbed face. Arthur Shaw . . . the Chief . . . these images of violence could become a habit. Not one he wanted to acquire.

The sky had paled, retreated. There seemed to be less traffic than usual, and when he switched off the engine outside Westcote Gardens he found that was all he remembered of the journey home. Awaiting the lift, in the lift, he hoped increasingly for the respite of Hilary having gone to work, but her door opened without the least warning from behind it. She looked as ill as he had yet seen her, but smiled in relief at the sight of him, giving an unaccustomed wrench to his heart.

"Neil! I'm sorry about last night, but Dr. Yates called uninvited, and when he saw me he insisted . . . You're late, aren't you?" She was leading the way into the sitting-room. He said, as he sat down beside her on the sofa and put his hand in his pocket, "Actually, I've been out. It's ordinary enough now but it was a weird sort of a morning, red and grey. . . ." He was talking at random while he told himself it must be a complete deception, a complete lulling of suspicion, despite his steadily reasserting belief, once more in her presence, in her innocence as well as her ignorance. "By the way, I found this on the landing, thought it looked like you." Like a conjuror he exposed his palm to reveal the gold gleam, forcing himself to watch her face. It lit up, feebly, as she leaned towards his hand.

"Neil, how clever of you, I'd given it up. I missed it—oh, some time last week, and I would have been upset if other things hadn't . . ." She peered closer. "And the butterfly! That's amazing, it must have come off for me to have lost the thing. You've got exceptional sight."

So far he had done what the Chief would expect. The Chief would now expect him to offer to put the earring somewhere for her, in order to return it unobtrusively to his pocket, then suddenly remember to make an unspecified urgent telephone call, and come back and keep her company until his official colleagues arrived.

What he did, as she put her hand out, was to close his fist and keep it clenched until, in slight curiosity, she looked up at him. "I can't give it back to you just now," he said. He saw the curiosity deepen, take over from the weariness, so that during the small operation of returning the earring openly to the envelope and the envelope to his pocket she became more and more her normal self.

"Why on earth, Neil?" She even laughed, looking into his face for a sign that he was teasing her, so that the wrench turned in him again, and more painfully.

He had alerted her now and he must go on. And yes, he had never intended that anyone but himself should thrust her into understanding of her latest dream.

"I'm not officially concerned in the investigation of Peter's death," he said gravely, and against the noisy chime of his pulse in heart and temple, "as you know." He took her hand between his, and it must have been his tone, because with his repetition of the familiar words the hand tensed. "But this morning I agreed—I had to agree—to play a brief part. To deceive you for the only time. But I didn't agree to undeceive you when—when my job was done. I'm doing that off my own bat."

"What is it, Neil? What are you doing?"

The dullness of her voice made him hope she was too exhausted to feel either his treachery or the full impact of the coming blow.

"I didn't find that earring on the landing, Hilary, I didn't find it at all. The police found it on the carpet in the room where Peter died, they found it the next morning."

She turned to him with a dreadful energy.

"But—that's impossible! I had it last week, I wore it on—when was it, Wednesday, I think—yes, it must have been because I noticed it was missing while the police were here—that first time—I put my hand up and . . . and couldn't worry about *that*."

He wished the police were there now, hearing it as it was. Later, when she'd absorbed the truth, she might not sound so convincing.

He said quietly, "It would be impossible, yes, if things were the way you think they are. But I'm afraid, darling, you didn't dream that last time, that last dream, the night Peter died, you went home, and into the room where he was, and saw him, you were there. The shock affected you and you didn't want to believe it. But you did see him, and I wanted you to hear it from me, not from the others. You have to believe me, Hilary, you really were there. . . ." He wouldn't go on to the even more monstrous part of it, this was violence enough, but he kept going on with this, because there was no response and there had to be, she had to believe it, and then he could help her to accept it. . . .

But there was a response. Her hand was limp when he lifted it, her head had fallen against him, heavy. . . .

He didn't leave her until her breathing was quiet and regular and her pulse rate no longer alarming. And even then he rang her doctor first.

When he got back her eyes were open and as she turned her head to stare at him huge tears shook off on to the nubbly surface of the sofa beneath her cheek. He thought this was the best he could hope for, but she said softly, "I remember. I know."

He stroked her hair. "Do you?"

"Yes."

"Hilary. My Chief is on his way. You've heard of circumstantial evidence. . . . Nobody else is known to have been at the house, nobody else left anything behind. So they have to consider . . . they have to ask you to go with them to answer questions. Oh, darling, it's insulting to tell you that I know you didn't . . ." And perhaps more insulting than she could imagine, because did he know?

It was as ugly a sound as he had ever heard, and he tried to drown it with his head against her mouth, by gabbling on about all the innocents who had suffered until the truth came out. When she stopped groaning her voice was deep and strange, frightening him.

She said, "I could only dream what I would eventually see. Peter was dead when I got there. If that isn't true, then I'm mad. Mad."

He got to his feet and took her by the shoulders, trying and failing to meet her wide gaze. "You are not mad. The police have to cling to what straws they can find. They know one thing about you they don't know about anyone else, so they must ask you questions. If your doctor says you're fit enough." He hadn't been sure she was hearing him, but she said, still in that voice which so horrified him, still without moving more than her lips, "I'm fit enough. Not that it matters. The real thing, and the dream. I can't seem to feel the difference. But Peter's death didn't come into either of them, because I wasn't there when he died. Anyway, it doesn't matter."

He couldn't bear her stillness. He said, "It does matter. I'll make you some tea."

"Not just now."

He sat holding her hand until the doorbell rang. Her doctor, the Chief, and Bob Ryan were another trio on her step. There must have been something in Neil's face, because the Chief merely nodded when Neil suggested the doctor should go in first, alone. As soon as he was out of earshot Neil told the two policemen what had happened and how he had exceeded his brief.

"She claimed the earring in the same sort of way she's done everything else—pinpointed her discovery that she'd lost it to the first time Bob was with her. Then—I told her where it was found and the only thing that could mean, and she passed out. I know, I went too far but the claim had been made and I stake my career on the certainty that she won't retract it." Perhaps he was growing a bit less single-minded, this was the first time he had thought of the implications for his career of the extra thing he had done. And he hadn't thought, either, of what he might be giving away. "I'm quite good at that sort of thing," he went on, forcing a lighter tone, "and it was saving you a second nasty job." Something in his Chief's impassive face signalled he was getting away with it. He returned to the facts. "When she came round she said she remembered, said she knew. Knew that she must have been there, I mean. When I told her the rest—why she had the edge on everyone else as a murder suspect— she said her husband was dead when she got there, or else she was mad. Said it quite calmly and quietly, except that there was something different about her voice. . . . Governor, it can't be as simple as that; everyone will have to be careful."

"The doctor's with her," said the Chief, but shifting about the narrow hall so that his shoulder tipped one of the small pictures on the wall behind him. "Anything else I should know, Carter?"

"I'm trying to think."

He was trying to think whether to tell about her pregnancy, or rather, knowing that he should and trying to do it. Before he said any more Dr. Yates came out to them, stern-faced.

"Chief Inspector, I think you should know that Mrs. Shaw is pregnant—in the fourth month"—had the Chief's eyes swivelled to Neil? —"and that although she appears calm and rational, she's in a state of shock. My professional advice is that she be taken to hospital, for tonight at least."

"May we talk to her there?" asked the Chief humbly.

"If you must. But nowhere else, and only for moments at a time."

"Hospital it is, then. Carter, thank you, you can go now."

Neil had started for the sitting-room, his second involuntary action in the triangle of himself, the Chief and Hilary.

"Of course, Governor, I'll just tell Mrs. Shaw I'm off." He didn't look at any of their faces, but no one made a move. Hilary was as he had left her, lying full-length on the sofa staring at the ceiling. He crouched beside her. "I've got to go now. The doctor's advised a short stay in hospital. For the baby as well as for you. You know I'll come and see you if I can."

"The vase is the answer. Find the vase." The same unfamiliar deep tones. She turned her head and looked at him without expression. He sensed a figure in the doorway and got to his feet. It was the doctor. Neil hardly hesitated as he went out past the Chief and Bob Ryan, home. He poured out some brandy because of the fluttering inside him, drank it pacing the flat and stopping every few minutes to look through his Cyclopean eye. He didn't know how long it was before the front door opposite opened and the cluster of pygmies, Hilary upright in their midst but heavily attended, made its way to the lift and disappeared. He could not have imagined anything more consoling than the coincidence of Cathy opening her door as he opened his. They were standing staring at one another, Neil still with his glass in his hand, when another movement made them both turn. Miss Prince's door had opened too.

"Mr. Carter, Miss McVeigh, good morning," said Miss Prince nervously, registering Neil's glass and then keeping her eyes off it, "I thought I heard . . . I was wondering how Mrs. Sharp—"

"Mrs. Shaw is all right, Miss Prince," said Neil soothingly. "But you did hear some activity. In fact she's gone to hospital for a few days' rest. The strain, as you can imagine—"

"Indeed I can!" Miss Prince was eagerly indignant. "But are you quite sure there's nothing—"

"She has actually gone, Miss Prince, thank you, you're very kind." While he was talking he shut his front door behind him and walked up to Cathy, past her and into her hall. Catching his purpose, Cathy clicked the door to on them both.

"Neil . . ." Leaning her back against the door she had a smothered giggle, her hand to her mouth, a knee drawn up to her chest, like a little girl. But her eyes were large and alarmed.

"You're hysterical," he said, briefly smiling.

For once he led the way into the sitting-room.

"Not really, it's just Miss Prince." She straddled the sofa arm. "Neil, has Hilary really gone to hospital?"

"Yes." He told her everything that had happened. "I want that diary now," he said finally.

"It depends on the balcony doors. You know Miss Prince has the extra front-door key. And Hilary may have taken the diary with her."

"I doubt she was fit enough. And if she thought of it, she'd probably decide it was safer at home." He laughed uncomfortably. "Will you try, Cathy?"

"Of course."

He followed her outdoors, to the corner of the building, watched her open the door which led to Hilary's part of the parapet which edged the whole building.

She was back quickly, holding a stiff-backed exercise book.

"In its usual place. Oh, Neil, isn't this—"

"If I don't take it now, Bob Ryan may well take it in the next hour or two. Mine will be both the more sympathetic and the more interpretive eye. And just as fair, I hope."

"Of course, Neil."

He held the narrow door for her, back to her own territory.

"What are you doing, anyway, home at this time?"

"I had a free period, which was super, and so I thought I'd come home and paint." Cathy's small second bedroom was almost impenetrable through artistic paraphernalia, to the extent that her parents always slept in a hotel.

"I wish Hilary had let her mother come," said Neil. They were in the kitchen, where Cathy without asking him was spooning instant coffee into her unique cups. "D'you know their number?"

"Hilary gave it to me yesterday. As if she was afraid . . . Do you want to ring them?"

"I want you to, if you will. Not to alarm, not to suggest them coming, now. Just to tell them she's resting in hospital because of the shock, and so they won't panic if they ring and don't get a reply." In that dialogue there would be no one who knew about the baby. "Will you do that, Cathy?"

"Now?"

"When I've finished my coffee and gone."

While he drank it the diary lay unopened between his body and the side of Cathy's lilac armchair. He had an idea she was keeping her eyes away from it. When he got home he found himself going into his bedroom, turning back the coverlet, taking his shoes off, lying down on the bed and then, with a sense of preparations completed, opening the book.

CHAPTER 19

Poison . . . Jealousy . . . I hate you . . . Sometimes, just sometimes . . . We must hold on to our civilization. But sometimes I think the effort's going to break me in two.

So, was it too great, the effort, in the end?

Other things he might be thinking of, would inevitably think of, when . . . later . . . *Sweet? Neil Carter on his own is anything but . . . anything but . . .* No, not now, enough for now. But—*I like him better than I like Neil Carter.* Not now, for God's sake. *Gross bad taste . . .*

The matter in hand. *Poison . . . Jealousy . . . I hate you . . . I hate you . . . Something unscrupulous about him . . . unscrupulous . . .*

The front-door bell exploded visually into his labouring skull, he could see it, a spark shooting through the darkness. Had he been asleep? His bedside clock told him two hours had passed since he had come home, and that it was afternoon. But he had read what the exercise book contained.

He pushed it into a drawer, fell over his shoes and kicked them under the bed, tangling with the trailing laces, plunged his feet into slippers, smoothed his hair and the bedcover and staggered out into the hall.

Through the spy-hole it took him a few seconds to recognize Clara Shaw's caricature, and by then she had rung again.

"I'm sorry, I was working half-dressed and thought I should at least . . ."

There was no embarrassment between them at this mental picture. Yet he felt some awkwardness as she stood before him, smiling her crooked smile, and decided it was because he had just been reading about her. The sensation reminded him of once dreaming with ludicrous unsuitability about an elderly tea-lady at work, and of how he had felt next day when she handed him his mid-morning brew.

"Please come in. Have you had lunch?"

"Actually, no. I've been too bothered." Her smile had faded and he could now sense the tension in her.

"Neither have I. Do please join me with a cheese biscuit and—will you have a drink?" He looked at her again. "I suggest brandy. You know about Hilary?"

"The police rang the shop and told me, good of them. I didn't exactly understand."

While he poured drinks and assembled the snack he explained some things.

"They really haven't arrested her, then?" She sat down heavily beside her tray, her colour brighter than usual, her hair perhaps more untidy. Her bosom, for the most part behind a pink crepe blouse, swung against the table edge as she leaned forward to butter a biscuit.

"Heavens, no! I suppose the category is helping the police with their inquiries."

"Neil Carter!" She let knife and biscuit fall to her plate. "That's pretty close to an arrest. I can't let it go any farther."

"And how can you stop it?" But he knew, from the little he knew her, that she must have something intelligent in mind.

"Oh, I can stop it. You see, it was me. Hilary may have been there, she may have—seen Peter. But she didn't kill him, I did. If not the coronary."

He knew he must be looking stupid, but for a few moments he

was unable to find anything to say. She looked back at him, despite everything still a reassuring presence.

He managed eventually a quite relevant remark.

"Why are you only saying this now?"

"Because I didn't think there would be any need to say it at all. It's only because the processes of the law seem to be closing in on Hilary. Poor love . . ." It was impossible not to keep imagining the heads of less confident individuals against that large front. He had been somehow surprised when Hilary had told him Clara and Arthur Shaw had no children.

"What are you saying happened, then?"

She finished half a biscuit before replying.

"Oh, I did go to the shop that night, Neil Carter, as I said I did. But before going home I called in on Peter to see how he was—we knew he'd cried off the City dinner because of not feeling well. He came down to let me in but I had to help him the last part of the way back up the stairs, and by the time he was in his chair again he was pretty well *in extremis*." He tried to gauge the style of her narrative as some sort of a clue to its value, and found the word *casual* in his mind. "You probably don't know it, but I'm a nurse by profession, and after his first mild attack Peter asked me in secret to despatch him, if I was in a position to, should he ever suffer a major cardiac arrest." She took a deep, bosom-jangling breath, and another biscuit, and Neil realized that for all her apparent openness it was impossible for him to know how she felt. "Well, it was pretty clear that if he survived this attack it could only be with massive deterioration. And so"—she held out her free hand as if in vague illustration—"perhaps in the moment when he might have been dying naturally, perhaps a few seconds after he *had* died, without stopping to think, I just—took his throat in my hands and pressed. . . ." Briefly she closed her eyes.

"Wouldn't it have been—better," asked Neil, "to ascertain first whether he was already dead?"

"Undoubtedly," she said, stung. "But I told you, I just did it. I just—tried to put an end to the struggle as quickly as I could."

"And then ran away."

Colour surged in her face. But she said quietly, "Yes, that was about it. I saw the marks of my fingers. And then for the first time I thought of murder. And then I thought . . . What benefit to anybody for me to be involved?"

"Might have been of benefit to Anthony Carey?"

"Oh. Carey."

"Would you be telling me this now if it was Carey helping the police with their inquiries?"

"I shouldn't think so." She was busy over her plate.

"No?" He had to give her a chance to alter that.

"No!" She looked up at him, and at least there was defiance in her eyes. "He's nothing. Carey's nothing."

Everybody's something. He just managed to prevent himself actually saying the improving words aloud. They were uncharacteristic, but she had shocked him. A reaction stronger than his impression of a gallant attempt to help a friend in need. He had to have that impression to some extent, because of feeling that the confession had all the marks of a botched-up tale.

"So that's your story, and you're sticking to it." He smiled as he spoke, to give her the choice of being angry or amused. A flash of anger might have crossed her eyes, but she said, smiling back at him, "It is, Neil Carter."

"Does your husband know?"

She said quickly, "I couldn't hide it."

"Know that you've come to see me?"

She said slowly, "There hasn't been a chance to tell him, but he'd be even less—he wouldn't try to stop me. He would have done before, but now—"

"I understand. He doesn't go for Carey either, does he?"

She disregarded the question. "Can you help me, Neil Carter, can you?"

"Only in so far as I can direct you to the official channel."

"I thought you might—come with me?"

Now he did have a definable reaction, to his displeasure. A sense of satisfied vanity at this strong woman's plea. But he said firmly, "I'm sorry. It would look like gross interference on my part and I know you wouldn't want to put me in wrong with my colleagues. And you can cope admirably alone if you really have made up your mind to do this."

"To do this? You might have said, to tell the truth. It's the same thing."

"Of course."

"Tell me at least where to go."

He gave her the Chief's name and precise location. "I'll do one thing. I'll phone and tell him you crossed the landing for guidance, and give him the gist of what he's going to hear."

"That was really the most I wanted. Thank you." She drained her glass and got up, absent-mindedly brushing biscuit crumbs from her corduroy skirt to the carpet. He noticed the unevenness of her hem. "And Hilary's whereabouts too, please."

"I don't know. I'm not exactly in the official confidence. But I hope my Chief will tell you when you see him." As he hoped his Chief would tell him when he telephoned.

"It'll just be—an ordinary hospital?"

"Of course. Oh, I know what you mean." He smiled at her. Somewhere among his complex series of reactions to Clara Shaw there was now disapproval, but it had not displaced a weird sense of what he thought was mutual appreciation. "But the most difference the police involvement can make will be in securing her an amenity bed."

"I'll go to your Chief now."

"I think you better had."

When she left he went straight to the telephone. The Chief was there. Neil told him about his visitor, and what to expect.

"What were your reactions, Neil?"

"Difficult to define. Her story was quite plausible, and yet somehow glib. It gave me the impression of being made up to protect Hilary but I didn't get the expected reaction of admiration for loyalty and courage."

"That could be you."

"I suppose it could. Anyway, you'll make your own assessment. I certainly didn't feel she was playing games. She's worried. She almost told me she wouldn't have bothered to own up if it was Carey as suspect number one. I felt I was learning more from that, actually, Governor, than from what she had set out to tell me."

"Learning?"

"That she really could be ruthless, whether or not she has been as regards her brother-in-law. Is it in order to ask for Mrs. Hilary Shaw's temporary address?"

"Oh, in the circumstances, I think so, Neil," said the Chief, revealing it.

"Thank you, Governor." He wouldn't stop to wonder how much he had recently given away. "And to tell her—"

"I don't think there's any reservation on anything you might tell her," murmured the Chief. "Come and see me in the morning."

He thought he had had a lucky break when he saw Dr. Yates outside the Sister's office, talking to the Sister. But before they had done more than acknowledge one another the Sister said, "Oh yes, Mr. Carter, I can let you see Mrs. Shaw for a few moments."

Still trying not to wonder if all along he had been less clever than he had imagined, or the Chief more so, he followed her along the corridor. Hilary was alone in a small room, lying still with open eyes. When the Sister said Neil's name she at least turned her head towards the door.

"I'll leave you a few moments. But gently, Mr. Carter."

"Of course."

He pulled up a chair and leaned over to kiss her forehead through the ruffled hair.

"Thank you for coming, Neil."

He hadn't been given a brief, or denied one. He recognized a moment of acute responsibility.

"Are you all right?"

She tried to smile. "I think I'm drugged. I don't feel dopey. Just remote." Her voice was still strange, but not so deep.

"The baby . . ."

"It's all right, nothing to disagree with the baby, I made sure."

"That's good. Clara's just been to see me."

"Clara?"

He was aware of her body stiffening the length of the bed, but he went on. "She wanted to tell me what happened the night Peter died."

He repeated Clara's tale. Before he had finished the stiffness had resolved in a flow of tears.

"How absurd, Neil! But how magnificent!"

He was becoming intrigued as to why he in no way shared this reaction.

"Yes. If she wasn't telling the truth."

"Of course she wasn't! Clara couldn't . . . She was doing it for me!"

"You don't think she could have killed your husband, then? Not even to spare him?"

"To spare him," she whispered. "Perhaps . . ." He thought he could see hope in her eyes. "If she had—tried to help him—I could understand—and they wouldn't—"

"If she was telling the truth," said Neil, "I can't believe she would receive any sort of a harsh sentence."

He didn't think he could believe, either, that Clara Shaw had been telling it exactly as it was.

"Neil, it's grotesque—after all that's happened—but, that pact between them—I felt *jealous* . . ."

"I think that will do," said the Sister, at his shoulder.

"Of course. Thank you for letting me see her."

"Have you been upsetting her?" asked the Sister, seeing the tear
marks.

"I don't think so. Isn't it good to cry sometimes?"

"Sometimes."

"Goodbye, Hilary."

"Goodbye, Neil."

But when he was at the door she said his name again, in that
dreaded deep tone.

"All right," conceded the Sister.

He went back to the bed. "What is it?"

"The vase." She was staring at the ceiling. "The vase is the answer."

"Your husband could have sold the vase. Someone could have
come in while Anthony was out."

She moved restlessly.

"No. No. He would never have parted with it." Anthony Carey
had said that. "Somebody took it away from him. Not Anthony, and
I was the only other one. *And it was still there.* But I didn't. I
didn't."

"Please go, Mr. Carter," said the Sister severely. *Something unscrupulous about him* . . . Why had he had to learn bits of the diary
by heart?

He waited outside the door until the Sister joined him.

"Is she all right? I'm very sorry."

"I told Chief Inspector Larkin I didn't think . . . Yes, I've given
her another injection, she'll be all right. But I'm afraid I must advise
you not to come again, Mr. Carter."

It was the moment for turning to some of the things he had been
neglecting. It was eight o'clock when he got home. Once upon a
time, he would have rung Cathy's doorbell, but now he telephoned.
He fancied her response was guarded.

"Have you had your supper?"

A hesitation?

"No, Neil."

"I've got a home-made granary. Scrambled egg?"

And again?

"Yes, I should like that. Thanks." *Her Hero* . . .

"Now?"

"In a few moments." *Her passion for Detective-Inspector Carter* . . .

He started to prepare the eggs but soon took his straining ears along the hall to the front door. Despising himself, he applied his eye to his spy-hole. Cathy came out of her flat followed by Don Everett. At least he overcame the temptation to watch and listen to their good nights. He was in the kitchen when she rang his bell.

He thought she looked very much alive. Very young and radiant. But the image of Hilary's motionless white face was at present an indelible accompaniment to all other impressions. In the kitchen he brought Cathy up to date.

"Was the diary any help?"

Each time he thought of it, his first reaction was discomfort.

"I don't know, really. It certainly reinforces Hilary's insistence that she didn't consciously do anything. There's the dream, just as she told it, several times before the event. And there's evidence of a well-balanced woman who reacted as well as anyone could react to what happened to her. Here and there . . . she hates him, she wishes him harm. But it's the very least of things."

"I'm glad." She had kept her head averted all the time he was talking, and turned to him to change the subject. "I've got another commission."

As the evening wore on he became increasingly aware that her presence was enabling him to defer an unpleasant task. It wasn't until she had gone home to bed that he realized what it was: the prospect of Hilary's diary with the solitary night ahead of him. With particular reference . . .

He found it after a search. *I haven't been in his flat as yet. I'm a little curious, but not so curious as I am about Stephen. That sounds so perverse, it can only say something about my real priorities.*

There was, there must be, some sort of antidote. Furiously he hunted, hating himself for so much as turning a page. But he couldn't have seen one thing, without the other.

Surprisingly good salary . . . Stephen isn't curious . . . respects the personal barrier . . . He's so retiring!

But all at once his presence in her flat, his hand on her arm.

And she had said, Stephen's changed.

He would present himself next morning at the Stephen Elliott Gallery, or at whatever place the man might be, would discover something, if only the loss of his unworthy hope.

Meanwhile there was more to disturb than to sedate in the book under his hand. He searched again.

Arthur's living antithesis . . .

He put the book on the floor, spread the three-word refrain all over his mind, and fell asleep.

CHAPTER 20

He decided some time in the night that he would pursue Stephen Elliott, for the coming day at least, only as far as his North London gallery. The decision, he supposed, came from the vestiges of common sense which still surrounded his distorted vision of the man. And perhaps also from a feeling that if Elliott wasn't there, of which there was a sporting chance, it might be as well for the investigation, if not for his own blood pressure.

The tall, broad-shouldered figure was actually taking a picture out of the window. As Elliott straightened up, picture in hand, he saw Neil outside and his grave face brightened in what seemed like spontaneous pleasure. Before turning back to his client he signed to Neil to come in.

Neil walked about the display area, rather liking the effect of small brightly-coloured cubes building up such disparate subjects as tigers and trees, wondering on some indefinable pang of regret what Hilary would have made of them.

"I'm sorry, Mr. Carter, but without Hilary . . ." Stephen Elliott was at his side. "Mrs. Tilsley is, I hope, about to bring me coffee. Do come through and join me and perhaps we can manage not to be interrupted for a few moments."

Following Elliott behind a half-drawn curtain, Neil had to believe the man was at least creating an impression of rather particularly liking him. He remembered, reluctantly, his own instinctive first reaction. Elliott put his head round a door and called for a second coffee. They had scarcely sat down on two severe elegant chairs before an elderly woman with sharp red features and a noticeably collapsed figure appeared with a mug in either hand.

"Mrs. Tilsley, Mr. Carter," said Stephen Elliott.

"Good morning, I'm sure." The door did not quite close behind Mrs. Tilsley's low-slung posterior.

"I saw Hilary yesterday," said Neil, more uncomfortable than when he had faced Anthony Carey's gun.

"So did I," said Elliott eagerly. "I didn't think they'd let me in, but I suppose I was a bit insistent, and they went and asked her, and she said yes." The frown had appeared, which sat so externally on the pleasant features. "She's not well."

"No," said Neil shortly. "How much do you know about what's been happening to her?" Even as he spoke, he was surprised by such unsophisticated directness.

"Nothing, I don't think," said Stephen Elliott apologetically. "I can see that she's more than simply upset by her husband's death, and she's said a few things I haven't understood, but I haven't asked—"

"But you've been around, all of a sudden, since last Thursday. She said to me, Mr. Elliott, she said in so many words, 'Stephen's changed.' You'll have to excuse me, you and I both know that I'm not on the case, but as neighbour and policeman I can't help being concerned, and in this sort of context I can't let coincidences alone. Coincidences such as you happening to be in your doorway when she went by, happening to ask her in and offer her a job, happening to change towards her the moment her husband dies. . . ."

At least he was managing to say it quietly, calmly, almost smiling at the man as he let him have it, quietly, calmly. . . . He was awaiting his own regret for what he was doing. And the disdain, or rage, or at least amazement which must show in Stephen Elliott's face.

But Elliott was relaxing as hugely as his chair would allow him, pumping out a breath with exaggeratedly inflated cheeks and then smiling at Neil, suddenly without any trace of nervousness or apology.

"Yes, Mr. Carter, that's all absolutely true and you're quite right, it isn't any of it a coincidence, and I've been wondering why the official police haven't put it to me just the way you have done, because that's the way I've been putting it to myself."

"So you've got something to tell them? In that case I think you should telephone them now." Neil put his hand out towards the instrument on the table between them.

There could have been hurt in the eyes, but it quickly gave place to amusement. "Oh no, Mr. Carter, I haven't got anything to tell *them*. You've made me decide that I've something to tell *you*, but it isn't police business and I won't be telling you because you're a policeman, it'll be self-indulgence because I'm afraid of exploding and you've given me an opening. I feel a bit sorry you thought it might have something to do with . . . but as things are, of course I can understand." Yes, the man had been hurt, but in what must be his usual fair way, he had justified Neil's action to himself.

"Well, then?" invited Neil.

"I can tell you in one sentence, really." It was the only time he had seen the healthy brown face take on extra colour. "I was in love with her at first sight. To the extent of asking her to come and look round when I saw her through the window. Not in the least like me," said Stephen Elliott earnestly, "but she stood outside for quite a few minutes, absolutely long enough for me to be sure she really was the girl I'd always known. . . . It was extraordinary, really, how she just was the girl whose—well, whose picture I'd had inside my head as long as I can remember. I couldn't let her go, so I asked her in before I thought about it, and then asked her if she wanted a job. I did need an assistant, in fact, urgently, I was just going to advertise"—he pulled a rueful face—"I've wished since that I'd actually done so, so that I could have broken that chain of coincidence. I can't think why the police—"

"Because they find other coincidences more compelling," said Neil shortly.

"Yes, well, Hilary accepted the offer, but she made it pretty plain from the start that it was all business and I knew I must lie personally low. Luckily we had the Arts—sorry, that sounds pretentious, but it's a summing up—we had that in common to take us through idle moments and the odd lunch, and I suppose I hoped that eventually she would talk to me."

Which she might have done, reflected Neil, if she'd lived elsewhere. The bell on the shop door jangled. At least it had waited until Elliott's hardest part was over. Neil sat tight behind the curtain, monitoring one or two rearward creaks, until the gallery owner came back to him. It was immediately clear he had lost his fluency.

"Do go on," encouraged Neil.

"I would, but . . . You're not giving me any idea of what you're thinking."

It was as near as Neil had found him to a rebuke, and perhaps it was fair.

"I'm sorry, but that's my training. I assure you I'm listening with an open mind." As he spoke he was aware that Elliott's whole bearing had made that true.

"Well, when her husband was killed, and I saw her . . . I didn't *say* anything, of course, that would have been appalling, but I suppose I just stopped acting backward, I had to be *there,* even if in a dumb sort of way, I couldn't help it then, and I hoped something would get across of my concern at least, and make her feel better."

"I think it has." Neil had spoken before he thought, apparently pleasing Elliott.

"You do?"

"Certainly." Yes, he really did think so.

"I'm glad. For her, I mean. I wasn't thinking of me."

"But you should," said Neil. "When she's better. When it's all over." He was more surprised by this than by anything else he had said that morning. He heard himself going on. "Doesn't do to be too self-effacing."

"Sometimes it can be politic." There was a glint of humour. Half an hour earlier, Neil would have found words and look sinister in the extreme. Now he saw them as a desirable dilution of so much good nature. Stephen Elliott was suddenly looking at the diary beside the telephone.

"Heavens, I'm supposed to be in St. Albans. . . . I'll have to ask you to excuse me, the last thing I'd do from choice at this moment, but I'm late as it is. I'm very glad you came, Mr. Carter. Don't hurry away, have a proper look round." Elliott was ineffectually smoothing his hair, straightening his tie.

"Are you going to see Hilary today?" asked Neil.

"They said I could look in. Mrs. Tilsley!" Stephen Elliott had raised his voice, but Mrs. Tilsley was at hand in the doorway. "Oh, you're there. I'm off now, I've got John Edwards coming in about half an hour to hold the fort until I get back. If you wouldn't mind until then . . ."

"That'll be all right, Mr. Elliott, you better get going now."

"Heavens, yes! Goodbye, then, Mr. Carter."

Neil and Mrs. Tilsley stood watching him catapult through the door, whirl past the window.

"Too much to do," said Mrs. Tilsley oracularly. "Not enough help."

"We must hope Miss Fielding will soon be well enough to come back and help him."

Neil was aware of Mrs. Tilsley's sniff shaking her whole heavy body. "Won't be Miss Fielding, nor Mrs. Shaw, as comes back if Mr. Elliott has anything to do with it. If he has his way it'll be Mrs. Elliott. He's that besotted with her."

"Did he tell you?" Neil looked doubtfully at the close bright eyes and small pursed mouth.

"He didn't *tell* me. He didn't need to, did he?" There was a pause, but for effect rather than for an answer from Neil. "No, I could see it, the way he changed between when she was here and when she wasn't. A baby could have seen it. I hadn't thought Mr. Elliott was so—" Mrs. Tilsley wrestled with the complexity of her thought. Neil found the word *unsophisticated* and was wondering whether to offer it when Mrs. Tilsley triumphantly brought out the word *soft*.

"Ah, that's what love does, you see," observed Neil.

"That's what I told meself." Mrs. Tilsley's fierce gaze briefly modified in approval. "And I'd always been a bit sort of sorry that he never seemed to have no lady-friends. Not that Miss Fielding was ezactly a lady-friend, but 'e did seem interested in her. I'm glad he's talked about it—I couldn't 'elp hoverearing just now"—her glance did not waver—"Is Miss Fielding ill or summat? I read the papers and I must say it seemed a bit . . . one minute they say as the poor man had a 'eart attack, and the next he's been murdered. I must say—"

This was undoubtedly the moment for bringing the exchange to a close.

"It does seem to have been rather complicated," agreed Neil. "But it will all be sorted out soon, you'll see. Now I must go, too." He smiled encouragingly at Mrs. Tilsley, but she was realist enough to recognize defeat.

"Good morning, I'm sure." She turned from him as sharply as her lumbering form would allow, gathering up the mugs.

"Goodbye. Thank you for the delicious coffee."

But Mrs. Tilsley didn't turn back and he didn't need her any more, she had done the most she could do for him, destroyed his last vestige of doubt as to the *bona fides* of Stephen Elliott, forced him into line with Bob Ryan and Co., who hadn't thought it necessary even to ask Elliott those questions which Neil had just asked him. Only now, as he opened the gallery door and felt the sun on his face, did Neil admit to having been out of line with the official enquiry.

"I expected you earlier, Carter."

One of the difficulties with the Chief was not always knowing whether he was annoyed because of something Neil had done or not done, or because of something disagreeable which had happened to him elsewhere.

"You didn't specify a time, Governor, and I transacted some other business on the way here." Neil spoke crisply, purging any resentment which might remain with him as a result of the morning so far. And he felt better for having gone home again and stuffed Hilary's diary, in an envelope, through Cathy's letter-box.

"All right, Neil, it doesn't matter. How did you get on yesterday with Mrs. Hilary?"

Neil told him. "It fits with her other reactions," he commented, after waiting a few seconds in a silence the Chief didn't fill. "I don't think the Sister was very enamoured of my visit. Anyway, I'm not intending to try and see her again."

"I think that's wise, Neil. I'm told she seems better this morning, but we're leaving her alone for the moment, too. Did you know she was pregnant?"

He had learned to cope on a reflex with the Chief's lunges, even while in shock. "Her doctor let it out last night. Oh, you were there, Governor."

"Not," said the Chief irritably, "that she seems likely to tell us anything more than she told us at the beginning."

Because she can't. He realized the diary had finally confirmed his belief in Hilary's ignorance. But innocence was another matter. "Do you still not know whether you're pursuing a murderer or a would-be murderer?"

"Still don't know," growled the Chief. "I hate it when a bad business keeps turning into a farce."

Neil decided his Chief was out of sorts over the general fact of the Shaw case being on his plate.

"Mrs. Arthur? What are you making of her?"

The Chief exhaled an impatient breath. "There again, it's all ifs and buts. Nothing obvious. Nothing dovetailing. No way of proving whether or not she's suddenly telling the truth. Just the feeling that here's one more thing which doesn't fit."

"Doesn't fit?"

"Dammit, Neil, I suppose this is what you were saying, it doesn't seem to go with the woman. And yet—it makes sense, there aren't any gaps. But no real links, either."

"So what next, Governor?"

"We can only wait on Mrs. Hilary. Who won't tell us anything."

"Or can't."

"Or can't. I know, Neil. And we're trying to get at the whereabouts of the mysterious vase by trying to get at its history. Now, for goodness' sake go away and do something else. You should be grateful, you at least have the option."

There was an outstanding visit to pay in Bloomsbury. Perhaps not of any greater urgency than one or two others, but he chose it. Afterwards he crossed the road to the British Museum. He stood undecided in the great hall, until the unbidden dictum *Business before pleasure* came into his head, then climbed the stairs.

One Wedgwood Portland in protected splendour for all the world to see. Another . . . The second victim, fancied Neil, in the Shaw case. Missing, believed killed. Was there in fact no more now than a few sharp shards in a dustbin? Returned forever to the obscurity which only three people (smiling, he amended the figure to four, and then, frowning, to an unknown number of policemen and their harnessed experts) knew it had emerged from? Hilary had said it was the key, and she was right, of course, even the Chief and Co. knew that.

Had Hilary put it in a bank deposit, and buried her remembrance? Had Carey staged his going-over of her flat as an elaborate deception tactic? Such things were commonplace. Had Arthur Shaw's pale eyes lighted on it with more understanding than Neil had given him credit for? If the passionate statements were to be believed of both Peter Shaw's lovers, whoever knew the fate of the vase knew the fate of the man. . . .

Neil was on his way downstairs as he discovered why he had really come to the British Museum. He quickened his pace across the hall, through the bookstall and the postcards and past the looming Assyrians. Aphrodite and her mosaic, Apollo and his lute, the small bright room behind the curtain. But first . . .

He stood in front of her stone image, gravely admiring. He felt, even through his amusement, as if he was taking part in a small ceremony. He was alone among the statues, and he murmured his thoughts aloud.

"It's over, isn't it? You won't need to tell me. And you won't need me any more. I hope it helped. I shan't forget you, no man could. I may even come and see you here now and then." It wasn't all that crazy, really, it was only like talking to a photograph before tucking it away in a drawer. And he had a sense of gratitude to work off, it wasn't often things came to an end so easily and naturally.

He laid his hand against the cold cheek, then ran up the steps and behind the curtain.

In the bright centre of the room, in the morning of the world, stood the real, the original, thing.

Almost on tiptoe he moved towards it, round it, tracing its encircling mystery of gods and men, welcoming the lift of the heart it gave him, the revitalizing sense that none of his current preoccupations mattered, and that in the moment he was totally free.

CHAPTER 21

The short uneventful journey back to the office seemed the most cheerful thing he had undertaken in a long time.

"Any messages?"

"Just one, Governor."

The caller had left only a number, but the message said to ring back at once. Neil went to his own telephone. The ringing tone was quickly cut off with an abrupt "yes."

"Neil Carter here."

"Neil Carter. I didn't want it to be noted who was ringing you. But I need to see you. Is there a chance of your coming out to me?"

"Now?" There was no doubt about the voice, even though he had never heard Clara Shaw without seeing her.

"As soon as you can. If you can make it now, there'll be a snack lunch for you."

Sergeant Hislop, whom he had tended to neglect of late, was doing a cat's cradle meaningfully at him from his desk across the room, with string off a lately opened parcel.

"In the shop?" He pulled a conciliatory face at the sergeant.

"No, I'm at home. You know the address, of course."

"Of course. I'll come right away." He hung up.

"And will I come right away, too, Governor?"

"You won't come, Tim, I'm sorry, private business this, but you'll go. If you can disentangle yourself."

He gave instructions for a job which normally he would have preferred to do himself, from selfishness rather than policy. The sergeant was happy. They went down in the lift together, managing four exchanges of cat's cradle before reaching the ground floor.

The Arthur Shaw house was vintage Peter Shaw, but smaller and with only a path to the front door. As Neil rang the bell he saw a shape moving inside the long bay window at his right hand. Clara Shaw had been looking out for him.

She was at the door with the disconcerting speed of movement of certain heavily made people.

"Oh, thank you. I feel frantic."

Without actually looking more untidy than usual, she had an unaccustomed air of disarray, as if the slight displacement of clothes and hair had spread inwards. But cheese, pâté, tomatoes and a Thermos of coffee were set ready on a low table beside the gas-fire.

"How very nice."

"I don't like missing meals." For a moment he saw her usual smile. The room was chilly and the fire gently flamed. The furniture, including the armchairs, was too large for the space available, and of heavy design. Parental things to which Peter Shaw wouldn't have given house room but which Arthur would have been pleased to take. The forbidding accumulation was softened by an abundance of leaves and flowers. "No sun ever in here," she said. "Please sit down. Will you have a drink?"

"Only the coffee, thanks."

She poured some for them both. He had noticed before how unexpectedly slim and beautiful her hands were, with their unadorned oval nails and one plain gold ring. Her hands . . . someone's hands . . .

"What's the trouble?" he asked, when they were both supplied with food.

"They won't believe me!"

"They?" Through the gloom he thought there was panic in her eyes.

"Your colleagues. Your Chief. They think I'm—making a gesture. Neil Carter, I wouldn't! Oh, I'd do whatever I could for Hilary, I'd suffer for her, but I wouldn't pretend I'd committed her crime!"

"So you're saying you did it because it's true?"

"Yes. Yes. Of course that's why I'm saying it!"

"And why have you come to me?"

She smiled again, ruefully.

"There was just one face on which I did *not* see an expression of amazed admiration. Not that I'm saying I exactly saw belief and understanding, more like an open mind willing to be convinced. But at least in your direction there's hope. If I can persuade you that I'm telling the truth, then there's a chance that you can persuade the rest of them."

"You flatter me. Unless you have some sort of proof, I could talk to my Chief until I'm blue in the face."

Against the window he saw her shoulders rise and fall.

"I've thought and thought. I've gone over and over it all. How unfair life is! *I* should have been the one to drop an earring—or I could have dropped a scarf, or be seen. And the only thing I *had* got . . . well, it wouldn't have been significant in itself, but at least the fingerprints might have made them think but when I washed mine off—so very carefully, of course—well, I washed Peter's off too. And there just isn't anything else. Have another biscuit."

He waved the plate away. "Washed your fingerprints off . . . off what, for heaven's sake?"

"Hadn't I told you that? I suppose I didn't think there was any point in it. And perhaps . . . well, it didn't exactly show me up in the best light. I only took it from panic, and I didn't—"

"Mrs. Shaw, perhaps you'll tell me *now*. If I'm to help you, you have to tell me everything, and leave me to decide whether or not it's important."

"Of course, yes, I'm sorry. Well, when I got Peter upstairs and into his chair . . ."

"Go on." She was shaking her head, taking a great draught of coffee. Again he was reminded of a shaggy dog. "What is it?"

"Neil Carter, I—simplified my story last time. No, it was true, but I—shortened it because it didn't seem necessary . . . I'd better tell you everything exactly as it happened."

"You better had, yes. And right away now, please, or spontaneous combustion will take place in your drawing-room."

He even resented the seconds it took her to smile her acknowledgement of his little joke.

"When I got Peter upstairs and into his chair he seemed to recover somewhat. There was a sort of a vase on the table and after he'd sat down he picked it up and stroked it and then put it down laughing and asked me if I didn't think it was clever."

"Clever?" The pulse was in the back of his throat, painfully ticking.

"It was a black vase with white figures round it, classical-looking. He said it was a copy Wedgwood had made of a really old vase. Apparently they made some copies two hundred years ago, and those are very rare and valuable, but they've just started making them now again, lots of them, and didn't I think it looked good, considering it was all modern processes and two a penny. . . . He sort of pushed it into my hands, grinning at me. . . ." She paused and quickly ate half a biscuit. Neil decided she was a compulsive eater, it had struck him already that hers was the sort of fat which contained a slim woman. "He always used to tease Arthur and me about having no real taste. No feel for things, he called it, and I never minded, he could have been right. . . . Anyway, he kept urging me to look at the vase, handle it, didn't I think they'd been clever, but of course if one looked closely, et cetera, et cetera, and I just kept agreeing, anyway I was more concerned for him, and then he began to gasp again and I put the vase down and that's when I . . ."

This time, even through the gloom, she alarmed him as she sank back in her chair, and he threaded his way towards a familiar bottle on a side table, trying to contain his impatience. There were glasses and he poured a generous tot of the brandy.

"Here. Drink this." She did so, with immediate advantage, or perhaps she was already recovering. "Can you go on?" asked Neil, as unfeverishly as he could manage.

"Yes. I'm sorry. It's just . . ."

"Of course. I'm sorry to have to ask you."

"Neil Carter! You didn't, remember? I insisted on telling you."

She was all right. Impatience jerked in his wrists and ankles. He said, "Tell me about the vase."

She set down the glass of brandy, almost empty.

"As I was leaving I remembered it, and how my fingerprints must be all over it and I just grabbed it and tucked it under my arm as I—ran away was the phrase you used, and it was quite right."

"You didn't think . . ." He had to cough and start again, the pulse in his throat was so constrictive. "You didn't think of wiping it clean on the spot?"

"I didn't think of anything but getting out of the house. And murder. I told you, I'd started to think of murder, and Carey would be coming back, and anyway every moment was a danger, and so—

Neil Carter, I was just a living, breathing desire to get away. I didn't think, I acted."

"And when you got home, what did you do?" Absurdly, his eyes were raking the dim room as she drank the last of the brandy. On the table a glass tulip. Beside the fire, a gleaming brass bulb. A huge Victorian cut-glass bowl on the side table, near a green and orange faïence plant pot. A Chinese ginger jar on one side of the window. On the other, tucked away on a small table, half concealed by the feathery foliage which overhung it . . . But Clara Shaw, running round the curves of the drive, panic-stricken, stumbling perhaps—or perhaps thinking, why take it home, why take the trouble to wipe it clean when . . . *two a penny*—into a bush, over a wall . . . But the shape in the corner, dark, rounded, a white glint, must be a narrow neck because the stalks were fine, and upright . . .

Clara Shaw set the glass down, empty. "I don't know why I didn't just chuck it away. Being one of so many it would hardly have been traceable. I suppose I was just too het up. All I remember about getting home is the rhythm of my feet and my breath. Both getting louder. It was only when I'd calmed down a bit that I saw the vase on the kitchen table beside my handbag."

"And then?" He made himself relax his hands on the arms of his chair. The knuckles must be showing white.

She chuckled. She looked almost normal. "I washed it, and put some leaves in it. After all, it was rather pretty and I'd rendered it harmless. Arthur thought that was quite clever. It's there, in the corner. You look sick, Neil Carter? What's different?"

He told her, after he had asked her to give him a minute and had gone to squat reverentially in the window. He had learned Hilary's lesson, and he made sure with his eyes, touching only when he had done so, folding his hands round the curves for his own satisfaction.

He had to ask her if she didn't think the vase was beautiful.

"Of course," she said impatiently. "You'll have to telephone your Chief now, won't you?"

"Yes." But he sat down again to look at her. The next most amazing thing was that Clara Shaw hadn't flinched at the elegant confirmation of her story, rather she appeared triumphant, her doubt and depression gone, her shoulders silhouetted more squarely against the window.

"They'll have to believe me now!"

"They might think," pondered Neil aloud, on the very instant of being certain that Hilary was proved innocent, and that he had already believed her so, "that you agreed to provide Hilary with a hiding place."

He couldn't see any further change in her, but he had the impression her soft-surfaced body had stiffened.

"Do you really think I'm strong enough to carry that through?"

"Maybe."

"And that Hilary would go along with it?"

"Not that, no."

"No." She turned her head for the first time in the direction of the modest shape of whose presence in the room he was every second conscious. "It's a miracle it's there, I suppose. I may not have thrown it away, but I could so easily have dropped it or knocked it." Neil shuddered, involuntarily and to be noticed. "It's only a thing," reproved Clara, "but I suppose it represents a fortune for someone. Who?"

"That's not why . . . Yes, a small fortune. On the face of it, for Anthony Carey. But Hilary will contest the will, and there's no knowing at the moment how things will be apportioned."

"They'd better get it out of here, or it might get broken after all." He hadn't realized quite how bitterly she hated Anthony Carey.

"What time was all this?"

"I must have arrived about ten past eleven. I know I locked the shop up at eleven, I looked at my watch when I got outside, by the street lamp, and it's a ten-minute walk. It's all ten minutes—the shop to home, home to Peter, Peter to the shop, a sort of triangle."

"Late, wasn't it?"

"Not for this family. And Peter always waits—waited—up for his beloveds. If he hadn't felt like coming down he'd have thrown me the key or else said good night and I'm all right from the window."

"I wonder," thought Neil aloud, "what time Hilary arrived."

"Twenty-five to twelve. I looked at my watch again."

He leaned forward, trying in his astonishment to read her face through the gloom. "What did you say?"

"She arrived while I was there. After I'd—when I was about to run away. I was going to tell you and then you asked about the vase and anyway, it didn't add anything—"

"Tell me now."

"I heard a car and I looked round the curtain and saw Hilary getting out and walking to the front door, and I heard her opening it. I ran out of the room and into the bathroom next door and stood behind the door and heard her come up the stairs, very steady, and across the landing and straight into the sitting-room and then I heard her scream. And scream. And scream. And then I heard her running out and down the stairs and bang the front door and drive off, and I looked at my watch and it was nearly twenty to twelve." She leaned back in her chair.

"More brandy?"

"No, no. I'm all right."

"Had you taken the vase then? Did you have it with you in the bathroom?"

"No, Neil Carter." There was, he thought, a brief smile of ironic approval. "I went back into the sitting-room again—you know, that was in a way the worst moment—just to see, well, to see if there was anything different, and there apparently wasn't. And then I thought about the vase and then I grabbed it."

"She said," observed Neil softly, "the vase was always there, on the table, in her dream. It was the one thing she couldn't understand."

"She was right. It was there."

"Yes. Did you believe she thought she was dreaming?"

"When she looked at me and told me, yes. I was hoping, of course, that she wouldn't say anything about having been there. But when she said she had dreamed it . . . my scalp crawled."

He had to admire her stoicism. A world of horror must be in those three lightly offered words.

"'That it might be fulfilled that was spoken by the prophets.' She *had* dreamed, you know, many times."

"I know now." She leaned forward again. "So perhaps you can understand how I was glad for once that there was a Carey."

She knew he had been unable to swallow on that. Nor would he make a concession now.

"A scapegoat."

Without showing a reaction she indicated the table which held the vase. "The telephone's there. You can stand guard while you use it."

He almost fancied the vase gave off a warmth, but he had moved nearer the fire. The Chief had clearly come grudgingly to take his call.

"What is it, Carter?"

"I'm at Mrs. Arthur Shaw's, in response to a strongly-worded invitation." He glanced towards Clara Shaw, but she was not looking round. "Mrs. Shaw wanted to enlist my help in getting you to believe her story, she having the idea that I might have some influence with you." But he had enough good material without recourse to silly jokes. "I do believe it, Governor, because in the corner of her drawing-room here she has the Portland vase. She took it in a panic because of it having her dabs all over it, not knowing it was in the least valuable, and somehow it escaped getting broken. She'll tell you the whole story, of course."

"Of course, Neil." There was no expression in the Chief's voice. "You're sure it's the Portland vase, then?"

He suppressed his ridiculous indignation.

"Certain, Governor. I've been twice to the British Museum." There was no need to let the Chief know that Clara Shaw would be saying everything for the second time. "I'll wait here for you."

"For Bob Ryan," growled the Chief, "and an expert. By the way, Neil, the forensic boys have come up with their decision."

"Which is?" The itinerant pulse was thumping now in his breast bone.

"Death due to strangling. Although Shaw would probably have died, and could only have survived as a vegetable."

"Mercy killing, then? As intended." He said it to prepare her, and he thought her body had drooped. The Chief growled again, more ominously. "All right, Governor, I'll expect Bob Ryan."

He went back to sit opposite Clara Shaw. They stared at one another.

At last he said, "You understand, I think. He could only have survived as a vegetable. If he hadn't died anyway. Those are my Chief's words."

"But he was murdered. I murdered him."

"For his sake!"

But she continued to stare at him with wide, anguished eyes. At the height of her strange victory she was appalled by it.

She whispered, "Murder . . ." The ebony clock on the tall mahogany mantelpiece clanged one into the silence. She squared her shoulders. "They're coming to take me away."

"To ask you to go with them to answer some questions."

"I know. To help them with their inquiries." She half smiled at him, she had pulled herself together. Neil realized she had surprised him by even briefly losing her way.

"How long have we, would you say, Neil Carter, before anyone arrives?"

"At least a quarter of an hour."

"More coffee? There's still plenty and it's still hot."

"Thank you."

She poured coffee for them both. Sun was beginning to reflect off the leaves and pavements outside and the yellow light from one dazzling opposite window caught Neil in the eye. Even when he moved and it struck the wall behind him, the gloom where they sat was scarcely disturbed.

"If I asked you for a promise of secrecy," she said, leaning towards him, "over certain things which I feel moved to tell you, would you be able to keep it? Would you keep it?"

"I would certainly keep it if I gave it."

"I'd have to ask for it unconditionally."

"That's all right."

"Anyway, I assure you I'm not proposing to offer any sort of revelation to interest the police, so your official conscience won't be tried."

"I'm not worried. But be sure you want to talk."

"Oh, I'm sure."

"You'd better start, then."

"Yes." She set her cup and saucer down on the table beside her, made a lightning change in the order of her crossed knees so that the heavy calves shook, and leaned forward again. "It's simply that— well, I'd like one person to know the truth—the whole truth, that is —and I feel that person has to be you. I've felt—you have some sort of a quality, Neil Carter, which makes one want to tell you how things really were."

"Thank you." He was reminded again, of course, of Hilary—of Hilary telling him, and him alone, about the baby. And there had been other instances. He had never considered himself as having any special talent, but now it came to him, more as a recognition than a revelation, that perhaps his one abiding talent was to attract the truth. The possibility warmed him, reunited him with the bright sun so near and yet so far away. "Please begin."

"I don't even know," said Clara Shaw, "if I'm really going to tell you anything else about Peter's death, although your Chief might think . . . It's all a question of my sex, my own huge personal private libido." She flung back in her chair, smiling at him with her now familiar look of intimate but sexless understanding. "Always, Neil Carter, all of the time, everywhere. Not all men, quite"—her smile widened—"not you, for instance—and of course I know not you for me—but there are always enough. But never enough, you see. . . ."

He was seeing her in his mind's eye the one time he had seen her unobserved, in her shop. And having to ask her, out of a sudden acute curiosity, "And Arthur? With Arthur?"

The smile, the animation, vanished. She sat still and serious.

"No, not with Arthur. Well, with Arthur of course, but not because I want him, only because he occasionally wants me, and I am his wife. But make no mistake, Neil Carter, I want to be his wife, I want to be there. Because he needs me. I suppose that's my other need, to be needed." She smiled again, but with an effort, on this territory. "When I discovered that through my fault there would be no children, I knew I would always stay with the one person who would be like a child without me. So that my feeling for Arthur is one of the only two sensations which can't burn themselves out. You see, with me it's the beginnings which count, I get tired, have to move on, and so the better the beginning the quicker the end. I had no beginning with Arthur, there's nothing to get tired of, get sickened of, it's the one thing which is always the same."

She was staring at him expectantly. He said slowly, "As you say, this doesn't seem to have anything to do with your brother-in-law's death."

"It hasn't. At least I don't think it has. But it might seem . . . to someone knowing everything . . ."

Her expectancy was mounting. He heard himself saying, "Even with Peter."

"Yes." She sat back with a deep sigh. He thought this was what she had really wanted to tell him. "Even with Peter. And even after Hilary had gone and he was living with Anthony. Because it wasn't important to him, I want you to understand that. He couldn't love a woman any more, but he could sleep with one, if only on a reflex." Her laugh was shrill, disagreeable, far from her normal laughter. "Sometimes, when Anthony was away . . . But it wasn't important to him. He couldn't have anything more to do with Hilary, because that had been important. You must believe me that I was never any threat to Hilary. And never wanted to be."

"So I'm surprised," said Neil austerely, "that you took the risk."

"Oh, you don't understand!" He jumped, at the intensity of her protest. She leaned towards him, her hands between her large knees. "I told you, I told you there were two things which couldn't burn themselves out. One was to belong with Arthur. The other was to love Peter. To love a man. The one and only time . . ." The sun, now, had reached a mirror opposite the windows, and was reflected back into her face so that he could watch the gradual fading of her exaltation. "Oh, perhaps," she said, tiredly, "perhaps it's only because I never really got beyond the beginning. How can I be sure? But I must persist in believing that I loved one man. Was able to."

"Two, surely?" suggested Neil. She smiled again, sadly.

"Yes, two. The two brothers, between them, have been my life. Well, I have Arthur still. And no doubt the compassion of a nation —minus one." She showed her uneven teeth. She seemed to be entirely restored, appeased by her self-exposure.

He said, formally, "And this last time, Mrs. Shaw, when you visited your brother-in-law?"

She nodded. "You disappoint me, Neil Carter, coming back so quickly to your murder case. But I suppose I knew you would. No, not this last time. I just wanted you to know that there *is* another dimension, which *could* have been relevant. But isn't."

"Yet you've just been talking to me in such a way as to make me surprised that it isn't."

"That's easy, I'm a nurse. A sick man, thank God at least for that, has always been beyond my personal ambition."

"Thank you for telling me these things."

"Yes, I've finished, and there's nothing to thank me for, I wanted to, I've never talked about them to anyone else, ever, and it's done me good."

There was something more he wanted to know. "Is your husband aware of—how you live?"

"I don't know." She spread her elegant hands, smiling at his evident astonishment. "No, I really don't. Except Peter, I'm certain he didn't know about Peter. Otherwise I've never made a secret of the people I see, of my need for independence. But I've always shared his bed the nights I've been at home—which is most nights, Neil Carter, there being also mornings and afternoons—and Arthur has never asked me any questions. So—I don't know. And if things aren't put into words, they can be presumed not to exist."

"Yes." The idea was a not unfamiliar one.

"He has a thing about Hilary?"

She shrugged. " '*La princesse lointaine.*' The distant ideal. He hardly realizes it himself, although since she left Peter he's enjoyed his brotherly role." Again, as she leaned towards him, he felt that thrill of danger. "So you see now why I hate Anthony Carey. On behalf of two women."

A car door banged. Clara Shaw heaved slowly to her feet. Neil got up too. They were standing close to one another, but the slight physical gap was something neither of them would ever have the feeblest impulse to bridge. Neil realized the chief impression he had of her was strength. And ruthlessness. Like recognizing like?

She said quickly, "I suppose one of the things I wanted was to try and find out if my motives had perhaps been mixed."

"And have they?"

"I don't think so. But I still don't quite know. How can I know?"

Bob Ryan and a man whose name Neil couldn't remember were coming up the path. He let them in and satisfied the second man's immediately searching gaze. There was some balm in the awed extent of his reaction. He put the vase carefully into the soft-centred container he had brought for it, after Clara had snatched the fronds from his apologetic hand. She thrust them into the brass tub in the hearth, turned the gas-fire off.

"I'm afraid I shall have to ask you to accompany me . . ." Bob Ryan began, but she was already scribbling a note. She asked for a telephone number, added it to the note which she folded and propped against the ebony clock.

She was only a moment upstairs, and the four of them left the house together. She had put on a glamorous coat and almost tidied her hair and her face, whose focal point was now a bright slash of lipstick. Neil could see that she was attractive, as he could admire a Rubens without wanting it on his own wall. A sort of triumph in her bearing, she sailed down the path to the police car, the men in her wake. Feeling somehow that he and she had not quite finished, Neil sought her eyes as he took his leave, but she didn't look at him again.

CHAPTER 22

He spent the afternoon at his own work, then went home. It was almost six o'clock but there was no reply from Cathy's. Usually she was back by five. Sometimes, of course, there were staff meetings or other after-school activities. And there were bound to be evenings when she had engagements. . . .

He had just spread some work papers on his table when his own bell rang. Stephen Elliott stood beyond the glass eye, his caricature the least extreme of Neil's collection. Seen undistorted, he looked boyish and cheerful.

"Come in."

"Just for a moment, then. The thing is, I've brought Hilary home and I've only come to ask if you'll join us for a drink to celebrate her return."

"Return to health as well?"

The bright face clouded.

"It's a bit early for that, I'm afraid. In fact the hospital were all for keeping her a bit longer even though the police don't seem to want her at the moment. But when I'd talked to her and got her to promise to stay with her parents they agreed to let her go. And I have the feeling she'll recover in more—well, in more natural surroundings and away from where everything's happened."

"She's promised to go and see her parents?"

"Tomorrow. I'm sure it's best."

"And I'm sure you're right." He had a feeling there was more in his sense of relief than was immediately available to his understanding.

"You'll come over, then? In about half an hour?"

"Lovely!" His ironical manner was, of course, for his own amusement. "When did you bring her?"

"They let me wait while she got ready and we were here about four. I left her to rest while I went to relieve my Samaritan at the St. John's Wood gallery."

"You're an excellent employer," said Neil, forcing a grin.

"And now I count myself a friend as well." Responding, Stephen Elliott stepped back on to the landing. "I couldn't get any reply from Hilary's friend Cathy McVeigh."

Neil usually managed to think of Stephen Elliott's ignorance as his own strength. He tried to go on thinking it, to banish the ridiculous resentment at his all-round social exclusion by this best-intentioned of men. "She's probably not home from school yet. I mean, from teaching." Even if Elliott had ever encountered Cathy, he could have misunderstood. "I shouldn't think she'll be late." Why shouldn't he think so? He didn't know. Elliott could be right, in fact. He realized he felt bleak.

"I'll try her again later then, thanks. Now I'd better go back and see that Hilary's all right. She's still rather dazed, poor love, with everything. . . ." Tenderness, straightforward love, irradiated the handsome face. *I'll tell Stephen soon about the baby.* Stephen would weather it beautifully.

A few Lucky Jim faces into his bathroom mirror almost restored him, and an application to his papers, which became really absorbing just as he must set them aside.

And quickly. It was a quarter to seven.

Stephen Elliott, as he had expected, opened Hilary's door to him.

"Ah, good. We were beginning to wonder. But I suppose, in your job . . ."

"That's right."

His resentment had been recharged by the sight of Cathy in the sitting-room doorway. But the quizzical lift of her eyebrows could only be the expression of her surprise that she had not found him already there. With such expectation, she would hardly have rung his bell first. He really must stop seeing himself as the only person who could be disappointed.

Hilary was sitting in her grandest armchair, where he had never yet seen her, looking not ill but remote and beautiful. Her hair, her face, her pale dress, were immaculate. Neil hoped other people beside himself would bear in mind that the illness which no longer showed in her face might be manifesting in the supreme serenity of her manner.

The patio doors were open to the fine evening, and Elliott was busying himself with drinks, assisted by Cathy. It shouldn't have been difficult to ask Hilary to stroll with him on to the balcony. She agreed readily enough. As they went out he saw Cathy's head turn sharply towards them, and as sharply away.

They leaned on the rail, and he told her rapidly about the vase, and why it had been at Clara's. His relief, as his mention of the vase brought her face to life, was considerable. Probably Stephen Elliott was the best friend she could currently have, eager for her to get back to work, to the things which could never let her down.

"Oh, Neil! So you've actually seen it!"

"And felt it. With my hands and in my bones."

"I know *that* feeling." He welcomed the momentary renewed tension in her face.

"Of course you do. You taught me."

"I told you the vase was the answer."

"Did they say anything at the hospital when they—let you go?"

"Only that they were satisfied I'd told them all I could, or something like that. Not that Clara . . . So Clara . . . after all . . ." But she was indifferent again. She had absorbed all the shocks she could take which had to do with people.

"Clara has the shoulders for it," he said, nevertheless offering comfort. "She seemed—well, she seemed relieved to have her proof at last."

"I still can't believe it," she said dreamily. Neil thought it was probably as well for her that she was unable to try very hard.

"I hope the vase comes to you."

She shrugged. "As long as it's safe, and to be fair it will be safe with Anthony. If it did come to me, anyway, I'd pass it on to a collection. May I tell Stephen?"

"Not yet. Remember, the police haven't yet told *you!*"

She smiled, more warmly than Cathy, who was suddenly beside them.

"Neil!" Elliott was there too, offering him his gin and tonic. Neil advanced his glass against the other glass Elliott was holding.

"Stephen!"

Elliott put his arm gently round Hilary's shoulders and urged her indoors. Neil followed with Cathy, not touching her. Stephen guided Hilary back to the principal chair and Cathy flopped on to a pouffe, spreading her legs at their usual angle, the pose now obscured by the voluminous flowered cotton skirt which dipped between them. The gold of her cap of hair shone against the pale wall. Neil tried to catch her glance, re-affirm their conspiracy, but her eyes were sparkling about the room. He was reminded of her party those years of weeks ago, although something now was very different.

They were four people who in uncharged circumstances would have generated some interesting conversation. As it was, they didn't do too badly. After it had been established that Hilary insisted on driving herself to her parents the next day, they talked about painting in an overall pattern of question and answer between Cathy and Stephen. Neil had the strange sensation of things having imperceptibly but drastically changed shape, without knowing what it meant. When the front-door bell rang Cathy tripped off to answer it.

The resonant tones alerted them at once, so that Neil had several seconds to observe the bruised circles reappear under Hilary's eyes as her cheeks went white. Arthur Shaw overtook Cathy in the sitting-room doorway.

"Hilary! My dear!" His short steps took him quickly across the room. Neil saw the small movement with which she made sure his kiss fell short of her lips. "I went to the hospital and they told me you were home. Wasn't it a bit hasty, dear? I mean, you've hardly had time . . . Although of course I'm delighted that the police felt able to let you go . . . I mean, come home. . . ." It was the first time Neil had seen the man embarrassed.

"Have *you* been home, Mr. Shaw?" he inquired, recognizing his official voice as he heard it.

"I beg your pardon?" Arthur Shaw turned to stare at him. "Have I been home? I'm afraid I don't—"

"Since you went to town this morning? Have you been home, or been in touch with your wife?"

"Have you?" reinforced Hilary quietly. "Have you, Arthur?"

Arthur Shaw turned back to Hilary, from whom the question was acceptable, a slight softening visible on those singularly unrevealing features.

"No, my dear, I went straight from the office to the hospital. And then here. But I hardly see what it has to do with Mr. Carter."

So Arthur Shaw did remember his name. Neil said, lightly, "No, well, I happened to see your wife at headquarters this afternoon, and I just wondered if you had seen her since, or been in touch with her."

"I will no doubt see her when I get home," said Shaw with dignity.

When he got home he would see the revised note which Clara Shaw would have written when she went with a WPC to collect an overnight bag. Neil pictured it, a white square in the gathering gloom against the greater darkness of the ebony clock. Let him wait.

"I'm going to stay with my parents tomorrow, Arthur."

Neil saw the slight figure stiffen, the hands clench against the thighs.

"Oh, but surely, my dear, the police won't—"

"The police are pursuing their inquiries," said Neil, still official, "and they have the address."

"Even so, my dear," resumed Arthur Shaw, after the statutory look of displeasure, "I hardly think—"

"It'll do her good, you know," said Stephen amiably, but with a firmness Neil had to applaud. "The best thing, in fact. What will you have to drink?"

"Yes, of course, Arthur, you'll have a drink?"

There was a moment of hesitation, in which Arthur Shaw appeared to decide to make the best of what was available.

"Thank you, my dear, that would be most acceptable. Scotch and soda."

Rubbing his hands, he dropped on to the end of the sofa beside Hilary's chair. The clinking of bottles and glasses sounded loud in the silence, which tended to continue from all but the new arrival, who began to reveal a bizarre exuberance, sending his love two or three times to Hilary's parents, commiserating with Stephen on the temporary loss of his right hand, even offering some commonplace gallantry to the bright-eyed Cathy. Neil, the only one not involved in the performance, canvassed the possibility that Shaw had been drinking, but decided the strange elation came from some less exterior source. When Elliott went to replenish drinks Shaw leaned towards Hilary. Neil's trained ear caught the whispered invitation to dinner, and Hilary's explanation that she had already agreed to have dinner with Elliott. Shaw asked again, and the intensity of the renewed plea reached Neil across the room. Denied a second time, Shaw redoubled his alarming pleasantries. Neil was not surprised when Hilary left the room on a murmured excuse. Perhaps it was his belated realization that she and Elliott had arranged to spend the evening together which decided him to get up and follow her. Shaw got up, too, but Neil was nearer the door. As he went out he was aware of Shaw bouncing petulantly back on to the sofa.

He went straight to her bedroom and she was there, standing staring through the window. He pushed the door to, came up behind her and put his arms round her, rubbing his throat on her hair.

"I'm glad you're going home."

She turned to face him, raising her hands to his shoulders. "Yes, and perhaps I'll eventually be able to think of it as that. I did once."

"Are you really all right?" He knew of course that she couldn't be, but he wanted to hear what she would say.

"For moments at a time."

"And the baby?"

"The baby's fine. It's all going to be for the baby, from now on."

"I know." They looked steadily at one another. Neil thought he had probably been offering her the chance to say what she had just implied. "Goodbye, love." They strained against each other, chastely. "Don't give any concessions of any kind to your brother-in-law. And work as soon as you can."

"A promise, on both counts. I'll see you when I get back."

"Of course." They drew slightly apart to smile at one another, to share their gratitude that there was no misunderstanding.

"Goodbye, Neil." This time they kissed on the lips, stayed close for the final exchange of courage. Behind Hilary's head the door flew open, and Neil at last caught Cathy's eye, held it for a dreadful second as it went blank. Then she had gone, and he heard the front door open and close.

He drew away again, and she looked at him in surprise.

"Neil! What is it? You look as if . . . Oh, God, did someone . . . ?"

"Cathy. It was Cathy. She saw us. She's—gone."

"Gone?"

"Left the flat. She went straight out."

"Then for heaven's sake go after her."

"What?" But he was most fearfully and agonizingly anxious.

"Go after her. Go on, Neil. The quicker the better."

"But . . . you . . ."

"For God's sake, what have we been saying to one another? I have a friend, Neil, and a child. Go on!"

"Second sight?"

"Go on!"

"Love you!"

He kissed her forehead, was just able to register and approve the tone of her laugh. Then he was down the hall, out of the door. He almost cannoned into Cathy, who was coming from her flat and had put on a cardigan.

"Cathy! Why did you run off? I was just saying goodbye to Hilary. Goodbye. You didn't have to—"

"Excuse me, Neil, I'm going for a walk." It was like a bad dream, that Cathy should be looking at him so coldly.

"But, Cathy, I want to talk to you, please don't—"

"I'm going for a walk, if you don't mind."

"But I do mind, I mind dreadfully! Cathy, I didn't realize . . . please let me talk to you!"

"Look, Neil, I just want to go for a walk. On my own. All right?"

"But, Cathy . . ."

She had darted away from him, into the lift which had just disgorged two women who looked like Miss Prince and who were in fact ringing Miss Prince's bell. By the time he had fallen over the feet of one of them and apologized, the lift doors were closed.

He took the stairs at a run, clattering his way round their marble curves, feeling like a man in an American B-picture cliché situation, in so far as he felt anything beyond this awful anxiety. And this fantastic surprise which had winded him even before he began his descent . . .

He heard the lift stop at the third floor. He could beat it. The waist-high line which bisected the green marble wall began to waver as he flew past it, his feet and the echoes of his feet rang out together. He reached the ground floor and the lift doors a few seconds before they opened. They emitted a couple of unknown men, and Cathy. She checked when she saw him, and he rejoiced in the brief faltering of her face, but, hard-eyed again, she walked swiftly to the entrance. One of the men held the door for her, and Neil lost a little ground, but he saw her turning left out of the gates, skirt and shoulder-bag swinging, head held high. He hurried after her, caught her on the first corner.

"Cathy, please. At least listen to me for a moment. Please just listen to me."

"I'm not in the mood for listening, Neil." He thought her voice, really, was more tired than angry. Slightly encouraged, he went on quickly, "Answer me one question, then. Just one question."

"Well?"

"Why—now?"

"Why now what?" Although she had stopped, the upper part of her body was straining forward, her hair and her bag were still swaying.

"Well . . ." To his fury he was at a loss to explain himelf, wasting the precious reprieve. "Minding. And when you least have to mind. Hilary and I were saying goodbye."

"Well, yes. She's going away."

"No. Really goodbye. Finis."

"Look, Neil. It's nothing to do with me, but I've just suddenly had enough. I'm just suddenly tired of—of not having a life of my own." Fiercely, her eyes snapping, she said, "I'm just suddenly thinking about *me*." Behind the sparkle, partly causing it, were tears. Even as they gave him hope, for her sake he regretted the threat they posed to her dignity. Dignity . . . Cathy . . . He realized she was sorry for herself, a state in which he had never yet seen her.

She was walking on, while he was standing on the pavement, absurdly theorizing instead of—but he couldn't touch her, it wouldn't have been any less possible if she'd been under a glass dome. He hurried after her.

"All right," he said, keeping a pace behind, "don't talk, but please just listen. If things were the same I'd turn round and go home now and leave you to it. But they aren't the same—for me—and I must tell you, even though perhaps it won't make any difference for you—" He lost ground again as it swept over him that perhaps it really wouldn't make any difference for her, that perhaps she no longer cared about him, perhaps she never properly had . . . Don Everett . . . The second onslaught was his awareness of his conceit, his presumption . . .

He couldn't see her, she had turned the next corner. He took it at a run. An empty pavement . . . panic . . . but to the right was the enclave of a small garden with teak seats and roses, a place he had passed a hundred times and been vaguely aware of very old men staring into space. Now there was merely Cathy, sitting down . . . knowing that he must come and sit beside her.

Overflowing with gratitude, he did so, but a decent distance from the corner where she was taking up so little room.

"Cathy . . ."

"I'm in a poisonous mood. Full of self-pity. Not the least wish to justify myself. You should go home, Neil."

He was even more aware now of tiredness at the expense of rage. He said humbly, "All right, I will. If you still want me to when you've heard what I have to say."

She was silent. She was at least prepared to listen. "Thank you," he said. "Cathy . . ." She was completely motionless, expressionless. He didn't look at her again, but stared straight ahead, reading and re-reading the commemorative plaque on the red brick wall in front of him. "I may be too late," he said, "or I may never have been in time, but I've just realized that I'm madly in love with you. I even want to marry you. More than I've ever wanted anything before. And I've never wanted *that* before. I don't pretend I'm not amazed, I can hardly believe it, for the first few seconds I didn't *want* to believe it, but it's true—"

"Neil, for God's sake. I know you can be a brute, but this . . ."

She was on her feet, her eyes blazing at him, no fear of tears. Her look of hate and horror seemed to pierce his body. He leaped up and put out his hand, and as she shrank away he could hear the entreaty in his voice.

"No, Cathy, please, I mean it, I'm in the most deadly earnest. Cathy . . . even if you can't . . . please at least believe me, take me seriously. . . ." His voice actually cracked, let him down, unfamiliar springs welled behind his eyes. But he was grateful that her face, as it now was, should have grown blurred. "Cathy," he croaked, "I've never spoken like this to any woman in my life. I'll go on my knees if you like." As he said the words that old hand, his mind, was measuring her against the sensation of pure independence which had seized him the second time he had visited the Portland Vase, alone. Finding that she stood up to it, melted into it. "You *must* believe me!" he said, out of his ultimate certainty, and there must have been something in his tone at last, because when his vision cleared he saw that she was still standing in front of him, her face again wiped clear of expression.

"I love you," he said.

"So when did you stop loving Hilary?" She gave him no clue, in voice or face.

He tried to conceal his surprise, his inappropriate amusement. "I never loved Hilary," he said evenly, "or she me. I liked her and admired her and found her attractive. I think, at a bad time for her, I did her more good than harm." It looked as if he ought to try and get it over now. "Look, love, I've had affairs with a number of women over the past ten years or so, some of whom I've liked more than others, but none of whom I've loved. . . . It's not exactly a phenomenon, Cathy, you must have learned that."

He searched her face, realizing it was the only face there was. He had never felt like that about a face before. She smiled, and it was like the sun coming out, flooding him and the garden, St. John's

Wood and London. "It *is* absurd, Neil, so absurd it must be true. Whooo, I've got to sit down."

He sat beside her, still a little apart. She was very stiff and upright. He waited until she said softly, "So there'll be other Hilarys?"

"Ah!" He turned to look at her, and she looked back at him. "Tell me," he said, "if I was away from you and met a siren and—and—I never found the idea of a siren less attractive—what would you feel? It wouldn't have anything to do with either of us. Nothing else ever will."

"Oh, Neil!"

"I mean it. But I'm—"

"You. You're you. Oh, I know. I don't suppose I'd mind all that much, deep down. Oh, but"—in a rush—"I don't *know*. Perhaps I'd rather not be told."

"Oh, darling, what an appalling conversation . . ."

But perhaps he had merely been delaying the moment of that first rushing contact of arms and cheeks and lips, knowing that nothing thereafter could ever be like it. . . .

She laughed softly. "I'll tell you something. Hilary—well, of course, she never knew I knew about—you and her—but she used to tell me that—well, that she was sure you were—fond of me—you know—and how I ought to behave. . . . I was a bit shocked. . . . Perhaps I am a bit naïve. . . . But I'm not . . ." The words twisted under his ribs. He couldn't, or he didn't want to, ask her to expand them just then. And anyway, he was amazed at the other thing she had said.

"Hilary—thought that? How on earth?"

She smiled at him. He suspected she could be smiling at the jolt to his vanity. "Perhaps her second sight. I don't know. Anyway, she told me to go out with Don and appear cheerful and unconcerned."

"You did very well."

"Actually, it came to suit my mood. I got a bit fatalistic."

"Oh, my dear darling!"

CHAPTER 23

They decided to eat in the little restaurant next door to the flats, where Cathy told him Stephen and Hilary would be.

He found himself somehow glad when Cathy said on the landing, "No, don't come in with me now. I need to take a few deep breaths. Call for me in half an hour."

"When would you like to get married?"

She sighed luxuriously. He had to put his hand up and trace the curve of her jaw.

"I think I'd better take you home next weekend, Neil. Will you be free?"

"Yes. Yes." It would be interesting to observe the Chief's reaction to a situation so completely without precedent. "Must you have Winnie as a bridesmaid?"

"We'll see."

He kissed the tip of her nose and closed her front door on her.

Behind his own he couldn't keep still, lurching from room to room, openly smiling. He discovered that marriage in the abstract was no less a concept for hostility and suspicion than it had always been, while marriage to Cathy was a unique sunny upland towards which the path was as broad as his horizon. He kissed *en passant* the glass of the little watercolour of birds she had done for his birthday, retracing his steps to polish away the smudge of his exuberance. He was on the balcony, peering down at the small gardens and wondering which of the two flats would be the more desirable to live in until he bought a house, when his doorbell rang a long peal and an immediate succession of short ones. He couldn't see anyone through his spy-hole but the bell was still ringing and he cautiously opened the door. Cathy was leaning against the wall beside it, her face unfamiliarly red and white. Beyond, the door of Hilary's flat was open.

He had her in his arms, but she drew away.

"Neil. Come over. Quickly."

He felt for his key, pushed his front door to. Inside Hilary's flat she urged him by the hand towards Hilary's bedroom.

It was a hand he saw first, dangling over the edge of the bed. Thank heaven a man's hand, emerging from a man's jacket sleeve. Near by, on the floor, almost fitting into the pattern of the carpet, was a gun.

He was hoping before he was close enough to see, and his hope was realized because it was Arthur Shaw lying neatly on Hilary's bed, feet together, eyes staring at the ceiling with intensified outrage. The only memorial of movement was the left hand, clutching at the shirt beside the round red hole and the surrounding burn marks. There was no pulse. The only sign of upset in the quiet tidy room was a small vase and some short-stemmed, brightly-coloured flowers in a pool of water on the floor near the door. Cathy was leaning against the doorpost, staring at the bed. Neil supported her into the sitting-room and a corner of the sofa. He made sure there was no one else in the flat, had another look round Hilary's bedroom, and standing with his back to the body telephoned his Chief. Only then he returned to the sitting-room.

"All right now?" He sat down beside her, caressed her in the fatherly way he had once caressed Hilary.

"Yes. Oh, Neil!"

"What were you doing in here, anyway?"

She flushed, said quickly, "I just came to put a posy in her bedroom—if the balcony doors were unlocked, which they were, and I went through and—I saw him. . . . Neil, did someone . . . ?"

"No, darling, no. There is nothing more certain in this world than that Arthur Shaw blew himself into the next."

"But—why?"

"I don't know, but I can guess. However, there's a letter. There would be, of course. Under the pillow, wouldn't you know?"

"But you haven't read it?"

"I don't know why not. I almost did. I almost looked for a pair of tweezers and some cotton gloves. But if there's any justice at all, the Chief will allow me to look over his shoulder."

"When will they be here?"

"In no time at all. . . ."

He sat forward on the sofa, holding her hand.

"Look, Cathy, I'm going to ask you to do something very important and difficult." And he wanted her out of the place, for her sake. "Will you go down to the Green Parrot and find Hilary and Stephen

—and—oh, darling, do you think you could? Tell her? And of course tell her not to come up, and wait with them until I join you?"

"Neil!" But she hardly hesitated. "Yes, of course. Yes, I should think I'm the best one."

"I'm certain you are. Don't wait for me, if you're hungry."

"Don't be silly. Shall I go now?"

"Yes, I think so."

But she didn't move. "Neil, shall I tell them . . . ?"

He looked at her in surprise. "Well, yes!"

"About us."

"Oh, darling!" Apologetically he stroked her hair. "There's a taste of the real me, you see, already. It's just that my mind—"

"I know, I know, I'm not worried." She didn't seem to be, smiling at him so radiantly he had to look away.

"And of course tell them about us." He looked back at her, to show her the certainty in his eyes. "If I didn't have to bother with this just now I'd climb on to the roof and proclaim it."

"Neil! It's awful, but now the shock's worn off I can't really feel bad."

He stood holding Hilary's door until Cathy's door was open, then went back into Hilary's bedroom and absent-mindedly restored the incidental vase of flowers, absent-mindedly admiring them and wondering what they were. He tweaked up the corner of the pillow again, just to be sure of the white envelope. Arthur Shaw had removed the bedspread and, somehow pathetically, his shoes. The shoes were neatly together beside the bed, the coverlet neatly over the back of a chair. He had another systematic prowl of the flat, more slowly but still seeing nothing he could think of as significant, before going out on to the balcony consciously to breathe the evening air. He was out there when the bell rang. On the step were the Chief, Bob Ryan and an assorted team of specialists. The landing seemed thronged, especially as Miss Prince was just letting out her pair of replicas.

"Good evening, Mr. Carter," she said tentatively. "I hope it was all right, my letting Mr. Shaw in."

The two groups were for a few seconds frozen, staring at one another. Then the Chief said charmingly, "You let Mr. Shaw into this flat, madam, Mr. Arthur Shaw?"

Miss Prince acknowledged the charm with a degree of relaxation.

"Well, I don't know if it was Mr. *Arthur* Shaw. It was Mrs. Shaw's brother-in-law."

"That would be Mr. Arthur Shaw," said Bob Ryan. "What time was this, Miss Prince?"

"I'm not quite sure *exactly*, but I know Hetty and Mabel had been with me about a quarter of an hour and it was only five minutes or so since I'd heard people leaving Mrs. Shaw's flat. I was crossing the hall from the kitchen," added Miss Prince quickly. "I think it must be about an hour ago. My bell rang, and this gentleman was on the step, saying that he'd left his own key behind in Mrs. Shaw's flat and if I could possibly let him in to get it . . . which of course . . . on *this* occasion . . ." Miss Prince at last appeared to be aware of something unusual in the concourse on Hilary's step. "There's nothing wrong I hope? Mr. Carter . . . ?"

Neil was glad that the Chief answered for him, saying gallantly, almost jokily, "Nothing wrong so far as *you* are concerned, madam, of that I assure you. But I may want to talk to you during the evening. You'll be at home?"

"Yes . . . certainly . . . er . . ."

"Larkin, madam, Detective-Chief Superintendent. Now, if you will excuse me . . ."

The smaller party, abandoning thoughts of the lift, drifted dazedly back through Miss Prince's front door. The larger party shut itself into the Shaw flat, followed Neil into the bedroom. The Chief did the things Neil had done.

"You been in this room before, Carter?" asked the Chief, from across the bed. His eyes gleamed, Neil could only think at the unexpected opportunity for so splendid a question.

"Well, yes, Governor, I telephoned you from here once, if you remember."

The Chief turned abruptly away. "Anything different?" he asked the window.

"Only that vase of flowers"—Neil indicated as the Chief turned back to him—"lying here in this pool of water. Miss McVeigh from Number Thirty-six was bringing them in for Mrs. Shaw and dropped them when she saw the body. I picked 'em up, but of course I haven't touched anything else. Except the corner of the pillow, to find the envelope."

The Chief made a gesture to one of the men in the doorway, who retrieved the envelope in the correct scientific manner.

"How did Miss McVeigh get in?"

"Through the balcony doors into the sitting-room—the balcony's continuous all the way round the building. I'm afraid up here we don't always lock our balcony doors. They're brutes anyway. And this evening both Miss McVeigh and I had been having drinks in this flat and the doors had been wide open. They could have been left like that when Mrs. Shaw and Mr. Elliott went down to the Green Parrot—restaurant—next door. Oh, Arthur Shaw arrived while we were having drinks, had one himself. Miss McVeigh and I left him and the other two, so I don't know in what precise formation the party finally broke up."

"Hm. You and Hennessy look round the flat, will you, Ryan? Where's Miss McVeigh now, Carter?"

"She's gone down to the restaurant, Governor, to tell Mrs. Shaw what's happened in her bedroom and to suggest she doesn't come back up for the time being."

"Yes. I gather Mrs. Shaw's going home tomorrow. Whether or not we finish with the room, I think she'd be better off with alternative accommodation for tonight. Miss McVeigh put her up?" The gleam was still there.

"I should think, for an emergency, she could make a space between the canvases in her spare room."

"Good. Mercer, will you bring me the letter in the other room?"

Neil followed the Chief into the sitting-room. When they were alone he asked if he could read the letter with him.

"I don't see why not, Neil, but shut the door. Bob can see it in a moment."

Arthur Shaw's handwriting even at such a stage in his life was legible and elegant, his last letter tidily set out. It had no superscription, merely the address of Hilary's flat. On a synchronized reflex, Neil and the Chief looked at the angle of the chair beside the desk where they stood, made sure their hands and sleeves were clear of any surfaces.

It does not seem as if my wife's story will be believed, and Hilary Shaw will be convicted of an action she did not perform. There is one certain way of ensuring that the truth prevails, and that is for me to stake my life on it. So I hereby tell the whole truth, there being no further reason for my wife to suffer when she is innocent and can have no more incentive to protect what she no doubt rightly considers to be my weakness.

I am not ashamed of what I did, although I would not, I think, have done it without the opportunity of my brother's sudden illness. I killed him because he deserved to die, and in that final moment I wanted him to die more violently, more unnaturally, more as a punishment, than even the coronary thrombosis would inflict on him.

What I have decided to do is what I wish to do: Hilary is going away from London tomorrow, and I may well never see her again.

There followed the signature *Arthur G. Shaw*, and the date.

"What do you make of that, Neil?" asked the Chief.

"It makes me wonder how that bullet-hole could have been red. And yet . . . in his own way . . . the bastard suffered." And would perhaps be suffering still, if Neil had not withheld from him what he had learned about the Portland vase. Or if Shaw had thought about his wife rather than his inamorata and had tried to contact her. Neil didn't think he was going to feel too badly about his act of omission.

"That's about it, lad." The Chief straightened up, turned round to face Neil. "Well, I'm glad Mrs. Shaw is really free at last, and that she's going away from all this. Though I don't doubt she'll be back to her work in the end, and Stephen Elliott seems properly devoted. Might not be a bad thing, with a baby coming. . . ."

Revenge? How much did the Chief suspect Neil had held back from him? Neil would never know. But then, the Chief would never know the accuracy of his own suspicions.

"I'm certain she'll come back to work, Governor, maybe even before the baby. On the personal side I think it'll take a bit longer. And talking of personal sides, I have to ask you to congratulate me. I'm going to marry Miss McVeigh."

He would hardly have chosen the Chief to be the first to know, but it was an unmissable moment. His superior officer felt behind him for a chair arm. He stared at Neil while Neil counted ten, and then said in a comparatively weak voice, "Of course I congratulate you, lad, although I hadn't the faintest idea . . ."

"Neither had I," responded Neil, matching generosity with generosity. "I'm on stand-by next weekend. Can I change it so that I can be taken home to Mummy and Daddy?"

"I suppose so." The Chief was recovered enough to look normally grudging. "And while I think of it, I've something fresh to put on your plate."

"Yes, Governor."

Bob Ryan tapped at the door and opened it at the same moment. It could be that he looked slightly askance.

"I'll be off," said Neil. "See you, Bob."

Hilary, Cathy and Stephen were at a corner table. There was no food on it, only an almost empty carafe of wine with two glasses, and a brandy glass in front of Cathy. Neil looked at her searchingly as he slipped into the fourth seat, at last understanding his sensation of change: Cathy was now the one in sharp focus.

It was immediately obvious that around the table shock prevailed rather than sorrow.

"The main thing, Neil," said Hilary. "I'm so glad. I know how happy you'll be."

"Yes, congratulations," said Stephen.

"Thank you." He leaned over the table to kiss Hilary's hand. Then took Cathy's and began to chafe it as he felt the unnatural cold of her fingers.

"I'm sorry it was Cathy who found him," said Hilary. "Neil . . ."

"He took his own life," said Neil, "no doubt of that. There's a letter. No revelations, really. I'll leave it to my Chief and Co. to tell you." He held Cathy's hand on his knee. "Cathy, do you think you could put Hilary up for tonight? Even if they've finished with her bedroom, she'll hardly want—"

"I've already asked her, and she'll bear with the clutter. What is it, Neil?"

A couple had just come into the restaurant and were threading their way among the tables. The woman was plump, with untidy fair hair, wearing a shapeless brown cardigan. He remembered Clara, with shame both for his forgetfulness, and for his reluctance to hold on to the recall. He looked round the table.

"Clara."

Hilary said softly, "Oh, God."

They decided to sit through another carafe of wine, to give Cathy and Neil a chance to toy with some food and the Chief and his team time to finish in Hilary's flat. Neil went up alone, in case of encounters in the public parts of the building, and came down to tell them the coast was clear. He left it to Cathy to help Hilary collect what she needed for the night, and sat by his telephone constantly and fruitlessly ringing Clara's house until midnight, when she answered. He didn't recognize the soft, toneless voice. She told him they had roused her to tell her what had happened, and to drive her home.

"I won't come now," he said. "I'll come first thing in the morning. I hope you'll go to bed." His front-door bell was ringing.

"I'll go to bed," she said obediently, and hung up. He was too preoccupied to look through his spy-hole before opening the door. Hilary and Cathy were there to tell him they too were going to bed. In the circumstances, and in accordance with his will if not his inclinations, he said good night to Cathy on the landing. Without real distraction, he was able to tell her in lightning précis about the vase and Clara's story and the contents of Arthur's letter. When she had gone in he stood for a long moment in a sort of astonishment, looking at the closed identical doors.

CHAPTER 24

This time she took longer to open the door to him, and he heard her feet plodding heavily along the hall. His immediate reaction was that she had grown smaller. They didn't speak until they had taken up their former positions in the dark front room.

Looking at her slumped silhouette, he said gently, "They showed you the letter?"

"They did." He could not see that even her mouth moved.

"Did he—was there a letter for you?"

Even though Arthur Shaw hadn't come home, perhaps in a pocket . . .

"No."

"I'm sorry."

"Thank you. Nothing," she said, "there was nothing. Now or ever."

"You mustn't think like that."

"I'm not thinking, Neil Carter, I daren't think, I'm stating a fact." Still the same quiet voice. He felt he should try to rouse it.

"Will you talk to me? Tell me what really happened? You know, the last time we met you praised me for a quality I obviously don't possess: you said I attracted the whole truth."

"I should have said, the real truth. I told you far more real truths than I told you lies." Perhaps there was a trace now of energy. "All right, the part of it that was Arthur I said was me, but I told you what happened. And how—"

"But not *why*. All that speculation about your motives."

"I did speculate, Neil Carter, how could I not have done? I took what Arthur did on to myself because it's true that Peter had asked me to despatch him if he suffered a massive stroke, and with such a motive I couldn't be given more than a short prison sentence. But how could I avoid wondering not only whether I would in fact have killed him if I'd had the opportunity, but whether, if I had, there would have been some other motive besides obedience and compassion?"

"Such as sexual outrage? Yes, I understand. And that in the event the motive was moral indignation. And, I suspect, a lifetime of envy stretching a small mind further than it had been designed to go." She was struggling to her feet, and he pressed on. "Good God, woman, you can't taste dust and ashes for Arthur Shaw. Not you!"

But she had sunk back again in her chair. She said wearily, "You don't really understand, do you, Neil Carter? Arthur didn't leave me a note, but he left me the knowledge that he killed himself to escape me. He couldn't go on without Hilary, and he couldn't go on with me. Oh, I knew he was obsessed with Hilary, but I underrated it. I thought I still had a unique role to play. And I had no role at all." Her face twisted in a dreadful parody of her crooked smile. "What irony, Neil Carter. Arthur killed his brother because he thought he had dishonoured his wife. And his own wife . . . Prison would have been something. Being in prison I would have been doing something for someone. I always have to be doing something for someone, to justify being alive. But Arthur didn't want to adopt children. . . . Every moment I was in prison would have meant Arthur wasn't. Because of me. I would have felt I was still protecting him. But of course I was never protecting him, he wasn't really a child, I was smothering him."

"Don't say that, the note was quite clear. He killed himself because he was afraid Hilary would be convicted, and because he knew he was unlikely to see her again. And I think he couldn't live with her lack of affection for him. I'll acknowledge his obsession was way out of hand, but there was no hint that he wanted to escape from *you*. That's monstrous."

"Yes, monstrous. Because to him I was a monster. And if I wasn't, if it was the way you want to believe it was—then I was nothing to him at all. Still nothing. Whatever it is, it comes back to nothing."

She was hugging herself, rocking backwards and forwards. He felt desperate to distract her, if only because of his own discomfort.

"I would have half expected you to deny your husband's confession, go on insisting it was you. Protect his memory, at least."

He had to say it again, but the second time, to his relief, he caught her attention.

"Oh yes, perhaps I wish now that I had, I don't know. But to convince I would have to have denied the confession at once, and I was too shocked, and it was too late. Like a more famous lady, Neil Carter, who at least still had armies to command, I had no more spirit in me." He returned her smile, disagreeable though it was, as bracingly as he could manage.

"A spirit like yours doesn't die—just like that—for such a reason."

"How do you know *that*, Neil Carter? Such arrogance!" At last she was alight, a small fire had been kindled in the chilly room. "How do you know what foundations other people build their lives on?" Even in antagonism they were uncomfortably close. Yet it would have been impossible so much as to touch her hand.

He said humbly, "No, I don't know. But tell me one thing: don't you get any strength, courage, from knowing that you always lived in your own way, that you did—so many things—independently?"

"I didn't. I did them in the certainty of Arthur." She ran her hands through her untidy hair. At least it was an improvement on the huddled self-protectiveness which had been so fearfully unlike her. But he had been naïve to imagine there was really anything he could do for her.

"Yes, you're right. I don't understand, although I have tried. I'm afraid now I'm going to have to carry on to the office. My Chief has some new chores for me. Will you go to the shop?"

"I expect so. Don't waste your energies worrying about me."

"Tell me one thing before I go." His mind's eye still saw Clara Shaw hiding in a bathroom, listening to Hilary screaming, then to her own crescendoing footfalls and breath. "Who took the vase?"

She smiled again, mockingly. "One will worry about you, Neil Carter, only if you lose your business instincts. I took the vase. I think Arthur realized even before he got home what it might mean and I ran straight off to get it. I went on foot because Arthur had been on foot, and I could hide if I heard Anthony coming back. I was just taking hold of the vase when I heard a car and of course I thought it was Anthony until I looked through the window. Everything I told you was as it was. Or as it would have been."

"How did you get back into the house?"

"Ah yes. We had our own key to Holly Lodge. It seemed wiser not to mention it earlier—or officially. Of course I let myself in."

"No need to mention it officially even now. No need to mention that you were there at all."

She shrugged. "It doesn't matter. Nothing matters."

"Please. And there's always something. Conspiring to pervert the course of justice could carry a short custodial sentence." She didn't react. "Also, you have another visitor."

A slight figure was negotiating the gate.

Clara Shaw didn't turn round, or make the least move when the bell rang. Neil went to answer the door to Anthony Carey. He was in his grey business suit and looked worried, but all expression vanished as he registered Neil.

"Mr. Carter. More private enterprise?"

"In a way," said Neil cordially. "I came because I was so sorry."

"So did I."

They stared at one another, both relaxing.

"Forgive me," said Neil at last, "but I hardly think you'll be welcome."

"I don't expect to be, but as soon as I read the paper I had to come."

"Of course, the paper." He hadn't thought of it. "Did the Press apportion the murder? If not, I think I can tell you that Mrs. Shaw is innocent."

"I think I already knew. Even when the vase made me go for Hilary. It was the eyes, Mr. Carter, they had the fanatic's stare. I was always afraid of those eyes, and then when Peter died and the police eventually told me . . ." Anthony Carey closed his own eyes, to absorb the spasm, to complete for Neil a trilogy for his pity. "I thought you might have noticed."

"I ought to have done. What else do you know?"

"Only that she has lost two men. How is she?"

"Defeated. Awful to see in such a woman. But you know . . ."

"Peter told me. I must go in. She didn't always hate me."

Clara Shaw was sitting as Neil had left her, staring ahead. He stayed in the doorway as Carey went swiftly across the room, dropped into the other chair, leaned forward and took her hand.

"Clara," he urged. "I know. I know."

Her head stirred, a faint life showed in her face, uncertainty, suspicion. But her hand lay still in Carey's.

"Let me stay a few moments," he said, as if coaxing a child. "There are only the two of us."

The change from immobility to the violent working of grief was as sudden, as ugly, in Clara's face as it had been in Hilary's. Neil watched them for a few seconds, the shuddering, sobbing woman and the motionless man joined by their hands, then let himself silently out of the house and drove away. Anthony Carey had helped her as he, Neil, had been unable to do, even if she eventually recoiled. But he didn't know what would happen next, he never would, because he didn't want to see either of them again, he didn't think he ever again wanted to sit inadequately beside a suffering woman.

Telling the truth of it reduced to about a quarter of an hour the time it took to neutralize the Chief's displeasure that he had not presented himself earlier to learn of his new assignment. But when he tore home by tube at lunch-time he was glad there was going to be so much to do.

Cathy precipitated herself on to him in her very earliest and most youthful way.

"Neil! I was hoping . . . I've got cheese and biscuits and coffee."

"In a minute."

It took them several to get through into the sitting-room. The food was there on a tray, an act of faith for which he felt affectionately grateful. But the Chief had indicated a short lunch-hour would be advisable. He said, through his first mouthful, "Hilary get off all right?"

"She must have done, I had to be at school by nine."

"I see you've brought your posy back. They're pretty, those flowers, what are they?"

"Neil! Don't you know a polyanthus when you see one? There are a few things I may be able to teach you!"

"I don't doubt there are a lot." But he spoke absent-mindedly, aware of a warning signal flashing in his mind. "Where did you get them, darling?"

"From that bit of border downstairs which goes round the side—the draughty bit where nothing much seems to grow. The sweet things seemed born to blush unseen and I thought—"

"Cathy! How long have you been taking them?"

"Just a few weeks. Neil, you're making me feel I've stolen them, for goodness' sake!"

"Dear girl, you have. And almost landed me with an exceedingly tiresome case. Miss Prince came to me a few weeks ago and asked me to help her find out who was stealing her polyanthus—"

"*Her* polyanthus?"

"Cathy," he said patiently, "a few tenants' meetings ago Miss Prince asked for, and was given, the right to plant and harvest all that went into that wretched little border. But you never go to tenants' meetings."

"Oh, Neil! Well, I went to the first one after I moved in but since then I don't seem to have . . . but it still wasn't exactly stealing, I mean—"

"I advised her," said Neil, dead pan, "to take her complaint round to the police station."

"You didn't!"

"I did, too. For heaven's sake don't do it again!" But he had to start laughing, and then he couldn't stop. And as he laughed he felt himself recovering from the obscure blow to his pride which all morning had struck him anew with each thought of the two Mrs. Shaws.

"I could go and confess," said Cathy. "Yes, I'll confess!" Eagerly she leaned forward. "I should be home by five and I'll go over and confess and I'll ask her to come and have a drink with us to celebrate. After all, she does seem to have been mixed up in things round here just lately. Six o'clock?"

He wiped his eyes. "There's just a chance of six o'clock, if I go *now*."

They smiled at one another. "I'll take you out for dinner properly tonight. Be thinking where you'd like to go. All right?"

"Of course, I'd love it." But she was looking down at the carpet, making patterns with her toe. "Neil . . ."

"Yes, darling?"

"Neil, I did take those flowers into Hilary's last night, but it was a sort of excuse because I wanted—I wanted to see if she'd written anything new in her diary. Only because of being worried about her, I told you I never looked at the diary and I never did. But I thought if she had it might give some idea of how she really is. I knew she'd had a couple of hours alone before we all arrived and . . ."

"And?"

"As soon as I went in from the balcony I had a look at the most recent page."

"And?"

"There were just three words at the top. With yesterday's date."
She hesitated, her eyes bright with tears.

"Cathy, tell me!"

"Oh, it's all right, Neil, I'm sure it's all right. She'd written—it's silly, but I feel shy, somehow, telling you—she'd written 'My dearest child.'"

Eileen Dewhurst was born in Liverpool and educated there at Huyton College, and later at Oxford. As a free-lance journalist, she has published many articles in the Liverpool *Daily Post*, the *Illustrated Liverpool News*, *Punch*, and *The Times* of London. She has written plays which have been performed in England and is the author of four other crime novels, including *Drink This*. TRIO IN THREE FLATS is her second novel for the Crime Club.